THE SARGASSO SEA . . .

a huge eddy within the North Atlantic Ocean, was first observed by Christopher Columbus on his initial West Indies voyage. It takes its name from the floating seaweed called *Sargassum*, or gulfweed, a brown algae that is easily recognized by the many small berrylike bladders that keep it afloat . . .

While the waters beneath the seaweed might be hundreds of feet deep, the calm surface and floating vegetation give the impression of shallows—so much that Columbus reduced his westward speed for fear of running aground. The *Santa María, Pinta,* and *Niña* were becalmed and drifted there, entrapped by the yellow and green weeds for weeks.

Today, travelers in high-powered ships, in airplanes—and even in space vehicles—still enter the Sargasso Sea and vanish for all time.

No one knows why.

SARGASSO

EDWIN CORLEY

A DELL BOOK

Published by
DELL PUBLISHING CO., INC.
1 Dag Hammarskjold Plaza
New York, N.Y. 10017

ISBN: 0-440-17575-5

Reprinted by arrangement with
Doubleday & Company, Inc.
Printed in the United States of America
First Dell printing—May 1978

*This story is dedicated to my son,
Eugene Charles Corley*

PROLOGUE

The Sargasso Sea, a huge eddy within the North Atlantic Ocean, was first observed by Christopher Columbus on his initial West Indies voyage. It takes its name from the floating seaweed called sargassum, or gulfweed, a brown algae that is easily recognized by the many small berrylike bladders which keep it afloat.

Shifting currents impart a whirlpool-like shape and motion to the Sargasso, and objects are gradually drawn toward its center, where, as legend has it, century-old ships still float, rotting, eternally trapped by the matted weed and lack of wind to fill their sails.

The Sargasso's northern borders are marked by the upward eastern curve of the Gulf Stream and its western and southern extremes by the returning Gulf Stream and the North Equatorial Current. Since the Sea has no clear boundaries, maps have shifted it from place to place over the years, but it is generally accepted that its area is marked by 25° and 31° north, and 40° and 70° west, although these extremes are constantly being altered by winds and sea currents.

This "Graveyard of Ships" surrounds the deadly horse latitudes with their doldrum spells that last for weeks. These shipping lanes gained their name because Spanish galleons were becalmed there so long that Conquistador war-horses had to be slaughtered to save drinking water to support human life.

Modern historians of the sea have observed that most of the mysterious disappearances of seagoing vessels attributed to the "Devil's Triangle" actually took place within the Sargasso Sea.

Under the waters of the Sargasso lies a variegated seabed. The North Atlantic Ridge, a huge underwater mountain range runs north and south. Beneath other deep waters of the Sea are the sheer faces of the Bermuda Rise, and the Hatteras and Nares Abyssal plains. Extremes so great that they might divide the dark and light faces of the moon lie side by side under the floating sargassum.

While the waters beneath the seaweed might be hundreds of fathoms deep, the calm surface and floating vegetation give an impression of shallows—so much that Columbus reduced his westward speed for fear of running aground. The *Santa María, Pinta,* and *Niña* were becalmed and drifted there, entrapped by the yellow and green weeds for weeks.

Today, travelers in high-powered ships, in airplanes—and even in space vehicles—still enter the Sargasso Sea, and vanish for all time.

No one knows why.

PART ONE
SPLASHDOWN

CHAPTER 1

The panic button was not a button at all, but a bright red knife switch positioned at the top right corner of the communications console. No one remembered who had originally installed the first panic button in those primitive days of the space program when all communications originated from the first missile control center at Cape Canaveral, Florida. Although some gave the credit to Shorty Powers, he denied the honor, and there are no written records to prove or disprove the point.

The panic button—or switch—was caged with a protective cover which had to be removed manually before the switch could be thrown. Air Force Captain Richard Jakes had practiced that emergency procedure often, as had a dozen of his predecessors. His best time to uncage the switch and throw it was 1.2 seconds, which was plenty of time, because the audio and video delay through the communications console was set at seven seconds. The high-density chromium dioxide tape belt which revolved within the console was changed every week, to keep oxide wear from degrading audio quality. Pool video coverage was delayed by a thick metal disc which was synchronized with the audio tape by a servo linkage, keeping the delay for both within a thousandth of a second. A laser beam read the video signals and converted them into usable Radio Frequency output.

This console was the best-kept secret of the space program. While highly classified details of thrust tonnage, of lift-off velocities, of sensitive impact areas on the moon or one of the planets, while all of these eventually leaked, no one had ever uncovered the fact that as the world watched the U.S. space shots, everything that happened on screen or over the radio had occurred seven seconds earlier in real-time.

The console had been designed and built by one of Peter Goldmark's mad CBS engineers, who was paid ten thousand dollars for the work, and another twenty thousand a year for keeping his mouth shut. The silence also included a yearly visit to update and service the unit.

When Captain Jakes had been assigned to his twenty-four-month tour of duty operating the console, his first question—after he had signed the security statement regarding the equipment—was, "What the hell for?"

His predecessor, Major John Freeman, said, "Remember when the capsule burned on the pad and those three astronauts were killed? Suppose we'd been making an actual shot, sound and video running live in real-time. Sure, the public has a right to know. But who has a right to listen to what happened inside that capsule? We're not withholding information, we're delaying it so that if there's another foul-up, we can pull the plug before the whole world listens to three of our men dying."

Jakes accepted the explanation, and for the past eleven months had gone through the often exciting procedures of co-ordinating communications for the media, always aware that the panic button was there, ready to be pushed.

But it never had been, and the chances were it never would be.

Jakes chewed on an unlit cigar. He was trying to cut down on his smoking, but it was hard, especially when he was just sitting around waiting.

His hand touched the cage over the knife switch. There was no reason to expect that it would be needed today, or any day. Which was just as well. Because, in his training, when he had actually pulled the switch to observe its effect, all hell had broken loose.

Walter Cronkite, as usual, had the largest portion of the total viewing audience, tuned to the CBS network.

The graying newsman had been associated with the space program nearly as long as it had existed, and while the other networks tried various combinations of anchor men and guests, they rarely dislodged Cronkite's ratings.

This morning, against a superimposed background of the Atlantic, he nodded at the big color camera and, referring to his notes, said, "We'll be hearing directly from mission control in a few minutes. But most of the results are in now, and it looks as if this joint U.S. and Russian exploration in space has achieved even more than we had hoped for. The three American astronauts have been on the Russian space platform for exactly one week, and the co-operation between the two teams has been perfect. All of the scheduled experiments have been carried out, the photography with both film and TV cameras has been described as excellent, and in just a few minutes, both space vehicles will be leaving the platform, which is now being powered down, for their return to earth."

The scene behind him changed, and Cronkite now sat in front of the bridge of the U.S. carrier *New Orleans*. He noted this on the small monitor mounted in his desk, and said, "As you know, the carrier *New Orleans* is standing by in the Atlantic as prime recovery vessel. Her choppers are ready, the frogmen are suited up, and we're all awaiting the countdown for separation from the space platform and re-entry."

Off-camera, an assistant producer made a C symbol with his thumb and forefinger, and Cronkite took the cue, saying, "We'll return to the splashdown of Apollo 19 after this message."

There is a relatively new concept in television media buying known as "horizontal" coverage.

Reasoning that at any given moment viewers will be divided among the major networks' stations, except for those few watching PBS or local programming, and to avoid having a commercial switched out by a viewer searching channels for something else to watch, certain

advertisers will make a horizontal buy on all four networks. This means that the same commercial will run at
exactly the same time on CBS, ABC, NBC, and CBA,
plus whatever spot markets the media buyer feels he
can depend on to run the commercial in the right time
segment. So, no matter where the viewer switches his
tuner, he'll see the same message.

That is what happened at precisely 10:38, Eastern
daylight saving time this morning of the Apollo 19
splashdown.

Approximately a hundred and eight million viewers
watched a one-minute commercial announcing the new
adventure motion picture from Warners/Para-
mount/20th Century Fox, a twelve-million-dollar epic
called *The Bermuda Triangle,* starring Charlton Heston,
Steve McQueen, Ali MacGraw and Also Starring Mar-
lon Brando as the Captain of the *Flying Dutchman.*

Perhaps a million or so of those viewers turned to
their companions and said, "Hey, isn't Apollo coming
down right in the middle of that Bermuda Triangle?"

The Atlantic re-entry had been necessary, rather than
the more conventional Pacific splashdown, because of
the simultaneous separation from the space platform of
both U.S. and Russian vehicles. Actually, it mattered
little to NASA, since the Atlantic footprint was large
enough to offer little difficulty in an accurate landing
and recovery. The principal drawback in Atlantic
splashdowns was clearing the area of other vessels.
Since these are international waters, voluntary compli-
ance is necessary, but during the dozens of manned
landings there, no ship had ever refused to give way for
the splashdown.

Nor had any this morning. According to Rear Admiral Judson Walgreen, Captain of the *New Orleans,* a
circle of more than a hundred miles around the giant
nuclear carrier was completely free of other shipping.

His shipboard radar showed nothing in the area except his own escort vessels and sea return. So, when at
08:45 hours that morning he had reported, "Area clear

of traffic," to NASA, he thought he was telling the truth.

He was not. Two other vessels were within the splashdown footprint.

One had been authorized by the White House, unknown to either NASA or the U. S. Navy.

The other had not been authorized by anyone.

The private research vessel *Lamprey* was less than forty miles from the *New Orleans*.

Her Captain, Arthur Lovejoy, stood on the bridge and watched the light swells raise *Lamprey*'s bow against the heavy chain attached to a nearby buoy. The other men on the bridge knew him well enough to know that he was worried. Lovejoy's deep blue eyes were squinted, and his powerful jaw was clenched to restrain the friendly grin that was his usual answer to the world's problems. Jet black hair, sprinkled now with gray, topped the sunburned face that had stood ten thousand watches on bridges just such as this. Shifting his wiry figure, *Lamprey*'s Captain frowned.

The ship's mini-sub, *Yellowtail,* had been below for more than an hour—on what was intended to be only a twenty-minute shakedown dive.

Lovejoy leaned forward and tapped the dials of the power indicators on the bridge's main instrument panel. The needles did not move. *Lamprey* had been completely without power for half an hour. Not a generator, not a battery, not a single light bulb would make so much as a faint spark.

That was disturbing enough up here on the surface. But what was happening below, in *Yellowtail?*

The second unsuspected vessel in the splashdown area scudded along under the brisk morning breeze, sails set as strong as the forty-eight-foot yacht *Plymouth Hope* would carry under the self-steering. The mainsail was 310 square feet, the mizzen was 130, and the genoa staysail was 220. *Plymouth Hope* was heeled well over, and she was clipping along at more than eight knots, which would have pleased her skipper tremendously, if only he had been awake.

Set above Captain Richard Jakes's console were four color TV monitors. Three showed him the major network transmissions. The fourth was the pool feed from NASA. Since the pool feed was transmitting at real-time minus seven seconds, the three networks were tracking exactly with it, timewise. Only the tiny three-inch monitor mounted directly in the console showed Jakes the real-time transmission from the *New Orleans*. He had long since learned to watch it with one eye, while checking the others casually. It was rather like a ham radio operator taking down Morse code. while, simultaneously, carrying on conversation with a friend.

Jakes yawned. It was going to be a long day.

Walter Cronkite saw the red light go on, atop the #1 camera, the one used for close-ups, and he turned his eyes into its giant zoom lens.

"There's less than five minutes to separation from the space platform," he told his viewers. "You'll be hearing the countdown both in English and Russian, since the command centers are linked for today's re-entry of both vehicles. This is the final experiment in the joint program, and for the first time will give the two countries a direct comparison between their land and sea recovery methods."

The camera angle widened, and revealed Cronkite's guest, John Horne, recently retired from the Air Force, and himself a former astronaut.

Horne said, "I wish I were up there with those guys. This should be the last of the conventional missions. The space shuttle goes into service next year, and then we'll all be bus drivers."

Cronkite chuckled. "I doubt that. Colonel Horne, could you tell us what's happening up there now?"

Horne nodded. "Both spacecraft have sealed off their connecting links with the space station." He glanced at the Western Union clock off-camera. "In about two minutes, they'll unlatch the holddown clamps and squirt out just enough propulsion to swing them away from the platform."

Cronkite said, "I thought all that was done automatically."

"It is," Horne agreed. "But the Capsule Commander is ready to back up the automatics if there's any delay. The two vehicles have to drop to lower orbit by the time they pass over the Guam range. The Russians will go lower than our guys, to give them more velocity. They're trying for simultaneous landings, which is pretty tough. The Russians have quite a few more thousand miles to go, so they'll be coming in relatively fast and hot. It should be interesting."

The plastic bug in Cronkite's ear buzzed instructions to him. He nodded his thanks to John Horne, and said, "We've got signals coming in from the platform now. So let's switch to Houston Control Center and Colonel Scott Wallace."

The viewers saw a slight picture roll as the electronic magic of television transported them instantly from the Kennedy Space Center to Houston Control, in Texas. Actually, such a switch can be done without so much as a flicker of the TV picture. But the broadcasters had learned that viewers needed the picture disturbance to convince them that they had, indeed, traveled fifteen hundred miles in the flick of an eyelash.

Now they watched Colonel Wallace, a thirty-four-year-old "good old boy" from Alabama who had, as a youth, hung around Huntsville, shining shoes, selling papers, anything to earn another admission to the Space Center there. Finally, his always present face was recognized by a friendly public relations officer, he got an on-base job, and spent his high school years rubbing elbows with space experts. Untalented in science, he had a flair for publicity, and when he enlisted in the Air Force, soon began a fast-moving career in Air Force public relations that led, inevitably, to this assignment as spokesman for the NASA program.

He had to go into training every six months to retain

his thick southern accent, which, he knew, endeared him to the millions of listeners and viewers out there. At retirement after twenty years of service, only four years away, he'd still be a youthful thirty-nine, and as well known as any movie star. That exposure, plus the good connections he'd made in the past two years, would pay off handsomely.

Now, conscious of the pool camera's baleful red eye upon him, he looked up from a script that he did not need, but which assured his viewers that he was serious and careful about his work, and said, "Folks, we've got a little problem up in the Apollo capsule." He paused, just long enough to let the pang of fear touch his audience. Not too much, though. You could overdo it and get a backlash. "Nothing serious," he added. "Just a foul-up in communications. Both primary radios have failed because of an unexplained power outage." He gave the camera his famous Andy Griffith smile. It made his lower face look as if it were encircled with a necklace of teeth. "In other words, good friends, we blew a fuse." He held up a hand. "But not to worry. The backup radio's battery-operated and it's putting out a signal, not much, but enough for us to hear. Tell you what, let's listen in on Capsule Commander Buck Jones right now."

Lieutenant Colonel Jones's actual given name was Horace, but his friends had always called him Buck, after the cowboy actor, and since almost anything was preferable to Horace, he'd adopted the nickname gracefully.

His voice faded in, ". . . ninety seconds to separation. Except for the primary radios, everything is go in the vehicle. Now switching to automatic mode, and counting."

The taped counter voice, with its computerized slight Swedish accent, said, "One minute, and counting," and then began to countdown backward from sixty. "Fifty-nine, fifty-eight . . ."

Other voices overlapped the computer's counting along with it.

Scott Wallace gave a little grin. "Folks, the machines have taken over," he said. "But as long as they do the job, you and me can grab a little more time for fishing. Thirty seconds now, and everything's go."

He knew he'd get a jolt from NASA Director Ken McClure for the crack about the machines, but the people loved that sort of off-the-record attitude, so the hell with McClure. What was he going to do, fire his most popular commentator?

Jakes watched the four color monitors with one eye, and the real-time console monitor with the other. In his ear, a tiny speaker fed him the real-time audio.

"Separation," said the real-time Capsule Commander. On the big screens, that wise-ass Wallace was still joking about the machines taking over. A little clock was running inside Jakes's head. After seven clicks, the big monitors cut to animation of the two space capsules separating from the big platform 21,000 miles above the earth, and Buck Jones said, as if for the first time, "Separation."

Jakes nodded. Good. Now the capsules were officially on their way home, and he was the only one who knew that the announcement had come seven seconds late.

There were five men on the bridge of *Lamprey*. Paul Forsythe, co-owner of the vessel, and commander of its scientific studies, had come up from his cabin.

Forsythe was tall and weathered almost nut-brown by the ocean suns he had worked under most of his life. His six-three frame carried nearly two hundred pounds without a fold of flab. His hair was a chestnut brown, the ends bleached lighter by tropic suns. The wrinkles around his eyes and the laugh lines around his mouth not only did not make him look older than his forty-one years, but, strangely, gave him a younger appearance. The khakis he wore were well cut and pressed, but had been laundered so often that they were almost like suede. A careful observer would have seen tiny pinpricks on the collar where officer's insignia had once been attached.

Paul Forsythe was originally from International Falls, Minnesota, had joined the Navy at eighteen, and except for rare leaves, had not seen snow since. Which was fine with him. Paul had never been fond of the white stuff.

His voice was low and precise, with the flat midwestern accent that defies description, unless you would want to call it a mixture between Gary Cooper and Chet Huntley.

On the silent bridge, although he did not raise it above its usual quietness, his voice now seemed to echo off the useless equipment.

"What's going on, Art?" he asked of the Captain. "The ship is dead."

"Power failure of some kind," said Arthur Lovejoy.

Paul Forsythe shook his head. "Nothing's working," he said. "Not even a battery radio. It's like something drained every watt of electrical energy aboard."

Lovejoy nodded toward the open wing to the left of the bridge. Forsythe followed him out.

"You know where we are, don't you?" Lovejoy asked in an undertone that the crewmen inside could not overhear.

"More or less."

"Right in the middle of the Bermuda Triangle."

Forsythe made a "tccch" sound through his teeth. "Come on, Art. You don't believe in that fairy tale."

"No," said the Captain. "Not until now. But what's going on, can you tell me? Since when won't a generator brush produce electricity? Since when does every dry cell battery die at the same time?" He reached into his pocket and took out a strange-looking flashlight. The bulb was on top of what appeared to be a pistol grip with a large trigger. "This is an emergency boat light. You pump this trigger, and it produces enough juice to light the bulb. Watch." He began squeezing the trigger against the handle. A whining sound came from inside. But there was no light within the peanut bulb.

"It's defective," Forsythe said flatly.

"No," said Lovejoy. "I don't know why, but there's no electrical energy at all, stored or generated." He looked over the side. "And *Yellowtail* is overdue."

"They're below? Who authorized it?"

"You did. Last night. Remember? O'Keefe said he wanted to check out that new ballast distribution valve. You said okay."

Forsythe tightened his lips. Yes, he had approved the dive. But he'd assumed he would be notified before it was undertaken. He started to say something to Lovejoy, but did not. The Captain was not at fault here. This was between him and his headstrong mini-sub commander, Kenneth O'Keefe. *If* O'Keefe managed to get back. More than *Lamprey,* the mini-sub was dependent on electricity. Without power, the underwater explorer would power down and die.

Both space vehicles had passed the Guam range. The Russian capsule was nearly fifty miles lower than the Americans, and heading for the atmosphere three thousand miles an hour faster.

Radar tracking stations in Hawaii captured both vehicles and reported their sightings.

The transmissions from the Russian spacecraft were loud and clear. Those from Apollo 19 were garbled and filled with static. The only clear words that Houston could hear were, ". . . A-OK."

Jakes heard the transmission twice—once in real-time, and seven seconds later, on the pool transmission. He smiled.

As far as he knew, this was the first time anybody in the space program had used "A-OK" in more than ten years. That Colonel Buck Jones must be a real old-fashioned duck.

Scott Wallace reported, "As I said earlier, we have radio problems with Apollo 19 but the San Diego tracking station has just reported that the capsule is exactly on course, with splashdown estimated in around twenty

minutes. The nuclear carrier *New Orleans* is standing
by approximately a hundred and ten miles east of the
Florida coastline, north of the Bahamas. The past few
recoveries have demonstrated the ability of our computers to drop the space vehicle within a few hundred
yards of the recovery ship. Let's see how much Buck
Jones can shave that distance."

He paused, watching the animated display on the
monitor before him. It showed the artist's version of
Apollo skipping along the very top of the earth's atmosphere. Wallace had never flown in a space vehicle. He
wasn't sorry to have missed it. Privately, he knew his
claustrophobia would probably have made him useless
on a long mission. Even the few flights he had taken in
a jet fighter as an observer had left him weak and
drained—not from fear of a crash, but fear of himself,
of his own uncontrollable responses.

"The new heat shields allow a much faster re-entry,"
Wallace went on. "Instead of a full orbit, Apollo can
come down in less than eight thousand miles if necessary, and that's a big safety factor in case of emergency.
Today's splashdown, however, is a normal orbit and at
this moment is going strictly according to schedule. We
can expect splashdown in around seventeen minutes
and except for our radio problems, the mission is going
exactly as planned." He went on, describing the recovery operation, and at the same time keyed the "network
alert" button under his desk. This warned the TV people that he was going to be switching off in a moment or
two, and gave them time to get their anchor men ready
with guests, or visuals, or prepared commentary.

In most cases, the alert gave the networks notice that
he would be returning to the air in a few moments with
new information. Not so this time. All the alert signified
this morning was that Scott Wallace badly needed to
take a leak.

Although the "Morning" show had already gone off
the air, except for its videotape replays for Mountain
and Pacific time zones, hostess Gloria Mitchel was still

in the CBA Fifth Avenue studio. She had just finished taping an interview with Norman Mailer in which he spoke glowingly of the huge novel he had been writing for the past six years. When the camera light went out, she thanked Mailer without enthusiasm; his *macho* attitude toward women turned her off, and she had tried to make that point come through during the interview, although, in honesty, she had to admit that he had met each veiled attack with good-humored jabs of his own.

While removing her makeup in the handsome dressing room CBA had provided for her, she watched the coverage of the Apollo splashdown without real interest. Space was old hat now. It was like anything else in show business. It came on strong, peaked with high interest, sustained for X number of seasons, and then— bang! Out to pasture along with Matt Dillon and Miss Kitty.

Gloria gave NASA spokesman Scott Wallace a glare when he informed the unwashed millions that the mission was going exactly as planned. She knew, and detested, that Central Broadcasting Associates was the only "network" not taken seriously by the NASA bureaucracy. Oh, CBA was accorded the normal press courtesies, and co-operation, but it was common knowledge that while CBS, ABC, and NBC were watched simultaneously at Houston Control, CBA was not. On a visit to NASA Director Ken McClure last month, Gloria had concluded their taped interview by presenting him with a handsome Sony color receiver. She laughed at his surprise when, switching channels, he discovered that all thirteen UHF tuner slugs had been replaced by ones that would only pick up Channel Five, CBA's Houston affiliate. Sweetly, Gloria had said, "Now maybe you'll watch us too, Mr. McClure."

The Director took the joke well, and promised her that he would. But, of course, she told herself, he wouldn't. Not until CBA broke that magic number of a hundred member stations.

Idly, she switched the dressing room set over to CBS

to see what Cronkite was doing. She came in right in the middle of a John Horne comment.

". . . we've had radio problems before. And Houston Control has informed us that while we're having difficulty hearing Apollo, the crew can hear Houston loud and clear."

Cronkite said, "I suppose this is a clear reminder that, no matter how accustomed we've become to trouble-free missions, space is still a hostile environment, where anything can go wrong."

"So what's new?" asked Gloria Mitchel, switching back to her own network, where one of her two cohosts, Woodrow Johnson, was giving a color filler on food in space.

Her lip tightened. When Woody Johnson had been moved up from the drama desk of the local New York City station to take the place of *Morning*'s departing Seth Williams, the brash young man with his full red beard and suitcase filled with electronic wizardry had seemed refreshing. Now she wasn't quite so sure. He seemed to be getting more than his share of air time recently, and that was something that could not be allowed to continue. She had the word of Walter Wylie, her producer, that Woody would remain secondary to Gloria and her long-time partner, John Francis. Privately, she was aware that John had been concealing a serious illness from the network for more than a year, and increasingly she had been filling in for him on difficult location assignments. Francis saw it as the generous assistance of a co-worker; Gloria saw it as an opportunity to help consolidate her position as television's most important woman, with the obvious exception of Barbara Walters. And if they broke that hundred-station mark this year, maybe she would see what she could do about shaking up "Barb," as Miss Walters liked to be called by her friends.

Gloria switched to Channel Four, to see what John Chancellor was doing on NBC. His guest was Buzz Aldrin, and they were talking about the impressions of the Supreme Power Aldrin had sensed in deep space.

Gloria Mitchel sighed. Next time, if there *was* a next time, she'd show them how to anchor a space shot.

Sir Roger Lean came awake suddenly. Something was wrong with *Plymouth Hope*'s course.

He rolled out of his gimbaled bunk and, barefooted, padded up the three steps to the yacht's teak deck.

Even before he reached the cockpit and glanced at the compass, he knew from the angle of the sun, high overhead, that *Plymouth Hope* was headed west, with all sails aback. While he had slept, the yacht must have been hobbyhorsing, bringing her head up into the wind, where she had fallen off onto the other tack.

Lean released the main boom. The mainsail came over fully and he wore the yacht downwind and put her back on her easterly course. After breakfast, he decided, he would inspect the self-steering again. It had been wearing rather more rapidly than he liked, and small errors quickly magnified themselves into large ones. The last thing he needed, approaching the horse latitudes, was an unreliable self-steerer, because that would mean that he would have to heave to every time he needed sleep, and there would go the race.

He smiled to himself.

What race? At seventy-one, he had sailed so many races that he felt himself always in one, but this was no race, not in the ordinary sense. Instead, it was what he intended to be his farewell voyage to familiar ports and those old friends of spray and wind and deep blue water. There was no finish time to beat; no crossing record to surpass.

Roger Lean, stark naked on the sun-heated deck of the *Plymouth Hope,* yawned and stretched. It was going to be another slow, lazy day.

Wrong.

Aboard *Lamprey,* lights flashed on, and a transistor radio began to blare out a Spike Jones rendition of "Glow-Worm," with pistol shots, soprano wails, and various horn bleats sharing the audio spectrum with the closing words of ". . . and lead us on to —Love!"

"What the hell?" said Paul Forsythe.

Captain Arthur Lovejoy said, "We've got power back."

"How?"

"Who knows. Let's try to reach *Yellowtail*."

Lovejoy switched on the underwater communicator, which used a low-frequency LORAN-like transmission to carry voice communication to underwater vessels.

"*Lamprey* calling *Yellowtail*. Come in."

Kenneth O'Keefe's flat voice responded immediately. "This is *Yellowtail*. I've been calling for half an hour. Where have you fellers been?"

"Right here," said the Captain. "We had a power failure. You're overdue. What's happening?"

"Nothing serious," said O'Keefe. "Tell you when we get topside."

"How about telling us now," said Forsythe, taking the microphone.

"Negative, boss," said the mini-sub commander. "This is a party line, remember?"

"Okay. But move it. Hey, Ken, have you had any power problems?"

"Not that I know of. Why?"

"Never mind. Come on home. The coffee's on. *Lamprey* out."

"*Yellowtail* clear."

Paul Forsythe replaced the microphone in its magnetic clamp on the side of the radio. His eyes were hooded as he stared at nothing.

"What?" asked Lovejoy.

"Hell, I don't know," said Forsythe. "I've just got this hunch that something's wrong."

"Hunch?" said the Captain. "Paul, we've had half an hour of unexplained failure of all our electrical equipment. If that's not something wrong, you tell me what is."

"Let's have some coffee," said Forsythe. "Before O'Keefe gets back and drinks it all."

Walter Cronkite said, "Well, they're on their way back, John. There's no power they could use to get back up again even if they wanted to."

"No," said Horne. "But this isn't quite as critical as the high-speed landings from the moon, when there was always the possibility of a skip-out if the speed was a little too great on re-entry."

"Still, John," said Cronkite, "this is the most exciting part of a flight for an astronaut, isn't it?"

"Right. The view out the window is fantastic. The air molecules are hitting the heat shield, shoving those temperatures up to around three thousand degrees Fahrenheit, and you get this red and orange and green effect. It's like a big rainbow wrapping you up inside itself. And it all turns into a plume in back of you. It's something to see."

"Well," said Cronkite, "we'll soon be seeing the actual landing by parachute. I'm assuming they're going to be on target. All of these Apollo landings have been. The weather is good, out there in the Atlantic, off the U.S.S. *New Orleans,* and we're going there now for a report from the *New Orleans.* Our CBS newsman David Bennett is the pool reporter, and he'll be coming up in two or three seconds."

The scene switched from the two men to a long shot of the flight deck of the carrier. Hundreds of men in their dress whites waited, not quite in formation, but close enough to form ranks when given the order.

"Captain Baker," said a radar signalman. "Look at this."

The communications officer of the *New Orleans* peered at the blue-green scope of the radar unit.

A large blip was registering at 0.19 degrees.

"Where did that come from?" Baker asked.

The signalman spread his hands. "I don't know, sir. One minute the screen was clean. The next, there it was. It didn't come up on us gradually, sir. It just appeared."

"Submarine?"

"It might be."

"Keep monitoring," said Baker. He reached for the special telephone that would connect him directly with the bridge, and pressed its alert button.

"Admiral? Captain Baker. We've got an unidentified blip around forty miles north, well inside the recovery area."

He listened for a moment. Then: "Yes, sir."

Minutes later, he heard the roaring whine of jet engines as anti-sub planes took off from the hastily cleared flight deck.

"What's happening now," said John Horne, "is that they're in blackout. It began around half a minute ago. Of course, communications have been poor anyway, because of the radio failure aboard the capsule. Normal radio blackout is caused by the ionization of the air particles around the spacecraft. There's nothing physiological that happens to the crew, it's just an electronic shield around the spacecraft which radio signals can't penetrate, so they can't talk to the earth, nor can the earth talk back to them."

Cronkite nodded. "In the early days of space flight, with the Mercury missions, we always waited very tensely to hear that you guys had come through that blackout. Now we're so used to it that the suspense is sort of gone."

"It ought to be a soft landing," said Horne. "There shouldn't be very much roll out there in the water. They've only got three- to four-foot waves, which is virtually nothing for the middle of the ocean."

"Just good sailing weather," said Cronkite, chuckling.

"Right," said Horne. "Twelve to fifteen miles an hour in wind. That's great sailing weather."

"I'd like to be out there with them, wouldn't you?" asked the newsman. The tiny earpiece buzzed at him and he made a little gesture, indicating to Horne that he wanted to continue. "We've just gotten word that the Russian cosmonauts have landed successfully four hundred miles southwest of Moscow. The Russians

have sent good wishes to the astronauts for a soft landing."

Gloria Mitchel, watching—having abandoned the
rather bland coverage of her own network—sat up in
the softly lit dressing room at CBA headquarters.

Her hand stabbed for the telephone, and when she
found it, without taking her eyes off the screen, she
said, "Give me Wylie, fast."

When her producer came on the line, she said, "Walt,
call it female intuition, but I've been watching the
splashdown and something's not kosher. No, I don't
know what. Let's play it safe. Get us a camera and authorization to break network coverage if we come up
with something. And get me a clear line to Steve Gaines
in Jacksonville. Gaines. He's that kid who monitors all
the space shots, remember? We did an interview last
month."

Wylie said, "The one who got in all that trouble for
breaking the NASA relay codes?"

"The same."

"Okay," said the dour producer. "It's only our jobs."

Gloria hung up without answering. Her eyes were
held fascinated by the apparently normal coverage on
the TV screen. But underneath, her instincts told her,
something unusual was either happening now, or about
to happen.

Without being consciously aware of it, she began putting her camera makeup on again.

Walter Cronkite told his viewers, "We just got word
from radar tracking that they're running about eighteen
hundred feet long, that's barely a little over a third of a
mile, from their estimated impact point. But, John, I
understand that the Apollo has excellent aerodynamic
characteristics, and that they can tweak out that eighteen hundred feet."

"That's a small number," Horne agreed. "Of course,
once they're on the chutes, the die is cast for splashdown, because of the winds, particularly the surface
winds. But right now the guidance system gives them a

display and if the crew wants to fly automatically or manually, they can tweak out that error, if they want to get it out."

"It doesn't exactly fly like an airplane," Cronkite said.

"No," laughed Horne. "But as we'll see, it's a much better airplane than it is a boat."

The TV picture switched to what looked like a white biscuit, pulsing against the blue sky.

"That's the spacecraft itself," said Walter Cronkite. "No sign of the chutes, though. What's that pulsing effect we see?"

"It's hot," said Horne. "As a matter of fact, when it gets in the water, it's so hot that the frogmen can't touch it for the first few minutes."

"By golly, look at that," said Cronkite. This was the secret of his appeal, Gloria Mitchel admitted reluctantly. His way of honest interest and amazement at new things, never jaded, never bored.

"There they are," said Horne. "There they are. The main chutes just popped at ten thousand, five hundred. All three are out and working."

"You can come down on two, can't you, John?"

"Very reluctantly," Horne said.

The camera showed the white-clad seamen on the flight deck of the *New Orleans* clapping their hands.

"A round of applause on the *New Orleans,*" said Cronkite.

There was a hash of radio transmissions.

"That was Houston CapCom telling them farewell," said the newsman, "saying they'll see them day after tomorrow, but now it's the recovery forces that are in communications with them, with three helicopters and the ground ships—"

"I've always said, Walter," Horne put in, "that no matter how much we see from the spacecraft, those three parachutes are the most beautiful sight in view."

"They should be splashing down in just about a minute and a half," Cronkite said.

"No word yet from the crew," said another voice, that of pool reporter David Bennett.

The long-range cameras showed the Apollo capsule impacting into the deep blue water of the Atlantic.

Cronkite said, "And the splash, and they're back!"

Gloria Mitchel's phone rang. She answered with, "Yeah?"

The nineteen-year-old electronic genius in Jacksonville, Florida, Steven Gaines, said, "Hello, Miss Mitchel. They just splashed down."

"I know," she said. "Stevie, I've got a feeling that something's gone wrong. What do you think?"

He hesitated.

"Well—"

"Go on. I don't expect proof."

"That radio story bothers me. I mean, there's no way both main radios could go out. Unless somebody did something to them, that is."

"Are you copying their transmissions?"

"No, and that's funny, too. Mostly, I get better reception than Houston." The boy laughed. "And that burns them up. But today, everything from the vehicle has been hash."

She decided. "Steve, you keep listening. And keep this line open. We're paying the bill. I'm going up to Studio B, and I'll talk to you from there."

"I don't know," he said. "I got in a lot of trouble after that last interview. The government wanted to grab off my decoder, until I proved that I'd designed it myself, and that it was better than the one NASA's using."

"Five hundred dollars worth of parts," she said. She had learned that money itself meant nothing to the boy. But a credit account at an electronic wholesaler . . .

"Okay," he said. "I want to hook up a microwave link with the NBC satellite."

"Good for you," she said. "Try to find out what's happening, huh?"

"Okay."

She hung up, gave her face a quick check in the mirror. The hair job was starting to wilt, but that was too bad. She would ask Barney to soften the lighting with nets, and that would make her presentable. After all, she was a newsperson, not an actress.

"Stable Two," said Horne. "The capsule's upside down, as usual."

"Is it very hot in there, John?"

"Not too high, temperature-wise. But sort of a stuffy, humid environment. Once the flotation devices turn her over, the valves will open, and they'll get fresh air."

"I've just got the figures on how far Apollo is from the *New Orleans*. Nearly four miles. That overshot wasn't tweaked out after all, it appears."

"There we go," said Horne as the capsule was turned over in the water by what looked like two huge balloons. "What took so long, and you can see them, are all those nylon lines from their parachutes. They should have been cut free. In a strong wind, they'd make the spacecraft sail just like a boat, and the frogmen can't swim fast enough to catch up."

A huge chopper hovered just over the Apollo. Three Navy frogmen leaped out and splashed into the water near the capsule. They ducked underwater as an inflated rubber collar fell down from the chopper.

"You know, as we get to the end of this Apollo era," said Cronkite, "with a hiatus before we fly the first shuttle mission, you can't help but think back to events of the past, almost forgotten in these fifteen or sixteen years. Remember when Gus Grissom's Mercury capsule sank, and it was a very narrow escape for Gus?"

Horne said, "*He* almost sank, too. He had trouble with his life jacket, and his suit was leaking water."

As the Navy SCUBA divers encircled the capsule, Cronkite said, "Well, we learned our lesson. Now those frogmen get that collar around the spacecraft to keep it afloat. Also, the opening of hatches, the timing of that is a little different."

"No matter how you cut it," said Horne, "this isn't a

safe place to be, a hundred miles out in the ocean, and that's a long swim for anybody."

"We still haven't gotten voice communications with the crew," said Cronkite, "but there hasn't been any reference to there being a problem of any kind."

"What happens now," said Horne, "is that the frogmen get that collar around so that when the hatches open, the spacecraft is not going to fill with water and sink."

Watching the color photography transmitted by microwave from a hovering helicopter, Cronkite said, "That frogman in the yellow suit, what's he doing?"

Horne said, "He's plugging in a portable telephone so they can talk directly with the crew before they pop the hatch."

It was at precisely that moment when Jakes, in the Houston communications center, felt a chill against his neck, and realized that something was very wrong.

He heard Colonel Horne say, ". . . before they pop the hatch," from the CBS monitor, but on his own internal real-time monitor, he could see, and hear, the frogman vainly trying to communicate with the crew inside the Apollo.

He uncaged the panic button, the first time he had ever done so for a real emergency. There was no time to consult his superiors. Jakes had exactly seven seconds to decide whether to throw the switch or not. He sensed the clock in his head running, as he tried to make a decision.

The seconds were ticking away.

"Miss Mitchel?"

"Yes, Steve?"

"I don't know what's happening out there right now, but I just noticed something. I don't know how I missed it before. Maybe because I never monitored TV and the NASA signals at the same time."

"What do you mean?"

"You TV people aren't working in real-time."

"*Real* time? What other kind is there?"

"You're getting your audio/video on a seven-second delay. You know, like when you're doing a live call-in show, and you want to be able to kill the circuits in case somebody says something dirty?"

"I see," she said. Dimly, she remembered something called a "tape delay" on one of the small radio stations she'd worked at before coming to New York.

"I've got Houston on one channel," said the boy in Florida. "But they're seven seconds ahead of the stuff they're relaying to the pool coverage."

"How nice," said Gloria, making a note on one of the three-by-five file cards she used for reminders. "Thanks, Stevie."

"No sweat. I'll keep listening and—" He paused. Then: "Oh, oh."

"What?"

"Something's wrong. They're blowing the hatch from the outside."

Gloria did not hesitate. She lifted her head and shouted, "Walt! Get me on Standby."

From the control booth, he answered, "Standby in ten seconds."

Yellowtail was docking with *Lamprey*'s underwater chamber when the Navy jets arrived.

They screamed in, barely a hundred feet above *Lamprey*'s mast. On the bridge, Paul Forsythe was sweeping the radio band, trying to find the frequency the jets were using.

He hit it on their second pass. The lead plane's pilot, Commander Preston Martin, was broadcasting, ". . . yourself. Repeat, identify yourself. You are in a prohibited area."

"This is a U.S. survey vessel, *Lamprey*," Forsythe replied. "We are operating in these waters under authorization of the Department of Energy Resources."

There was a pause, then Martin said, "Hold your present course. You are in a NASA splashdown area."

"Roger," said Forsythe. "We know. But we have White House clearance."

"Maintain present course," repeated the Navy pilot.

On his tiny monitor, Jakes saw the frogmen blow the Apollo hatch. On the network feed, the frogmen were still speaking inaudibly into the telephone they had plugged into the capsule. So far, nothing bad enough to warrant hitting the panic button had happened.

But now that the hatch was open, and the frogman in the yellow suit was peering inside, Jakes watched with his hand trembling on the switch.

"Holy shit," said the frogman, clearly. "The capsule's empty. The Devil's Triangle is at it again."

The frogman slipped, and fell into the water. Another man took his place, leaned inside the capsule.

Jakes gave a sigh. This was the day he would earn his salary.

He threw the red switch and, just as he knew it would, all hell broke loose.

CHAPTER 2

To the millions watching television, less than a second after the frogmen blew the Apollo hatch their TV screens went blank for a moment, then were filled with a "STAND BY—NETWORK DIFFICULTY" card.

The time was exactly 11:06:47 Eastern daylight saving time. Network technicians scrawled in their logs, "Lost all signal from downrange."

His cuing button buzzing in his ear, Colonel Scott Wallace signaled the networks that he was ready to come on camera, and the three major nets switched to him immediately. CBA did not.

"We're having a little transmission difficulty on the *New Orleans,*" Scott said blandly. "It's hard to believe, but it looks as if somebody accidentally unplugged the main antenna cable. Stand by, we'll resume coverage of the splashdown in just a few moments."

The angry bee in his ear wasn't saying anything about main antenna cables. Scott recognized Ken McClure's normally jocular voice, now drawn tightly and speaking very fast, ordering, "Stall them, Scotty. Tell them anything. We need five minutes."

Actually, five minutes would not be long enough. When Jakes pulled the red knife switch, he had set several events into motion. First, he disconnected all audio and video feeds from downrange. They could not be reconnected without a complicated rewiring procedure. Second, he had destroyed both the endless tape loop and the video disc inside the console, wiping out any information that might have been recorded on them before he'd hit the panic button.

Finally, he had activated monstrous jamming transmitters located on Merritt Island in Florida, which blanketed the microwave frequencies from downrange to prevent any unauthorized receivers from picking them up.

This, of course, put young Steve Gaines out of business. But not before he had relayed what he'd heard in real-time to Gloria Mitchel in New York.

White-faced, she sat in the CBA news center. She didn't have much, but it was more than anyone else in the TV world had.

This was it. The big break reporters search for all their lives.

Her lips moved silently. Watching from the control booth, producer Walter Wylie smiled. He had, from years of observing performers through thick glass, learned a fair amount of lip reading.

Gloria had just whispered, "Okay, Barbara Walters, move over."

She looked at him, tapped the lavalier microphone suspended from a cord around her neck.

He nodded, gave her a signal to say that the mike was live.

"Put me on the air, Walt," she said. "Flash announcement. Something's happened to the astronauts, and we're the only ones who have it."

He glanced at the master network feed monitor. He grimaced. Then he pressed his talk-back button and said, "Hold on, baby. Ninety seconds. We just went into the number one commercial cycle."

Gloria bit back an angry reply. She was a professional. The network would interrupt its most important news broadcast, it would cut into the Super Bowl seconds before the final gun, it would even pre-empt Billy Graham, for a hot news flash. But never, not ever, would a bought-and-paid-for commercial be chopped.

She nodded. "Ninety seconds," she repeated.

That lost ninety seconds cost her the biggest news break of her career.

* * *

Agent Albert Hochling, who had been assigned to monitor Steven Gaines's telephone during the Apollo mission, had heard the call come in from Gloria Mitchel. On his hot line, he immediately contacted his superiors in Miami, and reported the conversation as it went on.

When he got to the part about the seven-second delay, his supervisor said, "Oh, Jesus."

Hochling said, "I'm looking into the main box. I can burn out his line by reversing polarity."

"No. Not since Watergate. Keep monitoring. I've got to get Washington in on this."

He reached the Director almost at the same moment as that when Captain Jakes hit the panic button in Houston.

"Ten seconds," said Walter Wylie.

Gloria Mitchel nodded. She moistened her lips.

"Five. Cameras on."

She looked up at camera #1. The Cyclops eye of its twenty-to-one zoom lens glared at her.

She smiled at it. You had to love the camera. It was sensitive, it could see your thoughts, and what it saw, eighty million viewers saw too.

Wylie gave her the "Go" signal.

"This is Gloria Mitchel," she said, directly into the all-seeing eye of the Philips color camera. "We have just learned that there's serious trouble with the Apollo splashdown. When the frogmen opened the capsule just minutes ago—"

A loud buzzer interrupted her.

The red light on camera #1 went out.

"Hold it," Wylie's voice grated through the talk-back speaker. "Gloria, don't say another word."

"But—"

"Shut up! Cover your notes. I don't want to know what you were going to say. We've been cut off the air. Attention, crew. Everybody get out of the studio. Right now. Leave your cameras heating. Clear out."

The floor director said, "Hey, wait a minute, Mr. Wylie, we—"

"Anybody who's still on this floor in the next five minutes will be put under arrest. As for you and me, Gloria, we're already there."

Numbly, she said, "Why? Who?"

"I just had President Foster himself on the line," said the producer.

"But—he can't arrest us."

Wylie chuckled. "Stick those notes down your bra so I can't see them, and come tell him that yourself. He wants to talk to you."

NASA resumed pool coverage of the splashdown operation some six minutes after the initial blackout.

Colonel Scott Wallace, his voice tense, apologized and said, "While we were off the air, the frogmen who were about to enter the capsule hatch were ordered not to do so, by Capsule Commander Jones. Apollo 19 will be taken directly aboard the *New Orleans,* where the crew will disembark for medical checkups and debriefing."

The camera shots from the carrier's deck, and from airborne units, showed the frogmen waiting, perched on the doughnut-like flotation collar that had been fastened around the bottleneck top of the capsule. The yellow-green dye marker, automatically released on impact, streamed away from the bobbing capsule, whipped into colorful bubbles by the downdrafts from the chopper blades.

Jakes had moved to a backup console. This one, however, operated in real-time, with no delay capability. Jakes was still trembling. He listened to Wallace's commentary and wondered how long they'd be able to get away with it. After all, sooner or later that capsule was going to be opened again.

Jakes had read several of the Bermuda Triangle best sellers, particularly the one by Charles Berlitz, which he found to be the most informative and, at the same time, literate. A careful, scientific man himself, he was forced to admit that some of the incidents which had occurred off the east coast of Florida seemed unexplainable. But often the unexplainable was simply the undocumented. Nature and science were not that far apart; both had invisible, often confusing, rules and laws that confounded the layman, yet were clear as printing when understood.

So, although he had no first-hand experience in the subject, Jakes did not believe in ghost ships; he doubted the existence of alternate time-planes; he could not accept the presence of UFO's, "collecting" sample specimens of humanity to be shipped off to some distant planet; he refused to believe in sea monsters, or "blue hole" vortexes that sucked down vessels without leaving a scrap of debris.

In other words, according to Jakes, the "Devil's Triangle" was just a big chunk of unpredictable water, with a hell of a lot of air and sea traffic, some of which crashed or sank.

Still, he mused, as Scott Wallace's voice droned on, describing the slow progress of the *New Orleans* toward the floating Apollo capsule, he *had* heard the crewmen broadcasting from the capsule during reentry, just before radio blackout. There was no way for them to get out of the capsule before splashdown. The hatches had been dogged down, and were blown from the outside by the explosive bolts. And once that had been done, the three men who should have been inside, alive or dead, were missing.

He watched the network coverage. The NASA cameras were now being very careful not to show the side of the capsule which had the incriminating open hatch. And their positions were farther away than the network technicians liked, he could tell. They were using electronic blowup and enhancement techniques to take the small image transmitted from downrange and fill the screen with it. But the image quality suffered and Jakes was sure that no casual viewer would penetrate the fraud.

How many people knew, he wondered? He did, and

NASA Director Ken McClure. The six frogmen in the water. The electronics men aboard the *New Orleans*.

Probably not Scott Wallace, who operated naturally in the delay mode without ever realizing that he was seven seconds behind the real world.

But that was still too many; no secret could be kept with so many people in on it from the beginning. Not unless they were all kept locked up somewhere, and of course that was impossible.

"Mr. President?" asked Gloria Mitchel.

It was his voice; she recognized it instantly.

"Good morning, Miss Mitchel," said Howard Foster. "Thank you for giving up your 'scoop' for the good of the country."

"I didn't have any choice," she said, not without bitterness. "You pulled the plug on me."

"Let's say I suggested to your news director, Mr. Abernathy, that it was in the national interest. Let me add, Miss Mitchel, that so far as I know, nobody at your network knows exactly what went wrong with the Apollo spacecraft, and I'm asking you officially to help keep it that way."

"Why? It'll come out pretty soon anyway."

His voice hardened. "Be careful what you say, Miss Mitchel. This is an open line."

"So was the one I talked over to Florida. I'm not the only one aware of what happened, Mr. President. My source heard it on open radio channels—"

The President interrupted: "I've been advised of your source, and he'll undergo much the same sort of conversation that you and I are enjoying."

She managed a laugh. "Speak for yourself, sir. Look, you're busy and so am I. What do you want from me?"

"Silence."

"How long?"

"Indefinitely."

"I don't know. I'm sorry, Mr. President, but I'm not convinced that hushing this up is the best—"

"Miss Mitchel—Gloria—"

"Please call me Gloria," she said, trying to make light of it.

"Come down to Washington. I'll tell you what. *Air Force One* is on its way back from London. I'll divert it to JFK. Have lunch on board with the Secretary of State, and come here and we'll talk."

She almost gasped. "Mr. President, are you bribing me?"

He laughed. "Blatantly."

She said, slowly, "I accept. Can I bring my producer and a cameraman?"

"With the understanding that you may not get to use them."

"Good enough, sir. One more thing—"

"Ask."

"In private, you understand—can I call *you* Howard?"

The President laughed again. "Gloria, you can call me anything you want—"

"—As long as you don't call me late to dinner," she finished.

"Apparently we have the same gag writer," said Foster.

"I subscribe to Bob Orban's joke service," she said.

"The one who worked for President Ford?" He chuckled. "I'm into Woody Allen, myself."

"Mr. President," she said, "are you stalling me on this call?"

"Guilty," he said. "By now, you ought to be surrounded by FBI men. I'm sorry, but we want to keep you away from microphones and telephones."

"That's vintage Woody Allen, sir," she said, laughing herself at what she thought was a joke.

But when she hung up and, looking around the silent studio, saw the quiet men in their subdued gray suits, she realized that it hadn't been a joke at all.

The sub-chasers orbited *Lamprey* for half an hour, until the big Navy chopper arrived.

"Our landing platform will support you," radioed Paul Forsythe. "Come aboard."

"Thank you," replied the helicopter pilot. "I have a detachment of Marines on board, sir. Will you instruct all your personnel to assemble on deck, aft. Please do not show any weapons; our men are under orders to fire if necessary."

"Oh, hell, Commander," said Forsythe. "We're not flying the Jolly Roger. Come on the hell down and let's get this mess straightened out. You're safe on board as long as you don't eat any of the cook's flapjacks."

The twin-bladed Huron chopper dipped sharply and, as gently as a floating feather, lowered itself into the exact center of the circle painted on the landing platform mounted over *Lamprey*'s bow. By then, Forsythe had broadcast instructions to the crew to assemble aft; he did not make any mention of weapons. *Lamprey* carried none that he knew of.

The chopper blades were still spinning when the Marines scrambled out of the open hatch and took up positions around the helicopter, M-16 automatic weapons pointed at the sky, but obviously loaded and ready for business.

The Navy Commander adhered to procedure. He stepped lightly to the landing platform, saluted the ensign above the bridge, and then saluted Forsythe. "Permission to come aboard, sir?"

"You're aboard, Commander," said Forsythe. "Now, what the hell is all this about?"

"Can we go to your quarters? Or—"

"The galley'll be empty. Come on, we'll have a drink."

"Coffee would be fine, sir."

"Oh, sure. On duty. Okay, but you'll wish you'd taken the drink."

Forsythe led the Navy man below to the big dining room he had called the "galley." It was as far from any crowded Navy wardroom as a private railroad car is from a Pullman compartment. Rich brown wood lined the walls, and the chairs were soft and comfortable.

"I'm Commander Stewart, sir," said the Navy man.

"No first name?"

"Allen."

"Okay, I'm Paul Forsythe. Now, what the hell is this? Why did your planes heave us to?"

"You're in the Apollo splashdown area, Mr. Forsythe."

"I know. I have specific authorization to be here."

"There seems to be some confusion about that."

"Well, contact the Department of Energy Resources. I'm under contract to them."

"For what?"

"Deep bottom exploration."

"A hundred miles off shore? What are you looking for? Oil?"

"Commander, I'm looking for anything that will keep our factories open. Oil, coal, flammable seaweed, if necessary."

Commander Stewart gave a look of surprise. "Seaweed, sir?"

"Oh, hell, Commander, that was a joke. For seaweed, read any alternative energy sources I can find. Here's your coffee." He poured it from the Silex.

Stewart looked around. "I understand you carry a submarine aboard."

"A submersible, yes. Not a sub in the true sense of the word. But *Yellowtail* can explore the bottom down to around six thousand feet."

"Didn't this vessel formerly belong to the Howard Hughes organization? Wasn't it involved with raising a Russian nuclear sub in the Pacific?"

"No, but that's a common error. *Lamprey* was built to my specifications by the Osha Shipyards in Yokohama, Japan. This is her maiden voyage. The Hughes underwater exploration vessel was scrapped last year in Italy."

"Why?"

"Ask the Hughes company."

Forsythe had poured himself a light scotch and water. He toasted it toward the Navy man. "Come on, Commander. You didn't board me to get a history of *Lamprey*. What's up?"

Stewart put down his coffee, untasted. "I'm sorry, sir. I was under specific instructions." He glanced at his watch. "By now, your entire crew is under arrest, and my staff are in control of this vessel. I must ask you to come with me."

Forsythe fought down anger. "Where? And under what authority?"

"I'm acting under the orders of Rear Admiral Walgreen, Captain of the U.S.S. *New Orleans*."

"They don't apply. I'm in international waters. You don't have any jurisdiction out here."

The Commander drew a flat .45 automatic. He did not point it at Forsythe, but it would not have taken much of a movement to do so.

"Please come along, sir," said Stewart. "The Admiral is waiting."

Sir Roger Lean did not hear the hail, but it would have been hard to ignore the shot that the cutter fired over his bow.

He dressed himself in faded blue jeans, cut off raggedly just below the knees, and came boiling up out of the cabin, still holding a shaving brush, heavy with white foam.

Peering at the Navy cutter, he shouted, "Good morning! Why are you shooting at me?"

"Heave to," called the cutter's skipper through a loud hailer. "We're coming aboard."

Lean stiffened. "In a pig's arse you are!" he said. "I fly the British flag on the open sea, and no one boards my vessel without permission."

"Heave to," repeated the cutter's skipper.

"Up yours!" called Sir Roger Lean, disappearing below again.

He was gone for perhaps two minutes, while the cutter circled, giving occasional hoots on its signal horn.

When Lean reappeared, he was fully dressed, which included his Royal Navy jacket with its five rows of ribbons and the gold braid that ran up the sleeve almost to his elbow.

In his right hand, he carried an ancient 12-gauge over-and-under shotgun. It was broken at the breech.

He held up two red cylinders. "Buckshot," he called. "Carry them for sharks." He stuffed them into the breech, clicked the shotgun closed, and cocked both hammers.

"Break off your attack," he ordered, "or I'll fire upon you."

He held the shotgun ready, aimed at the water between the two vessels.

"We're the United States Navy!" hailed the cutter. "You're in a restricted zone."

"I'm on the open seas," replied the old sailor. "State your business, or be gone. You have ten seconds."

He lifted the weapon slightly.

Lean saw hurried activity on the cutter. Someone seemed to be shouting into a radio. Someone else started to reload the small deck gun that had apparently been used for the original signal.

"Leave that gun alone," Lean shouted.

He fired a round of buckshot into the air.

The sailor retreated into the cutter's cabin.

The skipper of the cutter hailed again. "Sir, Rear Admiral Judson Walgreen, Captain of the nuclear carrier *New Orleans* sends his personal respects and invites you to join him aboard his ship at your earliest convenience."

"Why?" demanded Lean.

"We've had an emergency out here," said the Navy man, "and the Admiral wants to ask your help."

"Why didn't you say that in the beginning," asked Lean. "Can you give me a tow?"

"With pleasure," said the cutter's skipper. "May I suggest, sir, that you stow that scatter-gun?"

"Certainly," said Sir Roger Lean.

An official government limousine arrived at the CBA Building a few moments after noon. The driver wore the uniform of a chief petty officer in the U.S. Navy. He waited in the car, parked in a yellow zone, while his partner, a slim young man in a pale gray suit, entered the building, where one glance at his credentials sent him hurtling toward the thirty-fourth floor in the private elevator usually reserved for the Chairman of the Board.

Gloria Mitchel was ready; she always kept a fully packed suitcase in her office, complete with two changes, makeup, an extra set of the powerful contact lenses she needed to correct her short-sightedness, and a copy of the Modern Library edition of *Pride and Prejudice,* which she was determined to wade through before she died.

At thirty-one, Gloria had the kind of quiet, fresh-scrubbed good looks that weren't quite beauty, but were not often seen, either. Heads turned on the street, even in towns where her program had never been shown, so it couldn't be merely celebrity watching. She kept her private life submerged; *People* magazine had been vainly trying to get her to agree to a cover story for months, and were always turned away. Some said that it wasn't that she disdained the publicity, but rather that she feared what the energetic researchers might dredge up from her past.

Tall, slim without being willowy, she favored neat pants suits, basic black in evening dress, and comfortable double-knit slacks at other times.

Her dark red hair was her trademark; it had that natural, slightly waved look that achieved its naturalness by dint of daily sessions under the dryer. She was constantly experimenting with new gadgets to keep her hair under control on location trips.

"Toni is fine if you happen to be twins," she could say, "but give me a nicy swishy hairdresser."

Still, in her emergency suitcase, she had a hot curler and a can of the latest miracle spray, guaranteed to set a curl in a hurricane.

Walter Wylie was not so well prepared. His cries for help brought donations from other employees of a razor, some spray deodorant, and a ratty-looking Irish sweater.

Gloria's favorite film cameraman, Pat Crosby, was out of the building when all the action occurred. He had to be tracked down in his favorite Blarney Stone bar on Sixth Avenue, and rushed back to CBA, while his assistant packed up the tiny Canon Scoopic IV sound camera and dozens of rolls of magnetic sound-stripped 16mm color film.

The young man in the gray suit introduced himself as Secret Service agent Charles Reynolds. He glanced at his watch, said, *"Air Force One* will be touching down in less than an hour, so if we could leave soon?"

It sounded like a request, but everyone within hearing recognized it as an order. The words were spoken by Mr. Reynolds, but they had originated with the President of the United States.

When Pat Crosby was told he was going to Washington within the hour, he threw his head back and, addressing the air-conditioning ducts in the ceiling, cried, "Why me, O Lord? I've always been a faithful servant. Why me?"

And, answering in a gruff trick of ventriloquism, he assumed the Voice of God, and said, "Because, Crosby, you piss me off!"

Gloria said, "God will get you for that, blasphemer. Come on, let's put this show on the road."

The Navy driver had a small radio mounted under his dash. He spoke mysterious code words into it, and by the time they had reached the FDR East Side Drive, they had picked up an escort of two police cars with flashing blue lights.

"Hot damn!" said Gloria as they barreled through the Triborough Bridge toll booths without even slowing down. "I've always wanted to stiff these Transit Authority bastards. Imagine paying a buck and a half just to get to, for God's sake, *Queens!*"

Walter Wylie, smoothing back his black hair, said, "What did you do with your notes, Glor?"

"I ate them, what do you think?"

"Seriously," he said. "Be careful. It's bad enough that *you* know what happened. Keep us out of it."

Pat Crosby put on his standard Cary Grant impersonation. "Judy, Judy, *Judy*," he intoned. "Tell us all. Whose mail were you reading today?"

"Calm down," she said. "Just take it from me, we're on top of the biggest fucking story you'll ever see."

Crosby rolled his astonishingly blue eyes and made a wry face. "Such language, Miss Mitchel!"

"If you think mine is bad," she said, "wait until you hear what President Foster's going to say when I inform him that I mailed my notes to a trusted friend with instructions to open them and release them to the media if I'm not heard from within twenty-four hours."

"Holy shit," said Wylie. "You didn't!"

"I did," she said, settling back in the limousine's seat. She gave a little nod toward agent Reynolds in the front seat. He was scrambling for the radio microphone. "So, in the immortal words of Margo Channing, 'Hang on, it's going to be a bumpy flight.' " She laughed.

This was what counted. Not the money, not the fame. The *power!*

Captain Arthur Lovejoy fretted. He did not like the presence of armed men, even his own country's Marines, aboard *Lamprey*. He had accepted Paul Forsythe's instructions to remain calm and to accept orders from the Marine officer, but he was under no compulsion to enjoy it.

His instructions were simple. Stay away from the radios. Stay away from the engines. Sit down and do nothing.

This was a lousy beginning to what had looked like an interesting cruise.

They had taken delivery of *Lamprey* in early September. The months between then and now, the second week of December, had been occupied in final outfitting and in sailing the vessel from Japan to the Atlantic, then mating her with the *Yellowtail* submersible at a Norfolk, Virginia, dry dock.

This first shakedown cruise was scheduled to last only a week or ten days, and then the underwater survey would be undertaken in earnest. Lovejoy had been looking forward to the arrival of his daughter, Janet, who was taking a semester off from her studies at Penn State, where she was studying commercial art. And Paul Forsythe's photographer wife, Beth, had cut short her *National Geographic* assignment in Brazil to join *Lamprey* the week before Christmas.

Now what? They'd been given specific authorization to be in these waters. What had happened to all those glad-handers at the Department of Energy Resources, who had been so delighted that a private contractor had been willing to take on the incredibly tough job of exploring the ocean's depths? Forsythe had been told, in Lovejoy's presence, that the White House was solidly behind the venture.

Lovejoy looked up and saw a young Marine, his M-16 slung over his shoulder, leaning against the starboard rail with one boot resting on a polished hatch cover.

"Hey, sonny," called the Captain, "get your foot off that wood, unless you want to wax it down."

The Marine straightened. He gave Lovejoy a surprised look, then said, "I'm sorry, sir. I wasn't thinking."

"Nobody seems to be," groused Lovejoy.

Rear Admiral Judson Walgreen, who had served as a Lieutenant (jg) staff officer under Admiral Bull Halsey in the last year of World War II, had learned certain lessons well. He knew the importance of alternative positions of white-jacketed formality, combined with khaki baseball caps and fingers greasy from handling the machinery. All were tricks of command, and he also knew when to abandon them.

This was one of those occasions.

"Welcome aboard, Sir Roger," he said.

"Thank you for having me," said Roger Lean. "Some nice little dinghy you've got here."

"It serves," chuckled the Admiral. "Sun's over the yardarm, sir. Can I serve you a drink?"

"Gin and lime would be nice," said the old sailor. "I haven't tasted a lime since I left Martinique in October."

"October? You haven't been making very good time." Admiral Walgreen stopped. "I mean, you could have been home by now."

Lean nodded. "Yes. I crossed once in less than a month, but there's no hurry this time. I've been popping in and out of the various islands, you see. I don't know when I'll come this way again, so it's a good time to visit old friends, and charge up the memory batteries, if you know what I mean."

The Admiral handed him a tall gin and lime juice. "Yes, I think I do. I envy you. Sir Roger, I'm sorry to have interrupted your voyage, but we've had an unusual thing happen here this morning, and since you were in the area without specific authorization, I couldn't avoid this conversation."

"Admiral," said the old sailor, "I accepted your invitation because it was pleasing to me. Let's leave it there. Now, suppose you tell me your problem? If I can help, I will."

"This will go no further?"

"Naturally. Aren't you drinking?"

Walgreen shook his head. "Our Navy isn't as progressive as yours. Any grog on board is strictly for visitors. Sir Roger, we're out here as prime recovery vessel for Apollo 19, which splashed down just over an hour ago."

"Another one? Dear me, you Americans can't seem to stop leaping around in outer space, can you?"

The Admiral didn't smile. "After today, I'm not so sure," he said.

"What happened?"

"The Apollo capsule landed normally. Except that when we opened the hatches, we found nobody inside."

Lean sipped at his drink. "Odd."

"Impossible," said the Admiral. "We were in radio

contact with them just a few minutes before impact. There is absolutely no way they could have exited from the spacecraft, with or without parachutes. Yet—"

Lean nodded. "Yet they did."

"Or," said Walgreen, "something *took* them."

"Come, Admiral."

"You know we're within what is called the Bermuda Triangle?"

"Yes. The Devil's Sea, Limbo of the Lost, many names for the unexplained. More to the point, Admiral, we're not only within that controversial area, but at this moment, you're floating well inside what was once called the Graveyard of Ships, the Sargasso Sea."

He finished his gin and lime and put the glass down.

"Surely, Admiral, you don't think that *Plymouth Hope* and I have anything to do with this mystery?"

"No," Walgreen said heavily. "But the trouble is, I don't know *what* to think. And in a hell of a short time from now, I'm going to have to start coming up with answers."

"Naturally I'll help if I can," said the old sailor. He touched his empty glass. "Meanwhile, I wonder if I might have the other half to this?"

"There they go," said Colonel Scott Wallace. "Still inside their space suits and helmets."

The video showed three men getting out of the dripping capsule, which had just been hoisted onto the deck of the *New Orleans,* and saluting the ship's ensign. "Colonel Jones has reported to the NASA medical staff that the Apollo crew was inadvertently exposed to corrosive gasses during splashdown, and that they are remaining inside their space suits until those dangerous agents can be washed away in the high-pressure showers that are a standard part of crew decontamination. Otherwise, the crew are in excellent spirits, and glad to be back from this very important mission."

Captain Richard Jakes watched, in real-time, and thought, "Jesus, how can he get away with it?" Then, he realized, "Why, the poor bastard doesn't even *know!*"

It had not been hard to get three men aboard the Apollo to masquerade as the crew. What was difficult was finding three old space suits to conceal their identity, since examination of the spacecraft revealed that the three suits which should have been on board were missing, along with their Extra-Vehicular Activity oxygen and energy packs.

It was reasonable that the crew might have been wearing the suits, perhaps even with the helmets, during splashdown.

But it was impossible that they would have been attached to the EVA power packs. There simply wasn't room in the cushioned seats.

So it appeared that the crew of Apollo, sometime after their last transmission just before radio blackout—and before the splashdown—had gone EVA.

Except that was absolutely impossible without opening one of the hatches. And all the hatches had been dogged shut—one had to be blown by the frogmen—when the spacecraft hit the water.

It was almost as if something had reached through the metal walls of the capsule and *plucked* the three astronauts out of it, like a cosmic can opener removing prime anchovies from a tin without touching the capers or oil that surrounded them.

Secretary of State Sol Cushman greeted Gloria Mitchel warmly as she boarded *Air Force One*. "Good to see you again," he said. "What are you folks drinking?"

Wylie gave his order to the blue-jacketed Air Force steward. A martini. Pat Crosby had a dark beer, Cushman a scotch, and Gloria a Virgin Mary. To Wylie, she whispered, "Something stinky's up, and I'll be damned if I'll let them get me plastered before I find out what it is."

They were the only passengers. The press and official

personnel aboard the plane had been disembarked before the CBA car arrived at JFK's International Flight Zone.

Cushman lifted his glass. "Good luck." After a token sip, he leaned toward Gloria and said pointedly, "I understand that you're the only one here who knows what really happened."

Gloria nodded. "Right. Pat, Walt—would you mind?"

Wylie sighed and picked up his martini. "Come on, Pat. Summit time."

The two CBA men retired to the rear of the compartment, where, perhaps in defiance, Pat Crosby lit up a foul black Italian cigar.

"We've got ourselves a crisis," said Cushman. "Foster told me to level with you."

"The missing crew of Apollo?"

Cushman nodded. "It's no fake. They're really gone. Nobody knows where, or how."

"What little I heard from my source," said Gloria, "was pretty skimpy. Do you have an update?"

"It's under heavy wraps," said the Secretary of State. "We've rigged up some kind of phony crew who debarked for the TV coverage, but our story won't hold up more than a few hours. Sooner or later, we're supposed to produce the real astronauts, which we can't. In the meantime, everybody's busting their humps trying to find out what actually happened."

"What *did* happen?"

"You tell me. The theories keep coming back to one thing."

"The Devil's Triangle?"

"Yes. Except that's impossible."

"Why?"

"Things like that don't really happen."

"No?" Gloria ticked off the points on her fingers. "Triangle, Devil's Sea, the Sargasso, call it what you want, but more planes and ships have disappeared in that area than anyone can count, let alone explain."

Cushman said, "The unexplained disappearances are precisely that: unexplained. Without witnesses, survivors, it's to be expected that there isn't a pat answer for every incident. For my money, most of the so-called Triangle mystery has been generated by writers and publishers trying to cash in on it."

"How do you explain six Navy planes vanishing without a trace of wreckage?"

"Flight 19? There could be a dozen valid explanations. But without proof of any one of them, the UFO nuts prefer to call it another Triangle mystery."

"So all of the events are coincidence and natural happenings?"

"Probably."

"Well," said Gloria Mitchel, sipping at her spicy Virgin Mary, "chew on this one. Flight 19 in 1945, and the Apollo 19 mission today both carried the same number. And most Triangle mystery disappearances happened within two weeks of Christmas, which—in case you didn't notice—is only twelve days away."

Calmly, Sol Cushman looked at Gloria, and saw a beautiful, ambitious woman with the face of an angel and the soul of a longshoreman. Smiling, he said, "Gloria, are you trying to tell me that you really believe in the supernatural?"

"Hell no," she said, laughing. "What I believe in is a good story."

CHAPTER 3

"Mr. Forsythe," said Admiral Walgreen, "may I present you to Sir Roger Lean?"

"My pleasure," said Forsythe. "Sir Roger, I'm a great fan of yours. I enjoyed your last book particularly. *In the Wake of the Cutty Sark*. That was quite a voyage, especially—" He stopped.

Lean finished: "Especially for a sixty-eight-year-old crock?" He chuckled. "Don't be embarrassed, Mr. Forsythe. I find it hard today to believe that I really did it, if you want the truth."

"You beat the *Cutty Sark*'s time from Sydney."

"By a few hours. Pure luck. Somehow I scooted through the doldrums thanks to a freak weather front that made up for several bad days of track, and the wind held, so I prevailed. Oh, I took all the bows gladly, but my wife, Diana, never lets me forget that I owe most of my fame to that old boy upstairs."

Forsythe asked, "Is your wife sailing with you?"

Lean laughed. "Never. The old gel gets deathly ill. Thank God she's not one of your Women's Libbers, or she'd get the notion that I only sail to get shut of her company. Truth is, I miss her dreadfully, particularly this voyage. Not for publication, you understand. I prefer to keep my hard shell image covered with antisocial barnacles."

Forsythe nodded, and turned back to the Admiral. "Okay," he said. "Why are we here?"

Shortly, Walgreen told him what had happened during the splashdown.

Forsythe listened, frowning.

"Do you know anything we don't?" asked the Admiral.

"I don't know if it's pertinent, but just about the time your capsule was coming down, *Lamprey* lost all power."

"Generator failure?"

"Worse. The batteries seemed to have become fully discharged. The hand-operated boat light wouldn't work. Nothing that had anything to do with electrical energy would function. The effect lasted for perhaps half an hour, and then everything came to life again. In a second or so, we were back to normal."

"Do you have an explanation?" asked Walgreen.

"None."

Lean cleared his throat. "Forgive me," he said. "But the more time I've spent at sea, the more I've discovered how little we really know. This area, as you undoubtedly know, Mr. Forsythe, is the infamous Devil's Triangle, where all sorts of strange things are supposed to occur."

"Supposed is the operable word," said Forsythe. "Nothing is unexplainable if you can break the code."

"Perhaps. But haven't there been numerous incidents of total failure of electrical equipment in these waters?"

"None that I've heard of personally," said Paul Forsythe. "I don't take the ravings of science fiction writers seriously."

"But you took your own power failure seriously?"

"Of course."

"Can you explain it?"

"Not just yet. But I'll find the cause."

"If you don't?"

"But I will."

The old sailor gave a gentle smile. "Once I had all your confidence, Mr. Forsythe, and perhaps a few stone more. But it has gradually evaporated as I encountered the unexplainable, time after time."

"Are you trying to say," Forsythe asked, "that you've been through similar occurrences?"

"Many," said Sir Roger Lean. "And men I would trust—not merely with my life, but with my honor— have related others to me."

"Gentlemen," said the Admiral, "we're all in a bind. Right now, I've got seventeen men aboard this ship who know what happened. Fifteen are my crewmen, including me. You're the other two. And if we don't come up with a good answer to give the President, we're every damned one of us under tight arrest."

"On what grounds?"

"Leave it to the President to think of some."

"Bull," said Forsythe. "Granted, something strange has happened. And, as usual, the response of the government is to overract. My ship happened to be somewhere in the area, ergo, I'm involved. Ditto for Sir Roger. Admiral, don't you characters ever learn from the past? The world's too small today, communications too fast, to succeed with cover-ups."

"You don't have to convince me," said Walgreen. "But I've got my orders, like them or not."

"As a rational man," said Roger Lean, "you can't believe that Mr. Forsythe or myself had anything to do with the disappearance of your three astronauts. We were nowhere near the spacecraft, which splashed down within view of your entire crew, and was never out of their sight. Both *Lamprey* and *Plymouth Hope* were miles away, with no communications with your men, or even physical sight of them."

Slowly, Walgreen asked, "Mr. Forsythe, what time did you say your power was restored?"

"At 11:03."

The Admiral nodded. "That was exactly when you suddenly appeared on our radar screens."

Forsythe stared at him. "We were well within range. Do you mean you hadn't picked us up earlier?"

"Not a blip. The signalman was very explicit. At 11:03 you appeared well inside our fifty-mile circle. His exact words were, 'like someone striking a match in a dark room.' "

* * *

When the camera lights went out, Walter Cronkite turned to his guest.

"John," he said, "something's gone wrong."

The former astronaut nodded. "I've got the same feeling. It isn't like NASA, to whisk those guys inside without a word."

The newsman said, "I think I'll make a few calls. Thanks for the help."

"Any time," said John Horne.

Major Bruce Coburn tapped Captain Richard Jakes on the shoulder.

"You're relieved," he said.

Jakes glanced at his watch. "You're early."

"I know. McClure wants to see you. Dick—it wasn't your fault, losing coverage, was it?"

"You heard Mighty Mouth Wallace. Somebody disconnected an antenna cable."

Coburn shook his head. "No way, and we both know it. Why are we using the backup console?"

"McClure's orders."

"Dick—you hit the button, didn't you?"

There was no need for Jakes to answer. All he said was, "Take my advice, buddy. Don't ask questions."

Coburn signed the duty sheet, and replaced Jakes at the console. As the Captain slipped into his blue dress jacket, Coburn said, "Good luck."

"Thanks," said Jakes.

He left the communications center. On his way upstairs to the Director's office, he was not really surprised when two armed Air Policemen fell in on either side of him.

Their "Good morning, sir," was polite enough. But he noticed that the flaps to their service automatic holsters were unbuttoned.

The *New Orleans* was steaming at flank speed toward Jacksonville. With Sir Roger's permission, an experienced crew had been put aboard *Plymouth Hope,* which was under tow by two Navy cutters.

Paul Forsythe had radioed orders to Captain Arthur Lovejoy, instructing him to head for Jacksonville and to await further orders there.

Air Force One paused only briefly at Andrews Air Force Base, while three unidentified men boarded, and had then taken to the air again.

Strategic Air Command bases around the world went to Yellow Alert, with a third of their aircraft aloft at any given time.

Eleven nuclear submarines disappeared beneath the waves of three oceans, and began silent running toward an unknown destination revealed only to their captains and to digital computer tapes that controlled their inertial guidance systems.

Hard missile sites buttoned up.

Only a few high-level officials were aware of the latest step toward war preparedness, and while they remained silent, each wondered, "Why?" Détente had apparently been working well; relations with China were placid; Third World nations had been indulging in their usual revolutions and bickering in the United Nations, but not with any more activity than before.

There was no way this sudden action by the United States would go undetected. Conservative estimates gave the U.S. perhaps half an hour lead time before the Kremlin became aware that the focus of power had shifted abruptly.

Then what? Would this provoke the Soviets into reacting with their own military posture?

And, most of all, they wondered why President Howard Foster had taken this action little more than an hour after three American astronauts had splashed down following what had been heralded as a landmark co-exploration of space with Russian cosmonauts?

The atmosphere in the main cabin of *Air Force One* was hushed; even Gloria had been stunned when, less than a minute after they'd landed at Andrews, the front hatch opened and President Foster hurried aboard, followed by Senator Jake Dobsen, Majority Leader, and Press Secretary George "Butch" Gribbs.

Foster was gracious and friendly to the four surprised passengers, but he was obviously in a hurry to join the Secretary of State in the presidential compartment.

"I need half an hour," he said, "and then we'll talk."

Gribbs stayed behind in the center compartment and accepted a martini on the rocks gratefully.

Gloria settled on the arm of his seat.

"Okay, Butch," she said. "Give."

"Don't ask me," he said. "All I know is we're on our way to Florida."

"Florida?" yelped Gloria Mitchel. "He asked us to come down to Washington. Nobody mentioned Florida."

"Settle down, girlie," said Pat Crosby. "I like Florida in December. Ah, Fort Lauderdale, nesting place of the wild poontang."

"We're being hijacked," Gloria protested. "I've got a show to do in the morning."

Calmly, Gribbs answered, "Let's all hope the country is still here to see it."

The two reporters studied him in the sudden silence that had swooped down over the compartment.

"Jesus H. Christ," said Walter Wylie, speaking half into his now empty glass. "I think he means it."

NASA Director Kenneth McClure was a short man with a shock of jet-black hair. He had a spring to his walk that belied his fifty-two years, and in spite of his dark blue business suit, one got the impression that Ken McClure would have made an excellent leprechaun.

Twice divorced, he now gave his love to his work, and his body to an assortment of willing companions, mostly "liberated," who agreed with his rather cynical attitude that pleasure is for sharing, and responsibility is for the birds.

McClure actually had plenty of regard for responsibility—except that he only used that word now in connection with his work. He had been a very good, but unambitious, project co-ordinator in the early Apollo program until the morning he discovered his second wife, Jenna, in a laughably compromising position with his best friend, Astronaut Jim Fowler. Instead of yelling, fighting, and accusing, something seemed to snap inside McClure's mind, and he turned and left the new split-level ranch forever. From that moment on, his work became the only thing that mattered, apart from the lovely companions of a week, or sometimes a month, but never longer.

And, of course, the daily bottle of Chivas Regal. It never clouded his mind, never fouled his breath, never staggered his step. But by midnight every day, another dead Indian found its way into the trash compactor, to be ground to tiny uncompromising bits before the cycle began again with scotch and coffee the next morning.

Few were aware of how heavily he drank. It never affected his work. McClure used the alcohol to take the knife edge off a too sharp consciousness that otherwise filled his days, and sleepless nights, with a constant mental ache. Perhaps, because of its dulling effect, he only operated at 80 per cent of his capacity; but 80 per cent of Ken McClure's capacity exceeded 100 per cent of most other men's.

Now, as he motioned for Captain Richard Jakes to sit down, his mind had raced far ahead of the conversation he was beginning. It had joined the President at Jacksonville, as his physical body would do in a few hours.

"Dick," he said without preamble, "you and I are the only ones who know out here in Houston."

"That's good," said Jakes. "I didn't think Scotty was in on it."

McClure made a half-smile, half-Bronx cheer. "Mighty Mouth? He wouldn't know an elephant if it shoved its trunk up his ass."

Jake smiled. So the "Mighty Mouth" nickname had found its way up here to the ninth floor. Maybe God was fair after all. It had always frosted him, how fast

Scott Wallace had seemed to be advancing, while harder-working, and more reliable men seemed to languish.

Jakes said, "How long do you think that Academy Award performance with three frogmen in space suits is going to hold up? Ken, sooner or later, somebody's going to want to see those astronauts face to face."

"I know," said the Director of NASA. "But Big F himself is calling the shots."

"President Foster? It's that serious?"

"Dick, our whole defense system is on Yellow. That's only a phone call away from Red, and we haven't been on Red since the Cuban missile crisis."

"Why? Because three of our guys turned up missing?"

"I don't know. Do you?" He paused. "Did the crew say anything that might help explain what happened?"

Jakes shook his head. "They spoke with us just before the ionization blackout. Then nothing. How could they have gotten out of that capsule?"

"Space warp?" asked the Director. "Time transference? UFO acquisition?"

"Shit," said Jakes. "Don't shove that Devil's Triangle stuff at me."

"They're shoving it at me," said the Director. "I'm sorry, Dick. I'm as much in the dark as you are. Big F wants answers, fast. And I don't have any."

"Me neither," said the Communicator glumly. "I guess I'm under arrest, huh?"

"No more than me," said McClure.

"Is that supposed to make me happy? That we're both in the same sinking boat?"

"Not boat," said McClure. "Airplane. You and I are on our way to Florida in ten minutes. Bring your toothbrush."

"I may be Air Force," said Jakes, "but I hate to fly."

"When did you discover that?"

"The day I found out that when the engine quits, you can't flap those wings and fly away home."

*   *   *

Russian Premier Mikhail Nabov stared at the report his aide had just handed him.

"Yellow Alert?" he said, not wanting to believe the words. "Worldwide?"

"Yes, Comrade. I am sorry."

Nabov waved aside the apology. What good does sorry do when the world's secure earth suddenly drops from beneath your boots?

"Response?" prodded the aide.

Nabov bit his lip. Could this be a test of his resolve by the Americans? Or merely a practice alert as part of training?

Neither supposition seemed reasonable.

To what were the Americans reacting? Except for the renewed fighting in Lebanon, the globe was remarkably free of strife this Christmas season. Nabov knew that the Soviet fleet had recently replaced their standard nuclear missiles with individually programmed MIRVs— each missile now carrying up to nine separate warheads, each aimed at a different target. But there was no way the conversion could have been detected by U.S. spy satellites—and, besides, the new warheads had now been installed for more than three weeks. It was far too late for a response.

"None," he told the aide. "Call a meeting of the Committee of Six for eleven hundred hours."

"Yes, Comrade," said the aide. He withdrew.

Nabov studied the completely empty top of his desk. He sighed.

"It is still blindman's bluff," he said. "Except, which of us is the blindman?"

Secretary of State Sol Cushman said, "We're moving too fast. I think this is a matter for the Executive Committee."

President Foster smiled. "The Rat Pack? No time, Sol. They're putting the screws to us. If we don't react fast, the whole ball game's up for grabs."

Cushman said, "But we don't have anything hard to go on."

"We've got enough to provoke our threat of nuclear response," said the President. "If we hadn't made that response, what would we be saying to the Soviets?"

"I don't like it," said the Secretary of State.

"Nobody likes it," said the President. "But these are the cards we were dealt."

"Gin," said Senator Jake Dobsen, speaking for the first time.

Foster grinned. "I'll have a little of the same. Only, make mine scotch. Come on, let's go soothe the members of the press before they castrate poor Butch."

"If you touch one piece of my equipment," young Steven Gaines said, his voice breaking, "I'll sue the U. S. Government for one trillion dollars!"

"I'm sorry, kid," said the federal marshal who had accompanied special agent Albert Hochling to the boy's student apartment near the university. "We've got a warrant to bring you in."

"Show me on the warrant where you can break up my gear," cried the boy. "I'll go with you. But keep your stinking hands off my stuff. I built it all myself, and I can prove it."

Hochling drew the marshal off to one side. "Don't make a fuss," he said. "Let's drive him downtown, and then you can come back and pack everything up."

"I heard that," said Steven Gaines. "And what's more, so did fifty or sixty people within a mile of this transmitter." Triumphantly, he held up the tiny Citizens Band transceiver he had built into a cardboard Marlboro cigarette box. "Ten-thirty-three, trouble at this transmitter. Does anybody copy?"

A man's voice said, "Wall to wall, kid. We heard every word. Don't let those gestapo bastards scare you. We've got three mobile units outside your front door right now. You federal creeps, hear this. We're taking videotapes, so if you push that kid around, your ass is mud."

The federal marshal's mouth gaped open.

Hochling, who had been around the new electronic culture longer, merely sighed.

"Smile," he said to the marshal. "You're on Candid Camera."

Captain Albert Lovejoy sat in the main galley of *Lamprey,* sipping coffee with the mini-sub commander, Kenneth O'Keefe. The underwater expert, his long blond hair brushed back casually from one eye, put a growl into his flat Nebraska voice as he said, "How the hell can they do this to us, skipper?"

O'Keefe was nearing fifty, but he had the hard-muscled body of a man in his thirties. He had been diving most of his life, a career that had, oddly enough, begun doubling for Lloyd Bridges in a television series called "Sea Hunt." O'Keefe resembled the actor superficially, and while Bridges did much of his own underwater work, there were always pickup sequences that didn't warrant paying the whole cast and crew. In the year O'Keefe had worked on the show, he became a fast convert to underwater exploration, abandoning his acting career to follow it.

Lovejoy said, "It must be something big, Keefer. Otherwise we'd hear Paul screaming from here to the White House. I got kind of pissed off when those Marines boarded us, but they're good kids, just following orders. So I guess it's best to hold back until we find out what the score is."

"No further word from the boss?"

"Only that he'll meet us in Jacksonville."

"Is this going to delay the full survey?"

"I hope not. Why? What did you find down there."

O'Keefe hesitated. "I sort of wanted to lay this on the boss first," he said. "He's earned it. We'd all of us be sitting on the beach if he hadn't put this operation together."

"I agree," said the Captain. "Let's wait."

O'Keefe made an impatient move. "Ho, ho. You know it's boiling up inside me like lava."

"Okay," said Lovejoy. "Let's *not* wait. Give, you crazy Irishman."

"A road," said O'Keefe.

Lovejoy stared. "A what?"

"A goddamned paved road."

"As in highway?"

"You heard me."

"That's crazy."

"No, it's down there. I put a zap on the inertial guidance tape. I can go right back to the very inch where I first saw it. Art, it's all crapped up with sand and kelp, and, damn it, aluminum beer cans, but it's *there*. An actual, honest-to-god paved road, just like Highway One through St. Augustine."

"You're sure?"

"What else could it be? A slab of concrete, wide enough for two cars. No superhighway, but obviously man-made . . ."

He paused. "Well, maybe not *man*-made. But sure as hell not created naturally, either."

"Underwater lava flow?"

"No way."

"Keefer, you've been reading too many of those Anthony Dix books about Atlantis and the Bermuda Triangle."

"You know I never read. Ruins the eyes."

Lovejoy stared down into his coffee mug. "Why didn't you say anything before?"

"You mean before they took Paul away? How? In front of that committee of Marines and Navy types? What business is it of theirs? Besides, they'd have locked me up as a psycho. No, this is ours, Art. Let's keep it on ice until they give us back *Lamprey*. We'll go on the full survey and really dig."

"Well, if you're right," said the Captain, "that sort of makes oil exploration look unimportant."

"Yeah," said the mini-sub Captain. "Maybe we'll make a movie instead, and all of us get rich."

"Wouldn't that be nice," said Lovejoy.

"Naturally," said O'Keefe, "I'd play the leading role."

"Without doubt," said Lovejoy. "Opposite Raquel Welch, of course."

O'Keefe leered. "We'll go for an 'X,' good buddy."

The Captain thought O'Keefe was joking about the movie.

He wasn't.

It was nearly midnight before everybody concerned with the Apollo 19 splashdown had gathered in a hastily commandeered Ramada Inn motel wing in portside Jacksonville, Florida.

Air Force One had arrived early in the afternoon, landed without advance clearance, and pulled to the far side of the runway, where government vehicles were waiting for those aboard to disembark without being seen by either the public or by airport personnel.

The short flight down the eastern seaboard had been a strained one; when President Foster and his group had joined the newswoman, Gloria's producer and cameraman, and the uneasy press secretary, the respect with which he was greeted was tempered by the urgency of the questions he was asked.

"Sir," said Gloria Mitchel, "you asked me to come to Washington. Now we're going to Florida. Why?"

"The game has changed," said Foster. "Mr. Wylie, Mr. Crosby, I'm sure you are aware that something very unusual happened during this morning's splashdown."

"The Russians pulled the plug in the Atlantic, and our noble spacemen went down the drain," quipped Crosby.

As the President frowned, Wylie said, "Hey, hey, hold it down. This is no joke."

"Thank you, Mr. Wylie," said Foster. "I'm afraid you're right. What happened isn't a matter for joking. You see, what your Miss Mitchel learned from a source in Florida was that, once it impacted in the Atlantic, the space capsule was apparently found to be empty."

Crosby straightened. "Holy shit," he said.

Foster went on: "Luckily, very few persons became aware that anything unusual had happened. Less than forty, in total. All of them, including yourselves, are under supervision."

"Don't you mean, arrest?" asked Gloria.

The President shook his head. "No. I'm no dictator, to deprive you of your liberty. When we have all given some time to this problem, if you find that you don't agree with the way I suggest the matter be handled, you can go right ahead and make your case to the public any way you please. All I ask is that you give me a chance to examine what has happened, and to propose certain responses. After that, it's up to you. Is that fair?"

Slowly, Gloria nodded.

"Thank you," said Foster. "Actually, there are presently three stories floating right now about the splashdown. The first is what a few people thought they saw—an empty capsule. The second story is the one we set up for the mass audience in order to buy time—that the three astronauts were coming aboard the *New Orleans* in space suits because they were contaminated by leaking gas within the capsule. Three Navy frogmen played the roles in backup suits that were aboard the carrier. Then there's the third story, the true one, which only a handful of us knew until this moment. It's the one we'll finally have to release, because it will be impossible to hush it up. We are only holding back until we are absolutely sure in our minds that we know what actually happened."

"When do we hear that one?" asked Gloria.

"Right now. You won't like it."

"Try us."

"All right. Our men haven't vanished into the Bermuda Triangle. But they're not safe aboard the *New Orleans,* either."

"Where are they?" Gloria asked softly. Her voice carried a threat. Either the President leveled now, or all deals were off.

He recognized the threat. And he answered her, and the others, directly.

"All three are dead. Fried to a hard black dust, inside the capsule. We don't know how, or why. But they didn't vanish. They were simply cooked down to a few lumps of what looks like coal."

CHAPTER 4

The two military men aboard Apollo 19 had both been married: Colonel Horace Jones to the former Barbara Fosse; Commander Joseph Pelham to the once Shirley Green. The Jones family consisted further of two boys, aged eleven and eight; the Pelhams were childless.

Civilian astronomer Dr. Sydney Loren was a thirty-six-year-old bachelor. He had lived in a Houston condominium near the Astrodome; the two military men owned homes, with heavy mortgages, in the nearby suburb of Pine Hills.

The First Lady, Patricia Foster, had flown to Houston at her husband's request. She arrived secretly, and awaited only a telephone call from the President to send her on one of the hardest missions she had ever undertaken, in more than thirty years of supporting Howard Foster's political life.

That of telling two unsuspecting wives that they were suddenly widows.

When Senator Jake Dobsen lost his deep Kentucky accent, it was a sign that things had gotten serious.

In the sealed-off conference room of the Jacksonville, Florida, Ramada Inn, his voice had the same clipped, accentless character of a good mid-Atlantic radio announcer.

"I'm afraid," he told Gloria Mitchel, "that I can't find it in me to be as charitable as the President. We're sitting on a matter of such great importance as to be a turning point for this nation if it's handled wrong. Under those conditions, I wouldn't hesitate for a second to lock every one of you up for the duration. I hope he's right in relying on your good sense and patriotism."

"My," said Gloria, "patriotism?"

"An old-fashioned word. But maybe you still believe in what it means, even if you sneer at the word itself."

Gloria flushed. "Senator, I wasn't—"

"Do you know why this country has lost so much ground in the past ten years or so? Because we've forgotten that we're a family. A family sticks together, no matter what. Oh, we have our private squabbles and even out-and-out fights, but when some outsider comes butting in, we join together. Or at least we used to."

"It's a little hard to join together to condone a My Lai," Gloria said. "Or a Watergate. We've had a President resign just one step ahead of getting kicked out of office. What are we supposed to do, stick our heads in the sand and pretend it never happened?"

"Of course not," said the white-haired Senator. "I'm not speaking of actions, but of *attitudes*. Under no circumstances should those despicable acts have been concealed. But what I'm not modern enough to understand is the apparent glee with which so many of our own people uncover such misdeeds."

Gloria murmured, "We have met the enemy, and he is us."

"What's that?" asked the Senator.

She smiled at him and said, "The gospel according to Chairman Pogo."

As the *New Orleans* cruised toward Jacksonville, a Navy chopper had airlifted Admiral Walgreen and his two "guests" on ahead to join the group waiting at the Ramada Inn.

Paul Forsythe was surprised, and pleased, to meet the President. The two men had lunched twice in Washington, while Forsythe was putting his *Lamprey* proposal into a final form for the Department of Energy Resources, and Foster had been very enthusiastic about it.

"This is a job that rightly belongs in the private sector," he had told Forsythe. "Whenever big government gets into something like this, it invariably takes twice as long, costs four times as much, and angers everybody it was originally intended to help." He had wished Forsythe the best of luck, promising to give that luck a little boost every now and then.

"Me and my big mouth," he now said, without prompting from Paul Forsythe. "How was I supposed to know that you'd be in the wrong place at the wrong time when all the wrong things happened?"

"No harm done," said Forsythe. "This was only a shakedown cruise."

The President seemed genuinely honored to greet Sir Roger. He pumped the old sailor's hand and said, "I'm sorry it takes a bad day like today to cause our finally meeting one another. Like millions of my countrymen, I hold you in great admiration."

"I'm flattered, Mr. President. The only fly in my pudding is that I'm positive when I try to dine out on this story, not a soul will believe me."

"That's the dark side," said the President. He looked around. "Admiral, are we all here?"

"Director McClure and one NASA officer have just checked in at Point Able," said Press Secretary Gribbs, before Walgreen could answer.

"Admiral?" persisted the President.

"Sir," said Walgreen, "I didn't realize that you wanted all of my crewmen who were . . . associated with the incident."

"Where are they?"

"Aboard the *New Orleans,* isolated of course."

"Under guard?"

"Yes," said the Admiral, in a voice so low that it was almost inaudible.

The President did not force the issue; he realized how repellent it was for Walgreen to place trusted subordinates under what amounted to arrest.

Foster turned back to Lean. "The dark side I mentioned, Sir Roger, is that I'm going to try to persuade everybody here to forget this meeting ever took place." He looked at his watch. "Give me half an hour, once our men from NASA arrive, which should be any second."

"My time is yours," said Lean.

"Yeah." Gloria mumbled to Wylie, "but mine is running out. If I don't get on a plane in the next couple of hours, I miss tomorrow's program, and wouldn't that put a smile on Woody Johnson's face?"

Wylie said, "Give Woody a chance, Gloria. He's learning. We all have to start somewhere."

"Let him start on somebody else's dime," said Gloria.

There was a tap at the door, and Ken McClure was admitted, with Captain Jakes. The Secret Service men were briefly visible through the half-opened door, before it was locked again from the inside.

"That's the lot," said Butch Gribbs.

"All right," said Foster. "Here it is. There's been a tragedy aboard Apollo 19. At first it was reported that the capsule splashed down empty." He looked around. "Some of you may still be operating under that assumption."

NASA Director Ken McClure nodded. "Captain Jakes and I. It was the Captain here who disconnected the downrange links before any transmissions were able to get out of the recovery area."

The President said, "Good work, Captain. You acted correctly. But later information indicates that the capsule wasn't empty after all. We don't know yet what happened, perhaps a leak in the heat shield, but apparently a momentary burst of heat, so intense that it literally vaporized our men, swept through the capsule during radio blackout."

Jakes looked puzzled. "That's dreadful, sir. But why did we hush it up? Why the masquerade with the three phony crewmen?"

"We had to be sure," said the President. "That's the danger of our open publicity policy. At first we thought we had a mystery on our hands, and naturally we didn't want that to start snowballing; by the time we discovered what really happened, the masquerade was already under way. We've delayed since to be absolutely certain. Jones and Pelham were married, and Dr. Loren has parents and other close relatives. My wife is already in Houston, to break the bad news to the wives when I so advise her."

"Oh, my God," said Gloria. "Poor Patricia."

"I myself will call Dr. Loren's family," Foster went on. "But only when I am positive in my mind that there is no doubt. The—remains . . . well, they're almost impossible to identify. We airlifted the best pathologist in Washington to the *New Orleans,* and he's studying them now. We'll know in minutes." He paused. "No, that's not completely true. We *know* right now. But we'll have confirmation before releasing the news."

Gloria said, "Excuse me, Mr. President, but what's the big secret? If we lost our men, and their families are notified, it'll get out whether or not I put it on the air."

"No one's stopping you from that," said Foster. "What I'm asking from you is your promise that you'll make no mention of this—"

"This cover-up?" Gloria provided.

"If you want to call it that. Our space program has always been open, and we'd like to preserve that credibility."

"How open?" she asked. "With a seven-second delay and a panic button to cut us off the air?"

"That's nothing more than you yourself do with your so-called 'live' interviews and call-in programming," he replied.

"But we don't hide the fact."

"Don't you? I can't recall any such programs announcing to the viewer that what's being seen actually occurred a few seconds earlier."

She colored. "It's assumed."

"And isn't it just as fair to assume, if in nothing more than humanity, that we might not want to broadcast the death cries of our men in case of accident?"

Sandwiches and drinks were brought in shortly after darkness; Foster made aimless conversation, skipping around from détente with the Soviet Union to the presumption that the Israelis were within months of testing their own nuclear weapons openly. But the impression was clear that he was merely marking time . . . waiting.

Gloria had asked, "Whatever's happening, I get first crack at it?"

"Only after the families have been notified," said the President.

"Fair enough. And I don't see any reason to mention this little side trip to Florida, if you want it kept secret."

"Thank you," said Foster.

Shortly before 8 P.M., the President gave a slight nod, and George Gribbs said, "Let's go outside for a few moments; it's not too chilly."

"Like hell," said Gloria. "I'm staying near the phone."

"Come on," urged the President. "We'll throw Butch into the pool."

"That's a different story," she said. "Right behind you, Mr. President."

The swimming pool was heated, and now steamed heavy fog into the air above the brightly lighted water. Foster made a gesture toward the floodlights, and a Secret Service man vanished into the pool house. The lights went out.

Sir Roger Lean stood close to Paul Forsythe and said, "He's waiting for something."

"You said it," answered Forsythe.

"I fear he hasn't told us the complete truth," said the old sailor.

"And what else is new?" Forsythe began. The words died in his throat.

Above them, the dark night sky suddenly blossomed with a huge globe of flaming yellow light. It grew, in microseconds, from an eye-piercing slash through the black velvet of the cloudless sky to a horizon-filling lightninglike flash that flickered and nearly died, then blazed again with twice the intensity.

"Holy Mother," whispered Admiral Judson Walgreen. "That looks like a nuclear blast."

"More than one," said NASA Director Kenneth McClure.

Pat Crosby made a dive for his camera, still in its gadget bag inside the conference room.

A Soviet Service man blocked his path. "No pictures," he said.

"Up yours," yelled the cameraman. He kicked the agent in the ankle and as the man went down, jumped over him and began fumbling in the gadget bag.

"Let him take his pictures," ordered the President. "That thing up there is hardly a secret from anybody within this hemisphere."

Crosby came out of the room, with his film already churning through the gate at twenty-four frames a second, with sync sound being recorded by the directional microphone mounted on top of the Canon Scoopic. Every time he got the chance, he let the lens drift down from the pyrotechnics to pick up a zoom close-up of the President. He hoped nobody would notice that he was also recording everything that was said.

"What in the name of God was that?" asked Paul Forsythe.

"A warning," said the President. "Let's go inside. I have some unpleasant calls to make."

"What about me?" Gloria Mitchel almost shouted.

"Butch, take her to the station. I have eight-fifteen, on the nose. We need thirty minutes to contact the Apollo families." He reached out and shook Gloria's hand. "You can go on the air at fifteen of nine exactly. And thank you."

"What about that, up there? What do I say about it?"

"What I said. It's a warning. That's all I know about it."

"You mean, that's all you'll say!"

"Gloria!" warned Walter Wylie, shocked and angry.

Foster said no more, merely went back into the conference room, walking like a very old and very tired man.

Gloria, who had followed him, asked gently, "Now you have to call Patricia?"

He nodded.

"So you're sure? The astronauts? They're dead?"

"They're dead," he repeated, and his voice was as bleak as the coldest tomb.

Premier Mikhail Nabov learned of the bright flash in the night sky less than forty seconds after it occurred.

"What could have happened?" asked one of his top advisors on the space program. "What was it?"

Without knowing he was repeating words that had been uttered half a world away, Nabov said slowly, "A warning, my friend; a warning that perhaps the fox has not been so clever after all."

"I am sorry, Comrade," said the space official. "I do not understand."

Nabov chuckled. "Be glad that you do not." His voice changed, and the sadness that had been in it vanished. "Advise me of any further activities."

He hung up the old-fashioned French-styled telephone without waiting for an answer.

Across Red Square, waiting in the apartment assigned to the account of the Bolshoi Ballet, Anya would be making tea. Even at sixty-five, he still came to her at least twice a week, and it had already been three days since his last visit.

"Not tonight, dear Anya," he thought. "Do your exercises like a good girl, stretch and preen that supple body, prepare to make an old man happy. Then, one day, you will be free to do the same for many young men, and my heart will go with you."

He reached under his desk and pressed the single button there that would bring all his aides to an immediate conference.

The important question right now was—are the Americans still holding at the Yellow Alert, or have they escalated to Red?

Premier Nabov sighed. "If they have gone to Red," he thought, "we are all lost."

Both the Pentagon and NASA denied there had been any nuclear explosion in outer space. While the bright flash was "still under investigation," it was the official position that a fast-moving asteroid had skipped into the earth's atmosphere and had been smashed down to its component atoms by friction and impact.

Privately, both agencies were well aware that the Russian space platform was no longer in orbit around the earth. Perhaps the asteroid had given it a direct hit. But that was up to the Soviets to conjecture about, if they chose to discuss it.

The Russians did not.

The mystery had barely had time to begin to deepen when the Central Broadcasting Associates network cut into the middle of their latest sitcom, "Cajun Bride," with a flash announcement from Gloria Mitchel.

"I'm in Jacksonville, Florida," she told viewers. "And I'm afraid I have very bad news."

At her request, the network was rolling the edited reel of splashdown tapes, and—sitting in the small booth in the Jacksonville television station—Walter Wylie was calling for cuts from the "talking head" shot of Gloria to footage that had been recorded earlier in the day.

Now the viewers saw the three parachutes of the Apollo 19 spacecraft deployed, against the deep blue sky above the Atlantic. Gloria, voice over, said, "At this sight, we all cheered, because it meant that our men were back home safe and sound."

The scene cut back to her. "But when the capsule was opened, it was at first thought that it was empty. So you saw these scenes—" Now the viewer watched what appeared to be three astronauts in space suits climbing out of the capsule on board the carrier. "They were fakes, because at first it was feared that the three crew members had somehow become victims of the mysterious Bermuda Triangle, in which waters the spacecraft had splashed down."

Her voice lowered. "In minutes, the truth was learned. A leak in the heat shield had sent flames reaching three thousand degrees Fahrenheit scorching through the capsule's interior. There were no survivors. In fact, and there is no easy way to say this, there were almost no remains, which accounted for the original impression that the capsule was empty."

The taped sequences continued, and Gloria gave the rest of the story, eliminating only the meeting with the President and his companions. She had timed it almost perfectly.

But Gloria had an extra bit of whipped cream for the newsbreak's wrap-up.

Against a Slo-Mo replay of the splashdown, she narrated, "As the price for space exploration, we have been prepared to pay—and have paid—the expected high costs of achievement. But as this latest tragedy rocks the nation, many are already asking—what about those unanswered questions? Why did a supposedly perfect heat shield fail at precisely the critical moment of re-entry? And why was that re-entry aimed at the most controversial spot of water in the world, the infamous Devil's Triangle, which is credited with the unexplained disappearances of hundreds of seamen and fliers? *Is* there some mysterious force that bends time and space, wreaking havoc on those unlucky voyagers who try to cross its boundaries? Only when we find an answer to this last question will we ever really learn what happened to the ill-fated crew of Apollo 19. This is Gloria Mitchel, inviting you to join me on the *Morning* program at seven tomorrow, when I hope to begin unraveling some of these many deviling questions about the so-called Devil's Sea. Our hearts go out to the families of the men who were lost, and it's my promise that I will devote myself to seeing that we don't lose any more."

President Howard Foster, watching on the monitor in the forward cabin of *Air Force One,* which had just crossed the invisible line that separates the coasts of Georgia and South Carolina, shook his head and turned to Jake Dobsen.

"You know, Jake," he said, "we're flying smack the hell through that Devil's Triangle right now."

"You keep on lying the way you been," said Jake, his Kentucky accent comfortably back in action, "and that devil's going to *get* you."

SPLASHDOWN   83

"I didn't have any choice," Foster said, reaching for a drink.

Dobsen passed it to him. "Yeah, I know. That's always the hell of it."

The Secretary of State came forward from the communications room.

"Oh, shit," said the President. "Here comes the Prophet of Doom. Is it bad, Sol?"

"Couldn't be worse," said Cushman.

Jake Dobsen took a big slug of his own drink. "Don't tell me the Russians are going to an alert."

"No, they're keeping a low profile. I don't think we've got anything to worry about there. They tried to pull a fast one, we nabbed them at it, and if we don't brag about how smart *we* were, they aren't going to be anxious to reveal how two-faced *they* were."

"Then what is it?" asked Foster.

"I've got tracking reports. Guess where the wreckage, or debris, whatever's left, is going to come down?"

Foster forced a laugh. "Please, God, right on top of San Clemente?"

"Negative. Within a hundred miles of our original Apollo splashdown zone, in the Atlantic off Florida."

"Oh, crap," said the President. "Here we go again with more of that Devil's Triangle guff."

"Don't take it so hard," Jake Dobsen suggested. "That Triangle guff is helping us get this foul-up so mixed up that nobody'll ever get close to the truth."

"You may be right," admitted Foster. "We've already got three versions of the story floating. More important, we bought the ten hours or so that we needed. Every hour from now on is pure gravy. And with any luck, the truth never *will* come out, or if it does, it'll be just as fantastic as all those other smoke dreams, and won't be believed anyway."

"Unless," said the Secretary of State, and repeated it: "Unless—"

"*Lamprey*," the President said.

"She's scheduled to explore those waters."

"It figures," said Foster. "This is the first goddamned

time we've ever gotten major industry and the government together on a project that might work."

"Too bad," said Cushman. "We'll just have to find oil someplace else."

Foster nodded slowly. "You're right. We can't take the chance. Get me Henderson—" He stopped, looked at his watch. "No, it's late. Contact him and the other key people in Energy Resources. Set them up for breakfast."

Jake Dobsen said, "What are you going to do?"

Glumly Foster answered, "What *can* we do? We're going to have to pull the plug on Paul Forsythe and his underwater exploration." He looked down at his empty glass. "Butch, get me a refill. I think this is going to be one of those nights."

"I'm right behind you, Mr. President," said George Gribbs, reaching for the scotch.

Waiting comfortably for the arrival of their respective vessels, Paul Forsythe and Sir Roger Lean sipped Navy Grogs and ate *ramaki* at Jacksonville's version of a Polynesian restaurant.

"This makes a pleasant break," said Lean. "I don't carry much in the way of spirits on board, principally because I lack the willpower to cork a bottle again once it's been opened."

"What's it like out there alone?" asked Forsythe.

"It's funny, y'know," said the old sailor, "but I've never really been sure. Oh, I've written about it, and spoken of it, but each day is so different and yet the same, it's almost impossible to sum them up with some simple label, like 'lonely,' or 'spiritual,' or 'boring.' It's all of those, yet more."

"I suppose it'd be silly to ask, 'Why?' wouldn't it?"

"No, but I'm afraid you wouldn't get any more complete an answer. One does what one must. Why did you embark on this fantastically expensive venture of yours? Surely the risk is far more than you can ever hope to recoup. Shouldn't the voyage of *Lamprey* have been funded by government?"

"No way," said Forsythe. He ate one of the *ramaki,* pieces of crisp bacon wrapped around chicken livers and water chestnut. "I'm for as little government involvement as we can arrange. We've built *Lamprey* because we see a need for such exploration, and while we're obliged to co-operate with government agencies, we're perfectly willing to take big risks because we're looking for big profits."

"But the cost must be enormous."

"Just under five million dollars, to date."

"With no subsidy?"

"Sir Roger—"

"Belay the Sir," said the old sailor. "I'm reluctant to use it, except that I feel honored because of the Queen's having bestowed the title. Remember Ian Fleming's James Bond? He refused the garter because he knew, realistically, that accepting knighthood would double the cost of everything from his abominable version of a martini, to his gratuity to the men's room attendant. It's an expensive three letters, Mr. Forsythe. S. I. R. I refer to them as Send Increased Revenue."

Forsythe chuckled. "Paul, then. Okay, Roger, what I was going to ask is, would you have accepted a subsidy to build *Plymouth Hope?*"

"Instantly."

"With this Catch-22—someone could then tell you what color to paint her, how fast to cruise, *where* to go, and how many voyages you cou'd make?"

"Under those rules? Of course not."

"My point is made," said Forsythe.

Shortly after midnight, Eastern daylight saving time, a hulking object, glowing pale red, spun out of a thunderhead above the ocean northeast of Bimini Island in the Bahamas, hit the water with a hissing impact that boiled thousands of fish in that first second, and sank out of sight as the shock waves of its arrival began to spread.

On Bimini itself, squatting placidly at the end of his fishing pier, jutting out into the bay at Alice Town, Joseph Horatio watched the meteor-like thing from outer space cross the horizon and disappear beneath it.

Horatio could not tell how or why he had known the object would be coming. Like everyone else on the island, he had run out onto the beach when the skies had blazed bright orange earlier in the night. But while most had disappeared back into their homes, or the rude bars, or the plush tourist cabins, Joseph Horatio had squatted down to wait.

He was very good at waiting.

Now that he had seen what he somehow knew he would, he got up, his old legs aching, and padded down the pier to the battered fishing schooner that floated there. He would take a few hours of sleep, and when the offshore breezes began in the morning, he would go and see what was waiting out there in the middle of the Sargasso.

CHAPTER 5

Beth Forsythe found out before her husband did.

She took the call in her regular room at the Carlyle Hotel in Manhattan. She had flown in from South America the night before.

The reporter who called her did it as a friend, not in search of a comment. Beth, who was packing, took the call in her bikini panties and no top, which was the way she usually lounged around the hotel room—always making sure the door was on its chain, of course. At twenty-nine, Beth had the fresh, scrubbed look of a young Ingrid Bergman. Her dark hair was short and practical, but still feminine. Her eyes were jet black, and surrounded by lashes that drove most fashion models insane with jealousy. Her well-muscled body was still slim and graceful—the hours of swimming with which she had built its strength had not contributed ugly knots to biceps or calves. Although Beth had been born of Lithuanian parents in Wilkes-Barre, Pennsylvania, she had no trace of the regional twang in her soft voice, which had already earned several hundred thousand dollars for its owner, narrating films about nature.

Beth began her career as an actress; by twenty she had discovered the camera, and only a year later started what was to become her specialty, underwater photography.

It was while photographing the nuclear submarine *Gettysburg* that she met its bachelor Captain, Paul Forsythe. Six months later, they were married, and in another year, Paul had been retired due to injuries received while trying to save a crewman trapped in a

missile silo accident caused by a violent sea that had
almost capsized the *Gettysburg.*

Paul had many civilian job offers; the one he accepted was to help design and build *Lamprey,* financed
and constructed by Saito Osha, owner of the Osha Shipyards in Yokohama. Forsythe's terms had been hard,
but fair: he would collect a living wage, but when the
vessel was commissioned he would be half owner of her,
hull, earnings, and salvage. Some called Osha insane for
giving away so large a share; the multimillionaire
merely laughed and pointed to Forsythe's record in underwater vessels, and reminded his critics that one
seemingly minor change Forsythe had suggested had
saved several million yen in construction costs.

Paul and Beth had a small apartment in Georgetown,
which served as a base for both, and as a home when
they were together in Washington. But in the past three
years, he had been in Japan much of the time, and between assignments for the *National Geographic,* she
joined him there.

Beth was quick to deny their marriage was in any
way similar to that of Shirley MacLaine and her husband, Steve Parker—in which the husband resided in
Japan while the wife worked elsewhere and came to Tokyo for occasional visits. "Steve and Shirley have something that works well for them," she said. "Paul and I
have something else, maybe a little more old-fashioned.
He's the boss, and when he whistles, I jump."

Her feminist friends criticized her for such state-
ments. "For one thing," said one, "it's just not true.
Beth's her own woman, all the way."

Beth had her own views about both sides of the
"equal rights" issue, but she kept them to herself, and
went about being her "own woman," in her own way,
frequently to the despair of all involved.

Now, as Harry Gould of the Washington *Post* told
her, "Honey, there's dirty work afoot," she listened
while her mind raced, searching for some way that she
could help. "Big F has everybody who's anybody in the
Department of Energy Resources up there at 1600 Penn-

sylvania, scoffing down sausages and sharpening their knives for your hubby."

"Please translate," said Beth, taking a long sip of the No-Cal ginger ale that was her most conspicuous vice. Once, a young doctor who had spent an afternoon with her aboard a friend's yacht had suspected acute diabetes and had ordered her to run, not walk, to the nearest hospital. Alarmed, she had, and tests revealed that all she suffered from was an insatiable craving for No-Cal ginger ale and that there was nothing whatsoever wrong with her pancreas, or (as leered a young male intern) anything else in the immediate vicinity.

"In plain English," said Gould, "the word's being leaked that ER's going to cancel the underwater contract."

"They can't!" said Beth. "It's already been signed."

"They will," promised the newspaperman. "What can Paul do, sue the government? Lots of luck."

"If he doesn't sue, *I* will," she said.

"Beth," said Gould quietly, "my ass is out a mile on this one. My source leaked it to me because he thought the *Post* might be able to keep them from screwing a good man."

"Can you?"

"I'm afraid not. We can embarrass them afterward, but that won't do Paul a nickel's worth of good. Get hold of him. This is the straight—" He hesitated.

"Straight shit," she provided.

"Nothing else. Maybe he can come up with something. Cover his ass some way. I'm sorry, hon. I wish I could offer more help."

"Harry—do you know *why?*"

"No."

"You're lying."

"Beth, baby, what I've heard I wouldn't repeat to a snake."

"I'm not a snake. Give."

His voice lowered. "There's been a leak, no accusation, no formal statement, mind you, that maybe what happened to Apollo 19 was somehow caused by all that electronic gear *Lamprey*'s carrying."

"Those rotten bastards," said Beth Forsythe.

"My sentiments exactly. There never will be a formal charge, you can bet on that because if there were, Paul would have to be allowed to answer it. But who can answer rumor, leaks, official 'No Comments'? It's bad, as bad as anything Nixon ever did. And that's what bothers me. This isn't like Big F. He's hard, but he's always been straight."

Beth asked, "When do they plan to release this—?"

Gently, he said, "The word is shit, remember?"

"Thanks. When?"

"Any minute."

"Then I can't even be there with him when he learns."

"Not unless you're Wonder Woman."

"I wish I were. My first stop would be the White House. Okay, Harry. Many thanks. You're a prince. I'll tell Paul that you came through."

"Tell him I'll pass on anything else that might help. But not to hold his breath."

"Bless you," she said, and hung up.

A ham radio operator next door to the Ramada Inn had hooked up a phone patch from Sir Roger's room to a telephone in the small town in Rigly, Wales, where Diana Lean kept up their modest white cottage near the beach. Her arch voice revealed none of the inner emotion she felt; Roger never liked histrionics.

"How nice to hear from you," she said. "I wondered if you were anywhere that way. Wasn't it dreadful what happened to those American boys?"

"Too true," he said. "Luv, this has cost me a few days, and I still want to put in at the Azores, so I am afraid this shall rob us of New Year's as well as Christmas. Can you forgive me?"

"Certainly," she said. "So long as you remember to smuggle my bottle of madeira."

"That's a good ducks," he said. "Please don't worry."

Her voice broke a little as she replied, "Worry? About you? That'll be the day."

"Well," he said, "take care."

"I shall," she told him. "Wear your sweater."

He chuckled. "Dear, I'm in Florida. It's warm here."

"Oh, yes. Silly of me. Then, don't get sunburned."

"Please call the children, tell them everything's going well," he said. "Kiss them for me."

"Yes, dear. Good-by."

"Good-by."

He hung up. His head was bent. Forsythe looked away.

Lean's voice brought him back. "This was damned decent of your radio enthusiast. What do you call them?"

"Hams."

"Please ask what I owe him. He must have gone to a great deal of trouble."

"I already know," said Forsythe. "It was part of the deal."

"Whatever, it was well worth it," said Lean, reaching for his wallet.

"Put that away," said Paul Forsythe. "It's going to cost you exactly one autograph."

"Dear me," said the old sailor. "Where ever did we get the idea that all which interested you Americans were the material things?"

"I think you harbored a disgruntled writer a few years back by the name of Karl Marx," said Forsythe.

William Postiglion's favorite maxim was, "Pictures are 10 per cent *film*-making, 90 per cent *deal*-making."

Nobody really knew how old "Posty" actually was. It was a matter of public record that he had been prominent in the original J. Arthur Rank Film Organisation in the forties, and he had been quite active in the phase-over to television production toward the end of that decade.

"Britain has two national treasures," he once said. "Larry Olivier and me."

Posty would have been right at home with the flamboyant Hollywood producers and directors of the thirties; he would have been more spectacular than De Mille; more inscrutable than Von Stroheim; and more socially conscious than Zanuck. All of these characteristics had found their way into the series of postwar films Postiglion had produced, particularly the series of North Sea adventures for Eagle-Lion.

Another of Postiglion's mottos was, "If it doesn't hit at the box office, change the title and send it to the Americas."

At the moment, Posty had two money-making television series in syndication in the United States; neither had earned out its shooting costs in the British market, and neither had found a network home in America, thanks to the self-serving network policy that virtually prohibited any shows, other than those co-produced by the network, from being aired in prime time. The networks justified this policy by pretending to control the quality of programming. Actually, it was a sophisticated kickback system, abhorred by everyone, technically and morally illegal—and overlooked by the FCC, who were too busy making sure that minorities were hired on a quota basis, and that no politician was ever bad-mouthed without being given equal time to answer.

Recently, however, producers had been side-stepping network control by selling directly to local stations in what amounted to a bicycle network, in which prints were shuttled from one outlet to another, just as the fledgling movie industry broke the monopoly of Edison and his patent-holders. Norman Lear's "Mary Hartman, Mary Hartman" had opened the floodgates, and now independent packagers were once again a growing breed, no longer on the endangered species list.

But William Postiglion still yearned for the prestige of the giant blockbuster theatrical film. Television was fine for keeping the office open, but give him the two-hundred-million-dollar blockbuster every time.

He had been given a chance to acquire ten points of the new Charlton Heston, Steve McQueen film, *The*

Bermuda Triangle, but he hadn't liked either the script or the point spread between the creative people, the money people, and the distributors. It seemed to his practiced eye that the last group had every opportunity to steal the first two blind.

If *Triangle* hit, there would be room for another picture, not a sequel—which usually died—but a different approach, one which could be sold on the promise "You thought you saw it all in *The Bermuda Triangle,* but only NOW can the real truth be shown!" It was a ploy he had worked successfully several times in the past.

He had gotten up early yesterday morning, to watch the Apollo splashdown. It was not Posty's habit to tell anyone, even his closest associates, what he was planning, so he had not mentioned what to him was obvious—but what everyone else seemed to be ignoring—that Apollo was coming down right in the center of the infamous Triangle.

When he had first begun visiting the film community in Los Angeles (Posty refused to use the term Hollywood; most of the major studios, he pointed out, were elsewhere—in Burbank, or Culver City), he had made it a point, in rebellion against the flamboyant dress affected by the film colony, to wrap himself in the most conservative of Savile Row. But now that producers had to spend much of their time at the bank, dealing with lenders, their dress had moderated, so Posty, in turn, had liberated his own.

Today, he wore a dashiki, which made him look somewhat like a giant watermelon in a mumu. His bald head glistening by the pool did nothing to reduce the comparison.

A young man wearing only the tiniest concession of a string *cachesexe* came out, carrying a red telephone, which he plugged into an outlet near Posty's beach chair. At one time, there had been permanent telephones, and high-fidelity speakers, on the pool deck. But in recent years, burglars had taken to coming over the fence and cutting the wires to steal anything that wasn't bolted down. It was shameful, Posty thought.

"Who is it, Jules?" asked the rotund producer.

"A Mr. Kenneth O'Keefe, calling from Jacksonville, Florida. I looked in the Directory; he has no recent credits."

"Collect?"

"Of course not, Billy." Only Postiglion's great good friends were allowed to call him Billy. Posty was acceptable . . . and, one day, he hoped, so would be Sir William.

He gave a deep sigh, that of a celebrity pursued relentlessly by his public. "Very well, Jules." He indicated an empty plastic cup. "Some more bouillon, if you please."

Into the red telephone, as Jules Clutens took the cup back into the half-million-dollar Bel Air house, Postiglion crooned, "Yes?"

"You won't remember me, sir. Ken O'Keefe. I worked on *Sea Hunt* for a while, and we met in Nassau. You told me to call you if I ever had an idea that would be right for films."

"*Sea Hunt?* Is this Lloyd Bridges?"

"No, Ken O'Keefe. I was his double."

"That was a very long time ago, Mr. O'Keefe. I am afraid—"

"Mr. Postiglion, give me two minutes."

Posty shrugged. "Why not?"

"I'm in underwater survey now. I'm in command of a submersible that can dive more than six thousand feet under the surface."

Postiglion sat up. "Go on."

"Sir, I know there's already a movie coming out on the Bermuda Triangle. But it's just Hollywood fakery. What would you say if I told you that I'm on the track of what's *really* out there?"

"A docmentary? I doubt that—"

"No. A big story, but based on fact. All the real backgrounds, all the wacky stuff that nobody'd ever dare to make up."

Keeping the interest that he felt out of his voice, Posty said, "And what, may I ask, is your place in this . . . far-out idea? Are you trying to sell me a story treatment?"

O'Keefe's voice was urgent. "Negative. Listen, ask around about the *Lamprey*. It's the only ship of its kind in the world. We're under contract to survey out there, right down *under* the Bermuda Triangle. But we're private operators, and there's nothing in our contract to keep you from coming along with some of your staff and looking around, know what I mean?"

"In search of a locale and a story idea, you mean?"

"To begin with."

"That sounds intriguing, I admit it. But, Mr. O'Keefe, what's in this for you?"

"Easy. A part in the picture, if you make it. I'm good underwater. And two per cent of the action."

Posty put a frown into his voice. "Two per cent of the profits? Mr. O'Keefe, these days very few top actors dare to ask for—"

"I didn't say *profits*. I've been around, Mr. Postiglion. I want two per cent of every dollar that comes in, right off the top, before those Beverly Hills accountants get a chance to pull their vanishing ink trick."

"Unthinkable," said Posty.

"Maybe. But I'll tell you what. You watch all the news shows today about the Apollo splashdown, and then you say to yourself, 'Ken O'Keefe knows what really happened to those astronauts.' You tell yourself, 'Ken O'Keefe's already found things under the Triangle that are unbelievable.' And then you suggest to yourself—"

"Enough," said the producer. "How can I reach you, if I should want to after I think this matter over?"

"Get Jacksonville Ship-to-Shore. Have them connect you with the *Lamprey*. I'm on board."

"Thank you, Mr. O'Keefe. Perhaps you will hear from me."

"In the next twenty-four hours, sir. Or I'll have to call Ivan Tors."

"That porpoise-trainer! What does he know?"

"The same thing you do, sir. How to make money-earning films."

"Very well," said Postiglion. "You may hear from me."

"Good," said O'Keefe. "So long."

That had been yesterday.

Today, as Postiglion soon learned, traffic was stacked up, waiting to talk with *Lamprey.*

Aboard the survey vessel, the morning began calmly enough. After breakfast, Paul Forsythe had gone to the harbor with Sir Roger and, because of some calls Forsythe had made earlier to a liquor store, a food market, and the best ship's chandler in the port, watched with pleasure as the chandler's crew loaded heavy cases and bags of supplies aboard *Plymouth Hope.*

"Dear me," said the old sailor. "Paul, you haven't."

Forsythe chuckled. "I'm afraid I have."

"You'll spoil me. How can I thank you?"

"When you have your evening's gin and lime, lift one up for me. I'd give my left nut to be out there with you. But if I can't go along, at least let me have the pleasure of knowing I helped out a little."

"Thank you," said Sir Roger. He looked out at the rising tide. Holding out his hand, he grumbled, "Well, until next time."

"Soon," said Paul Forsythe.

Lean would only accept a tow far enough to get off the lee shore. Then he cast free and, with a dip of his ensign, he and his little yacht were on their own again, sailing east into the very heart of the disputed waters called the Devil's Triangle.

Drinking coffee in *Lamprey*'s galley with Captain Lovejoy and Ken O'Keefe, Forsythe listened to O'Keefe's report.

"A *road?*" he repeated.

"A concrete highway, I give you my word," said O'Keefe.

"Did you get any pictures?"

"Videotapes. They're not too good. Frazier's working on the cameras now. The lens hoods have to be modified. They're letting in too much flare."

"Well, let's see what you've got anyway."

In the well-equipped room which housed *Lamprey*'s electronic gear, O'Keefe switched on a Sony color monitor and plugged what looked like an automobile eight-track tape into a small gray box mounted to one of the equipment benches.

"This is the third-generation Betamax video unit," O'Keefe explained. "Three hundred lines of resolution, which beats most 16mm color film. And the cameras need only around one tenth the light."

"Stop pushing Sony stock, and let's see what you found down there," said Forsythe.

O'Keefe pressed a button and the monitor flickered, then showed a greenish-blue picture of the ocean floor.

"Don't worry about those two white flares," he said. "They're caused by the lens problem. But here. See?"

Forsythe leaned forward and looked closely at a blurred, whitish outline half obscured by sand and underwater growth.

"Can you freeze it?" he asked.

O'Keefe hit another button, and the image became stationary, with a slight tearing motion along the top of the screen.

Forsythe examined the blurred surface, half covered by sand. "It's got a straight edge, all right," he said.

Lovejoy asked, "Is that important?"

"In something like this, it is. Nature almost never produces straight lines. Too bad there's nothing in this shot to give us scale. How wide is it, Keefer?"

"I'd guess eighteen, twenty feet."

"How far does it go on?"

O'Keefe hit the PLAY button, and the videotape began to unwind again.

"There," he said a few seconds later. "I'd say we found a section that was eighty, maybe eighty-five feet long."

"Can you locate it again?"

"No sweat. I beeped it onto the logic tape."

Lovejoy asked, "What's a highway doing underwater a hundred miles from the nearest dry land?"

"That," said Forsythe, "would be an interesting question to answer, wouldn't it?"

Just then, the first call came in. It was from Beth, who had gotten her emotions under control enough to risk speaking over the telephone.

"Oh, shit, Paul," were her first words.

"And a jolly good morning to you, too," he said, surprised. "What's up, hon? Are you in town?"

"No, but I'm coming on the first flight. Have you heard yet?"

"Heard what?"

"Then you haven't. Oh, balls!"

"Sunny, you're going to get cut off. Those Ship-to-Shore operators listen in."

"Screw them. Paul, that terrible thing that happened to Apollo 19—"

"I know, Sunny—"

"No, you don't! Will you shut up and listen?"

"Come on, Beth. Settle down. What are you trying to say?"

"They're hanging it on you. On your ship, I mean. *Lamprey.* Foster's cooking it up right now with the honchos at Energy Resources. Their story is going to be that your electronic gear screwed up Apollo in some way and caused—" Her voice broke.

Slowly, Paul asked, "Where did you get this?"

"From our Washington friend. You know who I mean. He's steady."

"Yes," Forsythe agreed. "But don't be so upset, hon. It's just not true."

"What if it isn't? They're going to cancel your contract."

"They can't. It's been approved all the way up."

"Don't be naïve. They can do anything they want. If I were you, I'd get back to sea. Who knows, they might even try to seize your boat."

"Honey, let me start checking this out. What time are you due in?"

"Noonish. But don't meet me. You'll be busy. I'll find you."

"Okay," he said. "Smile, Sunny. We'll get this straightened out."

"I hope so," she said. "You be careful."

"Love you."

"Ditto."

Before she hung up, Forsythe heard what sounded like a long sniffle.

"What's up now?" asked Lovejoy.

"Trouble in Washington. Listen, Art, I have to use this circuit. Don't you have another one on the bridge?"

"Yeah, B Channel."

"Get on it, try to track down Henderson at Energy Resources. He usually comes in early. Something funny's going on. Beth says they're trying to cancel our contract."

"Beautiful," said the Captain, leaving the room on the double.

Forsythe signaled the operator and, tersely, requested a person-to-person link with Saito Osha in Yokohama, Japan. Told there would be a wait, he thanked the operator and hung up.

Uneasily, O'Keefe said, "Paul, do you remember what we talked about up in Norfolk, while we were fitting out?"

Absently, Forsythe said, "You mean, making a movie out there?"

"Yeah."

"So?"

Taking a deep breath, O'Keefe said, "Well, I talked with a big producer yesterday. You've heard of him. William Postiglion. He's been looking for another angle to the Bermuda Triangle, at least that's what I saw in the trades, and—"

"Jesus," Forsythe snapped, "when the hell are we ever going to forget all this science fiction stuff about

that so-called Triangle? Keefer, we've got real problems—"

"I know we do, and this might help. Listen, he
sounded real interested when I told him about *Lamprey*
and *Yellowtail*. If the survey contract blows up, we
might hit him for a good charter fee, and a piece of the
action—"

Sourly, Forsythe said, "And you might get in front of
a movie camera again."

O'Keefe looked away.

Forsythe said, "I'm sorry, Ken. That was a cheap
shot. You do a good job here. It isn't fair to drag up the
past."

Before O'Keefe could answer, the telephone buzzed.
Forsythe picked it up. "Hello?"

"Paul? This is Noah Henderson," said a deep voice.

"Good morning." Forsythe covered the mouthpiece.
"Keefer, tell Art that I've got Henderson down here. He
can cancel his call." Back into the open mouthpiece, he
said, "I was just trying to call you."

"Oh?"

"Cut the shit, Noah. I heard on the grapevine that
something fishy happened this morning at that big
house down on Pennsylvania Avenue. Is that why
you're calling?"

"In a way, Paul. Oh, there have been some questions
raised about the possibility that your electronic gear
might have somehow affected the Apollo splashdown.
Very touchy, because, after all, it was my department
which authorized you to be out there in the first place.
Ultimately, it's my responsibility, and that's just what I
told the President. If there's any blame to be assigned,
my shoulders are broad enough to handle it."

"That's very big of you, Noah." Paul Forsythe could
see the burly Secretary of Energy Resources in his
mind—dark blue eyes always locked to yours, a hand-
shake that could crush a walnut, the deep voice that
radiated authority and confidence.

"No need for thanks. It's my job. But, Paul, the man
who has the responsibility must also have the authority.

You know my saying, there is no responsibility without authority."

"I've heard it often," Forsythe agreed.

"Well," Henderson went on, "since I've taken the responsibility for any—malfunctions, if you will—of the vessel, it's only logical that I satisfy myself that such malfunctions will not occur again."

"Meaning what?"

"Paul, I think the entire survey should be re-evaluated and certainly *Lamprey* must be gone over by the experts."

"When?" Forsythe's voice was harsh.

"Oh, don't worry, Paul, we're not going to swoop down on you this very afternoon. First, a study of the entire underwater project has to be done—"

"You've done nothing but make studies for six years. Now you need another one?"

Calmly, the Secretary went on. "And once we've satisfied ourselves that our goals, and methods for achieving those goals, are in line, we should all join in making absolutely sure that *Lamprey* is in no way a hazard either to herself, or to any other vessels, sea or air."

"Double-talk!" shot back Paul Forsythe. "How long is all this supposed to take?"

"The study should be completed by late spring or early summer. Say July. And—"

"In other words, you're calling off the project!"

"Why, Paul," said Noah Henderson, "we wouldn't do that. We have a contract."

"Where in that contract does it say that you can put us up on the beach for six months?"

Blandly, Henderson replied, "Well, naturally, I haven't even glanced at the fine print, Paul, because frankly I hadn't the slightest notion that there would be any friction between us over this matter of the *Lamprey*'s safety."

"She's duly certified," Forsythe said, "and every piece of electronic gear aboard is type approved."

"I'm sure that's so," said Henderson. "But one of our technical people brought up an interesting word this morning. Synergism. Two parts equaling more than twice the effect of one. The analogy he gave was that of one safe sleeping pill, combined with one safe drink. But because of synergistic action, the person might die."

"Henderson," said Paul Forsythe, "I don't know why you're doing this, except that you've obviously been ordered to. But I won't take it. You may not be familiar with our contracts, but I am. There's a pay-or-play clause in it. If you prevent us from doing our job, it's going to cost you."

"I won't deny that," said Henderson. "By all means, submit your bills to the General Accounting Office. They're slow, but they're very fair. I'm sure that sooner or later, you'll get every cent you deserve."

"And if we don't co-operate, your office might just slow down those payments, right?"

"Well, look at it from our side, Paul. If you delay us in carrying out the project in the way we see necessary—"

"*Me* delay *you?* It's the other way around."

"Paul, why don't you come up to Washington? We'll discuss this in detail. Over the telephone is no way to reach sound decisions. It's too easy for someone to get mad and hang up."

"You're fucking-A right!" yelled Paul Forsythe as he slammed down the receiver.

Navy frogman Eddie Cooper said, "I don't care what they say now. That goddamned capsule was empty."

"Eddie," said his section chief as the two drank 3.2 beer in the beer garden at the Jacksonville Naval Station, "it was dark in there."

"Not once I'd pulled the hatch."

"Yeah," said the section chief, "but then you fell off the collar, remember? Fonda was the one who actually leaned inside the capsule. And he says that he saw what was left of those poor bastards, only he didn't know what it was at the time."

"Is that why he got sick and had to be airlifted back to the carrier?"

"I don't know. But, Eddie, hold it down. You know what the skipper said. Talk to anybody about what happened yesterday, and your ass is mud."

"I'm not going to blab off to anyone," said Eddie Cooper. "But I'm not going to lie between you and me, either. That capsule was empty."

Flying back to Houston, Jakes asked McClure, the NASA Director, "What do you think about that theory of a survey vessel's electronic gear screwing up the splashdown?"

"It's possible," said McClure. His eyelids were heavy. He had, for perhaps only the second time this year, drunk too fast and too much, and he could still feel the poisons that had not yet been eliminated from his body. He had a powerful thirst, but knew better than to try to quench it. Two glasses of water, and he would be drunk again.

"How could a radio transmission damage the heat shield?" Jakes persisted.

"Not the shield itself, but it might have activated one of the explosive bolts, or one of the hold-down latches."

"Wouldn't that show up when they examine the capsule?"

"Sure," said McClure. "Give them time." His voice seemed unnecessarily harsh.

"Yeah," said Jakes. "Time. It seems like forever, but it was only yesterday."

"What time is it now?"

"Nearly eleven, Eastern. We may be in Central by now."

"Somewhere it must be past noon. Ring for the stew, will you?"

"Coffee?"

Slowly, the Director of NASA shook his head. "No work today," he said. "Let's have a couple of Bloody Marys!"

William Postiglion finally got through to *Lamprey*. He first spoke with O'Keefe, then was connected with Paul Forsythe.

Posty's first offer was the usual Hollywood "option" routine, in which the producer ties up everything in sight for a token payment which allows him to shop the property around town looking for a profit while risking only a few thousand dollars. Forsythe laughed at him.

"I don't know much about this movie bit," he said. "I might be willing to let you come out on a cruise with us to see what we've got to offer, but I won't give you any rights whatsoever until a subsequent contract is drawn up that is satisfactory to both sides."

"Suppose I were to charter *Lamprey* for a few weeks?"

"You couldn't afford it," said Forsythe. "We'd have to charge you around twenty thousand dollars a day just to move the ship and the submersible from one place to another. Any fancy stuff would cost more."

He thought for a moment, then added, "Still, O'Keefe recommands you highly. I'd suggest that, if you have real interest, you accept our hospitality, without risking a thing. That doesn't commit either of us, but opens the door for future action if we both want it."

"I accept!" shouted Postiglion, over three thousand miles of telephone wire. "And may I say, sir, what a pleasure it is to encounter someone who speaks his mind instead of creeping around the bush."

"That's 'beating' around the bush," said Forsythe. "But I know what you mean. Okay, O'Keefe obviously knows how to reach you. Get your people organized, and we'll be in touch."

"When?"

"A week or less."

"Better and better," said the producer.

"Okay," Forsythe said, "you'll be hearing from us."

He hung up in the face of Postiglion's chatter of thank-yous.

"Okay, Keefer," he said to the mini-sub commander.

"You may get back into the movie business after all."

"Many thanks," said O'Keefe. "As an agent's commission, you get ten per cent of all my starlets."

Forsythe's next call was from Wales. Diana Lean was calling the master of *Lamprey*.

Lifting the receiver, he said, "Hello, Lady Diana."

"Good day," she said. "I'm not sure what time it is there. May I speak with Roger, please?"

"I'm afraid he's not here," said Forsythe. "He sailed more than two hours ago."

"Dear," she said. "Can you possibly go after him?"

"I suppose so. Is there anything wrong?"

"No, not if you catch up with him before nightfall."

"That shouldn't be hard. He can't be making more than six or seven knots. Do you have a message?"

"Yes indeed. Tell Roger that I, Diana, instruct him not to turn north under any circumstances until after twenty-four hundred hours Greenwich Mean Time on Friday, that's the day after tomorrow. Can you repeat that, please?"

"Don't turn north until after midnight Friday."

"GMT. That's very important."

"Greenwich Mean Time. Yes, ma'am."

"That's very good."

"Would you like him to come ashore to speak with you?" Forsythe asked.

"No, that won't be necessary. Roger and I have had many of these . . . communications. He'll understand."

"All right," said Forsythe. "We'll send the launch out after him. He shouldn't be far off."

"I can't thank you enough," she said. "Please give my regards to your beautiful Beth."

"I will," he said. "Good-by, Lady Diana."

Only after he had hung up did he wonder how she knew anything about Beth; she hadn't been mentioned in Sir Roger's conversation on the ham radio phone patch.

*   *   *

North of Bimini, between the Bahamas and the Bermuda Rise, in the heart of the Sargasso Sea, something lay deep beneath the surface, on the sandy bottom. Still glowing a dull red, it sent bubbles rising to the light swell above, and dead fish floating up along the edges of the Gulf Stream.

The sea birds flew in great circles around the frothing sea, but none of them came down to eat the free lunch that had been spread before them.

The day was very hot for December.

LIMBO LEGENDS
FLIGHT TO NOWHERE: Jack Begley's Story

What was worst about it is that the war was already over, had been since September, and now all those guys got themselves killed in peacetime, damn it, and for what?

Look, I know I ain't much to look at now—I mean, when I go in a bar, the broads don't jump up and down and give me the eye. They don't even hustle me for drinks, now that my hair's mostly gone, and I guess you wouldn't call my waistline a spare tire, more of a whole set of four. But inside my head, I'm still twenty-two, and weigh a cool 161, and those silver wings ride high and proud on my khaki chest, the way they did down there in Florida in the winter of 1945.

Everywhere you look these days, somebody's putting out a book, and now there's a big movie, about what they call the Bermuda Triangle. I read some of them. No, I never saw the movie, who's going to blow five bucks? I'll wait until it comes on TV. Besides, the flying service keeps me pretty busy. I've got the biggest crop-dusting outfit in the Valley, and it's long hours. Dangerous? No, not unless those pricks at the Power Authority sneak up a new line without telling us about it. Of course, it's safer with the choppers, because we can come down over the edge of the field vertically before we start spraying. Trouble with fixed-wing birds is you have to make your approach, and that's when the power lines clip you in half.

What I'm getting at is, it's business, you know? Not like the war—I mean The War, number two biggie. Jeez, we were all like gods then . . . my waist was thirty, I could do twenty chin-ups without even breathing hard. I never got overseas—none of the trainees in my outfit did—we were ready to go, then they dropped the bomb, and there we were, all fired up with no place to burn. Kind of like rubbing up against a broad all night on the dance floor, and just when you're ready to head for the nearest motel, she splits without a word. Man, that is why they invented the word frustration. And I guess we had our fair share of it down there in Fort Lauderdale. We were assigned to the NAS—that's Naval Air Station —waiting for orders, only we all knew that was a phony deal, there weren't going to be any orders, except to sit on our duffs until the point system caught up with us and we could draw our discharges. And every one of us, like I said, sitting there with a hard on and no war to fight any more.

Anyway, it wasn't business as usual then, that's what I'm trying to say. We were, by God, Gung Ho, and if the Nazis and the Japs had quit, well maybe there was something brewing with the Ruskies. We got up just as early, we trained just as hard, and we made out like bandits with those local tomatoes, Winchell called them V-girls, and the pros called them something else, because all those amateurs had put the whores out of business, except for the few bucks they could hustle off the enlisted men.

But, shit, none of us thought of dying.

That's what pisses me about all of the crap I've been reading. Mr. Dix, I've got to tell you, I read a paperback of that last book you did about that so-called "Triangle." Pardon my French, but bullshitski. You and all those others, you write about Flight 19 like it was some kind of Chinese puzzle. I mean, five planes fly off and vanish, and then the rescue plane disappears too. Flying saucers, whirlpools in the sky, some science fiction kind of crap you call alternate worlds, you've all got some fancy kind of theory about Flight 19, and you're all of you wrong as hell, because you weren't there and you don't know. Buddy, you've been barking up the wrong orange tree, interviewing that guy who missed the flight, and those radio operators. Oh, they told you the truth, as far as they knew it. But they weren't there, and I was. Because, and here's what fouled you all up, there weren't five TBM Avengers on that flight, there were six, and I piloted the sixth.

What do you know about prop planes? Hell, today everything's jet. Well, you know what you can do with your jets. Sure, they're fast—so fast that you can't get an effective field of fire with machine guns or cannon, we sure as hell found that out in Vietnam, right? Choppers—gun ships, that's what put the fear of God into those gooks. If the Defense Department asked, which they sure in hell aren't going to or they'd have done it already, I'd tell them to shove their jets, except for flying defense above our conventional prop planes and choppers. Anyway, the TBM was just about the biggest single-engine job in the air. Her wingspan went fifty-three feet, and she pulled herself along with a 1600-horse Cyclone power plant. Even hauling two thousand pounds of bombs, she could top out over three hundred. And fully loaded, her range was more than a thousand miles.

Like I said, I was pilot. The other two men usually on board were a gunner and a radioman, except today I was shy my radioman, who hadn't come back from leave.

I guess you know the date better than me. You sure in hell made a lot more money off it. December 5th, 1945. Looking at the first peacetime Christmas in four years. What I wanted, if I could get my claws on it, for my old lady—my mom, I wasn't married then—was one of them new kinds of pens, the ones that would write under water, or through butter. Ball-points, they called them. Want a laugh? You can buy a ball-point today for nineteen cents. You know what they wanted for them in 1945? One hundred smackeroos, and that was before inflation, so you'd figure that to be maybe two and a half now. Anyway, the inside word was the PX—post exchange—would be getting a shipment in maybe today, and so I figured that while all the other guys were down at the base theater watching that new movie What Next, Corporal Hargrove, with that actor, what's his name? Oh, yeah, Robert Walker, he was married to Jennifer Jones. Well, during the movie, I was going to hit the PX and grab myself one of those ball-points for my mom.

Only, first, we had to fly our mission.

It was a milk run. Fly due east for 160 miles, north for 40 more, then southwest back to the base. A simple exercise in navigation. Why? Except for us trainees, everybody in the group had combat experience and navigation was old hat. And practically everybody had from 300 to 500 hours of flight time. Who needed to prove we knew how to follow a compass?

Well, we did. Remember, Gung Ho? We were, by God, heroes, and heroes flew. Christ, I wish I could get that excited about something now. I mean, then we had a purpose, we had a mission. Not just making money, not just putting in time until retirement. Sure, the flight was routine, but even routine meant something then.

Now, here's where all you guys have screwed up. Yes, the flight plan for Flight 19 called for five TBM Avengers. Four carried the full crew of three men, and the Flight Leader, Chuck Taylor, had only two. Fourteen men in all.

Where did I come in? I was the Bogey. It was my job to sneak up on the patrol and see if I could catch them napping. So, although I was attached to Flight 19, I wasn't carried on its flight plan, because that would have alerted Chuck. The whole idea was to see if I could jump them out of the sun, and get enough of them in my wing cameras to prove I would have shot one or more of them down.

That day was cold; a weather front had moved through, and the temperature was down around forty, with clear skies and wind gusts of maybe thirty knots. Good flying weather, but unusual for that time of year.

Taylor got his planes out on the flight line by 1330 hours—that's one-thirty in the afternoon, and they started taking off by 2 P.M. I was already in the air by then. Their first destination was an old wreck of a cargo ship just off Bimini Island in the Bahamas. I was up high, maybe nine, nine five, and I watched them make torpedo runs on the wreck, before they turned east again.

I maybe didn't mention, I had a gunner, but no radio-man. I didn't need one, since my part today was to be the Bogey, not to practice navigation. Staff Sergeant Benny Sakol, U. S. Marines. A hell of a kid. He re-upped, went to Korea, and bought the whole farm up near the Chosen Reservoir when the Chinks broke out and pushed the Marines all the way to the sea. They gave his old man a Navy Cross. Benny was one of the best. Too bad. It seems like they always get the good ones.

Anyway, I tracked Flight 19 for most of their eastward leg, and then when they made their north turn, I jumped them. I came down out of the sun, from the west, and went right through the formation. I got off bursts from my gun camera, and Benny was shooting from the back with a 35mm Leica. I mean, we creamed them. We never did see those pictures, but I bet I could have claimed three destroyed and the other two as possibles. They were fat, dumb, and happy, and Chuck Taylor must have learned a lesson right there and then. Too bad he never got to use it. He was a good pilot.

I had my radio on the short-range plane-to-plane fre-quency. The second time I buzzed Taylor, I held up the mike, and he got my meaning and switched over from his command frequency.

"Bogey, who are you?"

"Guess. You're dead, by the way."

"Begley! You prick."

"Next time, keep an eye on the sun."

"How many of us did you get?"

"Three for sure. The other two are probables."

"Cameras?"

"You know it."

He swore. "They won't let me forget this."

"Neither will I. You owe me a brew."

"I'll buy you a case if you deep-six those films."

"Negative. But I'll sell you enlargements."

He chuckled. "What now? You returning to base?"

"Roger. Any messages for the troops?"

"Tell them not to start the movie until we get home."

"Affirmative. Okay, buddy. Go win the war. I'm on my way back to base."

"Roger. Flight Leader 19 out."

"Bogey clear," I said, and just to show off, I put the nose up and did a half loop to change my course toward the west. I heard Taylor key his mike, although he didn't say anything, but the message was clear. BEEP-BEEP. Fuck you.

I glanced over my shoulder, and saw Flight 19 heading due north. Come to think of it, that makes me the last man who ever saw them. Me and Benny, that is.

If I'd gone straight back to base, I would have been there by 1530—three-thirty civilian time. But I had a hair up my ass, and my flight plan was open-ended, so Benny and me got that Avenger right down on the deck, and we started buzzing waves. I mean, so low that our prop wash kicked them up and slapped the water against our horizontal stabilizer. Unless you've flown low and fast over water, you can't imagine the sensation. It's like all those dreams you have when you're a kid, of soaring without effort or fear of falling. The water rushes at you from the front with all the speed of an express train, and blurs past your side vision, and the sound of the big Cyclone engine is reflected back at you from the ocean's surface, and short of screwing Rita Hayworth it's probably the best sensation you are likely to find, at least in the last month of the year 1945.

We horsed around like that for fifteen or twenty minutes, so I was still in the air when the first call came from Flight 19's Leader, Chuck Taylor. I didn't know Taylor all that well, but he was always a level-headed guy, and the urgency in his voice didn't seem right.

He broadcast, "Calling Tower. This is an emergency. We seem to be off course. We cannot see land. Repeat: we cannot see land."

I did some quick figuring. We should have been on parallel courses, me to the south, heading for base. I couldn't understand why he was so upset. It was too soon to expect to see land.

The tower came back, "What's your position, Flight 19?"

Taylor answered, "I don't know. I'm not sure of our position. We're not sure just where we are. We seem to be lost."

Lost! What the hell were they doing lost, with five qualified pilot-navigators on the mission, all presumably practicing their craft?

I keyed my microphone. "Flight 19, this is Bogey. Come in."

Taylor answered, "Begley! Where are you?"

"Due south, I think. What's wrong?"

His voice seemed to tremble. "I don't know. Everything's screwed up."

"You must be pretty close," I said. "You're coming in five by five."

The tower overrode his answer. "Flight 19, assume bearing due west."

Taylor said, loudly, "Shit, don't you think I know that? The only thing is, we don't know which way west is."

"Repeat transmission," said the tower.

"Everything is wrong," Taylor said. "Strange . . . we can't be sure of any direction. Even the ocean doesn't look right."

"Taylor, come in," I called.

"I hear you," he said.

"Can't you see the sun? Head for it."

"Negative," he said. "Can you find us?"

"I'll try," I said. "Give me a count."

"One, two, three, four, five, six . . ."

He counted to twenty, while I tuned the RDF. The Radio Direction Finder was actually a small loop antenna which showed a signal's strongest reception with a needle. After Taylor radioed, "Twenty," I called, "I think I've got you on RDF. I find you north by northeast, but on this frequency you can't be more than forty or fifty miles away. Can you home in on me?"

"Trying," he said. "But the needle keeps fluttering."

"Okay," I said. "I know pretty well where I am. I'll come to you. Just keep talking."

He did not seem to hear me. I climbed to two thousand and put the Avenger's nose at twelve degrees.

I switched to the tower frequency. "Tower, this is Bogey. Do you read me? Over?" Nothing. Static.

"How about you, Flight 19 Leader? Bogey calling." More static.

Benny cut in. "Lieutenant, look at that."

He was pointing over the right side of the plane.

Below, the ocean seemed to be curving up toward us. The water, from having been a deep blue, had become a whitish green.

"Surface winds," I said. "We'll go up another thousand." I slid the throttle control forward and climbed to thirty-five hundred.

I guess we must have flown for six or seven minutes before I heard the next transmissions.

"Tower, this is Captain George Stivers. Lieutenant Taylor has given me the command. It is 1625 hours. We don't know where we are. We think we must be two hundred miles northeast of base. We are very short of fuel."

The tower called, "Give us a long count, so we can get a position. Now."

Stivers did not answer for several seconds. Then, instead of counting, he said, "We must have passed over Florida and we must be in the Gulf of Mexico."

I hit my mike button and yelled, "That's negative, Flight 19. You're east of Florida, not west. This is Bogey. Over."

Another long pause. Apparently while the tower and I could hear the flight, they couldn't hear us.

Stivers said, "It looks like we're entering white water. We're completely lost." A long pause. Then: "Doesn't anyone hear us? Anyone?"

The tower didn't reply, so I did. "This is Bogey. I'm just a few miles south. Don't head east. Repeat, don't head east. You aren't in the Gulf, you're still in the Atlantic. Orbit your present position. Do you read me?"

My answer was nothing but silence.

I didn't know it, but up at the Banana River NAS,

which is now Patrick Air Force Base, serving the NASA base at the Kennedy Space Center, an old beer-drinking buddy of mine, Lieutenant Harry Cone, was getting his huge Martin Mariner PBM flying boat ready to go to the assistance of Flight 19. With a 125-foot wingspan, the Mariner had been built especially for search and rescue work. Her fuel range gave her a full day—twenty-four hours—in the air, and on board she carried every conceivable life-saving device known to us at that time. Rafts, floats, radio transmitters which went into operation automatically when they hit the water. The PBM was the nearest thing to a guardian angel available to those of us who flew over water.

With Cone at the controls, and twelve crewmen aboard, the Big Bird took off and headed for Flight 19's last known position. I must have been on the wrong frequency, because I heard nothing of the Mariner's flight until much later. But apparently Cone reached the area, reported negative sighting, informed the Banana River NAS Tower that there were strong winds at six thousand feet, and was never heard from again.

You expect that in wartime. Good poker friends cash in their chips, take off on a mission, and die.

But in the Christmas, peacetime season of December 1945? It was obscene, buddy. You're supposed to get your discharge papers, kiss the nearest blonde, and live happily ever after. Right?

Tell that to Harry Cone and his twelve men aboard the PBM, none of whom were ever seen again.

Tell it to Chuck Taylor, and George Stivers, and those other guys in the lost Avengers.

Or try telling it to me. Because I'm the one who came through it all, and sat here laughing my ass off while you guys made legends out of pipe dreams and garbled radio transcriptions.

Like I said, the water beneath us was all churned up as I tried to find Flight 19. But there didn't seem to be any drift to my course, as I held it steady on twelve degrees.

What I didn't count on was something going wrong with my own plane.

The first noticeable effect was with the radio. I lost all communications. Nothing but static crackled in my earphones. I tuned from one frequency to another, but they were all jammed with the sound of frying eggs.

I was concentrating so hard on the radio that it took a couple of shouts from Benny Sakol to bring me back to the cockpit of my own Avenger.

"Lieutenant, look!"

I lifted my head and saw, directly ahead, what looked like a silver-gray lens. It was a huge cloud, miles in width, but only a few thousand feet in height. And we were heading right into it. I had never seen such a formation before, and it chilled me, I mean to tell you.

There wasn't time to climb over it, I didn't want to turn aside, so I pulled back the throttle and began unwinding the altimeter. I got down to two thousand before the first gust hit us. It was like some invisible giant had stepped up alongside the Avenger and, putting all he had behind the bat, had tried to knock us out of the ball park. The plane shuddered with the impact, and loose junk flew all over the cockpit. I felt the tail come around, and for a moment the controls were gone, and I thought we were going into a flat spin. Then I got hold of a little vertical rotation, and put the nose down and saw, with amazement, that my airspeed indicator had dropped to less than forty knots. As we dove, however, it built up, and I don't mind saying that my stomach stayed in a whirl until we got over the stall speed again. The water, which seemed just yards beyond the whirling prop, had a whitish cast that was unlike anything I'd ever seen, and it seemed to draw me toward it, as if it would be a nice thing to just let the Avenger plow into it. But I shook my head, and hauled back on the controls, and the plane lifted its nose and we headed toward what I thought was north again. Except now the compass had gone crazy, and with its wild swingings I couldn't tell which way was north, east, or west. The eggs were frying louder than ever in my earphones, and most of the instruments on the control panel seemed to be doing strange things. The only one which behaved naturally was the ball-bank indicator, and I remember thinking that it was the only non-electrical gauge there.

Then, like a switch being pulled, the radio went dead. One minute, static—the next, nothing.

And the Avenger's engine quit. No backfire, no climbing of oil pressure. Just a sudden silence, the prop windmilling until I feathered it.

"Benny?" I said. But the intercom was dead too.

I raised my hand and pointed down with one gloved finger. We were going into the drink. It was his job to get the rubber raft ready. I hoped that he had seen me.

A while ago, I told you a lot of good things about the Avenger. Now let me tell you a few bad ones. For one, it has a glide ratio similar to that of a brick. Once you cut the power, there's only one way to go. Straight down. Another drawback, particularly for a Navy plane, is that it sinks. Instantly. I think at one time there were supposed to be flotation chambers in the wings, but they'd been taken over by fuel tanks and assorted hardware. The ditching drill for an Avenger was simple. Glide into the waves, and the second the fuselage touches the water, start swimming.

I'd never seen the ocean the way it looked that day. The water was a garish green, and so was the sky. We were below the wind, or whatever it was up there that had caused the long lens-shaped cloud. I heard the slipstream whistling past the canopy, and that reminded me to slide it back, to save time when we were in the drink. Our approach, now that we were gliding down at an alarming one foot down for every five feet forward, was amazingly smooth. The airflow nibbled at both of my cheeks, so we were theoretically coming in exactly upwind, the way the manufacturers recommended in their tech manuals. I wondered how many of those tech writers had gone out and ditched an Avenger to get their techniques straight.

"Brace yourself!" I yelled at Benny. Maybe he heard me.

You go in wheels up, and you try not to bounce too

often. If you don't break the fuselage in half, you float a few seconds longer. That can make all the difference.

It was smoother than I'd expected. Two small bounces, and then a shuddering, settling stop.

The ocean didn't disappoint me. It came over the edge of the cockpit almost instantly.

"Out!" I yelled. "This bastard's sinking!"

I heard some splashing noises. I hit the quick-release button to shed my back-packed chute, pulled the two cords to inflate my Mae West, and stood up in the seat, which was now half a foot underwater. There came a POP and a WHOOSH, and in the corner of my eye, I saw the bright orange of the three-man raft just behind the right wing. Benny was climbing in, sprawled out to avoid tipping the rubber doughnut with its fabric floor.

"Come on!" he yelled.

I didn't need any encouragement. I slipped into the water just as the Avenger sank under me, without a ripple. I guess I had been afraid it would create what you guys call a vortex and drag me down, but except for a slight washing movement around my ankles, I felt nothing. I paddled over to the raft, and Benny helped me get on board.

I lay in the bottom of the raft, catching my breath.

"Benny," I said, "if you bastards have been eating the emergency rations out of this raft, you and me are going to be very sorry."

He laughed.

"Lieutenant," he said, "don't worry. Even in an emergency, nobody can eat that crap."

Three hours later, a beat-up old wooden scow drifted toward us. It was manned by a tall black man whose face looked like a cyprus plank that has lain in the path of rain, sun, hurricane, and blowing sand for a thousand years.

"Please come aboard," he said. "I am Joseph Horatio of Alice Town, Bimini Island."

We crawled onto his boat, and because there wasn't any wind we lay becalmed for six days and seven nights, before a Coast Guard vessel searching for Flight 19 finally picked us up, and took us back to Florida.

We'd had food, and water, and enough stories from Joe Horatio to last a lifetime. I mean, he was a nice enough old buzzard, but he was cracked like a dropped crock. Look, here it was 1945, and he was telling us stuff that happened to him in 1860. Hell, that would have made him more than a hundred years old. Too bad. If you could find him, you'd have a book that'd knock their eyes out. Except that would make him more than 140 now, if he was telling the truth back then, which I have to doubt. Anyway, he was a good old geezer, and if not for him, I probably wouldn't be here now giving you the truth about Flight 19, and you wouldn't be giving me the thousand bucks which you promised, in case I have to refresh your memory.

Many thanks.

PART TWO
SEARCH

CHAPTER 6

Anthony Dix looked like a longshoreman, not a writer. His corduroy sport jacket must have been pressed at some time in its long and obviously disreputable history, but no one could have seen any evidence of that fact this morning, as he tried to ignore the insistent buzz of the telephone in the next room. Dix had turned off the phone in his office, but had neglected to silence the one on his secretary's desk. And today was her day off.

Dix had just finished typing his version of the interview Jack Begley had given him, and he wanted to proofread it now, with all the details fresh in his mind. So he ignored the telephone, and soon it stopped.

Dix was slim and wiry; his hair was thinning, but he gave it no mind. Sometimes he had half a beard, sometimes he was cleanshaven. It all depended on whether he had found a razor close at hand after his morning shower.

At thirty-one, Anthony Dix could afford the best—his earnings last year had topped a million dollars, all generated by his writings about such mysteries as UFOs and the Bermuda Triangle. To his mind, what he wore today *was* the best.

His shirt was a faded blue navy work denim, manufactured long before the days of permanent press, as its rumpled wrinkles testified. His trousers were blue jeans which were probably older than their owner; they had never seen concentrated bleach to turn them to their cherished pale off-blue—hundreds of washings had attended to that. Unfinished western boots were on his feet—wide, sturdy, ugly—and very comfortable.

In contrast to the writer's rough appearance, his office was elegant with velvet wall-covering; his desk was an old roll-top from Philadelphia—legend had it that Ben Franklin had once used it. A Tiffany Coca-Cola lamp hung over his chair, just high enough so that he would not hit it with his head when standing.

The telephone began to ring again. Dix threw down the manuscript. This time, he knew without thinking about it, the instrument would be more persistent. He lifted the receiver, said, "Dix."

Across the continent, William Postiglion bellowed, "Tony?"

"Good morning, Posty," said Dix. "If you're going to shout, why pay the long-distance charges? Just put your head out the window and yell in the direction of New York."

Dix's co-op apartment and offices were on the twelfth floor of the Dakota, on West Seventy-second Street; he had inherited the nine-room treasure when John Lennon moved some years ago.

"How's our story coming?" demanded the producer, ignoring the remark.

"Good. I've got some new stuff. And it'll cost you."

"I'll pay. What is it?"

"Something about Flight 19 that nobody else has found."

Posty made a derisive sound. "That one's been gone over pretty well. Charlie Berlitz used it in his book, so did John Wallace Spencer, and Richard Winer, and—"

"*And* Tony Dix," said the writer. "But believe me, my version's unique. I'll tell you all about it when I see you—"

"That's why I'm calling," said Postiglion. "Listen, I've got us an invitation to go out on the *Lamprey,* that survey ship that got mixed up with the Apollo splashdown. Do you want to come along?"

Without hesitation, Dix said, "Yes."

"Then grab the next flight out here. We'll have a fast

go-around with the majors, see if we can get the studios to put up some front money. If not—well, your publishers are rich."

"So are you, Posty," said Dix.

"If so," said the producer, chuckling, "it's because I never put a dime into one of my own films."

Despite her having urged him not to, Paul Forsythe went to the airport to meet Beth. He drove a rented Pinto, and cursed the little car all the way. With the tiny engine, pollution-control devices, and a carburetor that seemed to be designed to operate only with the throttle wide open, his drive to the airport was anything but pleasant.

But when Beth filled his arms, he felt the tensions wash away and he gave himself up to the enjoyment of having her near him and feeling her fresh toothpaste kisses against his lips.

"You shouldn't be here," she said. "But I'm glad you are."

"You look terrific," he said. Then, lowering his voice, "Let's go somewhere and screw."

"Oh, don't I wish we could," she said.

"You're kidding."

"On the plane. Instant Curse."

"That's life," he said. "I should have gone with Keefer."

"The mad U-boat Commander? Where's he?"

He explained about Sir Roger Lean, and the unusual call from Lady Diana.

"Oh, I know all about that," said Beth. "She's psychic. Didn't you know?"

"I've never met the woman," he said, trying to get the Pinto to stop flooding out. "But she seemed to know a lot about you and me."

"She's been in all kinds of stories, if you read that sort of stuff."

The car lurched forward, and he aimed it toward the airport exit. "You know I don't."

"Well, several times she's warned Sir Roger to stay

away from unpredicted hurricane areas. From thousands of miles away, mind you, with no access to weather information. She's all the rage in the ESP set."

He chuckled. "And here I thought that all she was is a nice old lady in Wales."

Beth pinched the inside of his leg. "Far from it. Some say the old girl's actually a witch."

He pinched back. "And you know what you are. If you're not buying, don't pinch the merchandise."

Beth leaned over and bit his ear. "I'm buying," she said. "But you'll have to put it in layaway."

Lamprey's launch, commanded by Ken O'Keefe, caught up with *Plymouth Hope* some twenty miles off the eastern coast of Florida. Sir Roger was in the cockpit, and he waved at them as they came in carefully, downwind, and tied up alongside.

"Come on board, Mr. O'Keefe," said the old sailor. "I know it's only five in the afternoon, but my lips have been puckering for some of Mr. Forsythe's excellent gin and tonic."

"That sounds pretty good," said O'Keefe. "I've got a message for you from your wife."

Ducking below, Lean called, "Hurricane?"

Puzzled, O'Keefe said, "What?"

Lean reappeared with two plastic glasses, a bottle of Gordon's Gin, and half a lime. He nodded toward a plastic ice chest near the wheel. "Tonic's in there, if you'll get it." He began slicing the lime. "Diana's got this sixth sense, if you will, about me when I'm out here alone. It's fairly easy, when I'm near a radio. She sends warnings. Usually about weather. Not always. One time, she warned me away from my position near Martha's Vineyard. Later that night, the *Andrea Doria* and the *Stockholm* collided and the *Doria* went down."

He had doused two handsome slugs of gin into the glasses, squeezed the limes, and thrown them in also. O'Keefe handed him a cold bottle of Canada Dry Tonic. Sir Roger wrinkled his nose. "Not Schweppes, but much cheaper." He finished the drinks, handed one to his guest. "Cheers."

Curious, O'Keefe asked, "What if you aren't near a radio?"

Sipping, Lean answered, "That's more chancy. I get peculiar dreams. Nothing definite, nothing I could point at and say, 'That dream tells me there's rough weather ahead.' But, while the dreams may be of home or of the land, or even of my youth, when I awaken I'll be uneasy. And that tells me that something's wrong. I discussed all this with a psychologist, and he advanced the theory that subconsciously I might have become aware of the weather changing, or through some other input of information, have been warned that there's danger ahead, and that I then relate it to my dreams and take proper action. But if that is so, how is it that when Diana actually reaches me over the telephone or radio, her own warnings are so accurate?"

"Spooky," said O'Keefe. "Well, her message this time is that you shouldn't turn north until after midnight Friday. Greenwich Mean Time. She said that was very important."

"Twenty-four hundred hours GMT Friday," repeated the old sailor. "Very well. That will put my easterly reach farther than I'd wanted, but I'm certainly not going to fly in the face of Diana's warning. Drink up, young man."

"Sir Roger," the younger man asked, "I know what you've done, in the past forty years. Was it worth it? All of that time, out here alone?"

The old sailor thought for a moment before answering. "Yes," he said slowly. "It's not the life for everyone, or even for few of us. But for me . . . yes. Yes. The sea and I have become lovers, and my wife is wise enough to look the other way and accept the portion of me which remains." He took O'Keefe's glass and began to build another drink. "Isn't that the way you've found it, lad?"

O'Keefe said, almost sadly, "Yeah. Except for two

things. You're up here on top, and I'm down below. And you've got Lady Diana. Me, I've got nobody."

Sir Roger Lean said, "Don't despair, O'Keefe. Loneliness is the sauce that puts tang to being together with someone dear. Without the long road to travel, the destination might not seem as precious." He handed O'Keefe another drink. "Here you go."

O'Keefe lifted the gin and tonic and said, "Cheers."

Noah Henderson, Secretary of Energy Resources, was connected to the President's private telephone.

"Forsythe's going to be difficult," said Henderson.

"How?"

"He won't let us beach him. He wants to live up to the contract."

"Stall him," said President Howard Foster.

"It can't be done," said Henderson. "Forsythe is just the man to go out and do the job anyway, whether or not we pay him."

Foster laughed. "Yes, damn it. That's why we picked him in the first place. Well, what *can* we do? *Lamprey* mustn't go out there."

"Perhaps we could send him someplace else to run a survey."

"Would he accept that?"

Henderson hesitated. "I'm afraid not. If we'd done it at first, maybe. But now he'd be very suspicious."

"All right. What about the ship itself? Are there any grounds to lay it up?"

"Only if we violate the law. She's sound, Mr. President. So is the equipment on board. Forsythe could hit us with a Show Cause order, and you know the temper of the Supreme Court today."

"Very well," Foster admitted glumly. "Noah, I don't know what you can do. But find something. Stop *Lamprey*."

"We'll be called on it."

"So stall the bastards. Buy time."

"Sir?"

"What?"

"What about the Russians? Won't they be out there looking around too?"

"They may want to," said the President. "But we'll protect our two-hundred-mile fishing limit. Do you read me?"

"Loud and clear," said Noah Henderson. "Very well, Mr. President. I'll see to Paul Forsythe."

He hung up the phone and stared down at his desk.

And, he thought, I'll see to destroying my career. But what choice is there? It must be done.

"It must be done," said Soviet Premier Mikhail Nabov.

His advisor on Naval Affairs said, "Comrade, the Americans have been very positive in enforcing their fishing waters since the Chile affair. Their claim to two hundred miles, while not approved in the world courts, is nevertheless an actuality. In addition, those waters are far too southerly to sustain the cover of a fishing expedition."

"I know," said Nabov. "But we must find out what happened to the space platform. We don't dare send submarines. They could be construed as a hostile force. A surface vessel, with suitable underwater equipment, is our only choice."

"In that case," said the advisor, "our fishery research ship, *Akademik Knipovich* is closest to the area."

"Is the vessel suitable?"

"*Knipovich* is one of our BMRT types," said the advisor. "More than three thousand tons gross. Eighty-four and a half meters long with a single diesel. Only thirteen knots top speed, which is a disadvantage."

The Premier shrugged. "We could not outrun their jet planes anyway. Continue."

"*Knipovich* carries underwater equipment, which must be winchlowered. But at top speed, they can be in Bahama waters by noon Saturday."

"Give the order," said Nabov.

*   *   *

Captain Arthur Lovejoy, hearing a footstep on the gangplank, thought that Paul Forsythe had returned with his wife. He went out to greet them.

Strong, slim arms wrapped around his neck, and he felt his face smothered with kisses.

"Daddy!" cried Janet Lovejoy.

"Jan. What are you doing here?"

"I cut school. What are they doing to you?"

Janet, slim and boyish-looking with her close-cut brown hair and clean, scrubbed face, had to look up almost a foot to meet her father's eyes. She had never topped five feet, and probably never would. Soaking wet, she weighed in at ninety-six pounds. But where Nature had skimped in her bosom and other curve-oriented locations, Janet had been blessed with a smile that ranged from trembling shyness to a wide, face-splitting beam that radiated happiness at the speed of light to every corner. Her nose was speckled with freckles, and her ears poked out too much, and her hands were too big, and everybody who saw her fell instantly in love.

"Come below," said Lovejoy, leading his daughter down to his quarters. "I didn't expect you, so things are messed up."

"As usual. Don't worry, Daddy. I'll get you organized."

"Good luck," he said.

"I asked before," she said, sternly. "What are they doing to you?"

"To me? Nothing. But I think Washington's putting the shaft to Paul."

"I thought so. What a bunch of blah. I'm surprised they didn't try to blame you for the recession too."

"Well, we're holding our breath. ER's trying to get out of the contract."

"Which means?"

"No job."

"Mr. Forsythe'll find one."

"Maybe. How about some coffee?"

She made a wry face. "Not until I make it myself. I've been on your boats before, remember?"

"Ships," he said.

"Where's Keefer?" she asked casually. Too casually, her father thought.

"Out with the launch. He had a message for Sir Roger Lean, who's out there somewhere in a sailboat."

"The guy who went around the world twice by himself?"

"Seventy-one, and still hopping."

"Oh, Daddy! I wish he was still here. He's my hero!"

"I thought George Burns was your hero."

"He is, but Sir Roger's a *sailor*."

Lovejoy gave her a hug. "Still crazy about the swabbies?"

"I am," she said. "Now, where do I sleep?"

"Take this cabin," he said.

"No. It's the Captain's cabin, and you're the Captain. How about crew's quarters? I don't mind sharing."

"Maybe you don't," he said, grinning. "But I do."

"We've got co-ed dorms at the school now."

"I heard."

"No like?"

"No like."

"Don't you trust your little girl?"

He patted her trim behind. "I trust you all the way. I just don't trust those other characters."

"I can handle myself."

"Okay. But you'll do it in Cabin Three. Alone."

"Am I putting somebody out in the cold?"

"Just a crewman who doesn't belong in there anyway. We've let some of the hands use the cabins until the scientific staff reported on board."

"Why can't the crewman and I double up?"

"You try it," he said, "and I'll paddle your tail."

The wind was strong, and as Joseph Horatio guided his sloop away from the pier at Alice Town, he glanced

back. Nobody had come to see him off; they hadn't for
many years.

Some said he brought ill fortune to Bimini. They
spoke of his long friendship with Adam Clayton Powell.
Hadn't the Congressman fallen into disgrace, and ill
health, and eventual death?

Yes. But, Horatio contended, those events were or-
dained. What he had been able to do, as they occurred,
was to give the unfortunate man companionship and a
sense of belonging to the mainstream of time.

Joseph Horatio had never been more than poor, but
in his long life, he had known many important men. He
never intruded on their lives, never sought their help,
never accepted money. But, merely by being there, he
had shared moments with the great which still lived in
his fertile memory.

He still remembered, with pain, the day in Charleston, South Carolina, where he had been born, and lived
as a freed slave, when they came and, weeping, said,
"They've shot the President! They've killed our President."

And, uncomprehending, he had looked up and said,
"Boy, I don't believe you. I can't believe you." He had
seen, then, the tears in their eyes, and had whispered,
"Why, is Mr. Lincoln dead?"

CHAPTER 7

Noah Henderson had moved fast. He, as did most of those in the inner circle close to President Howard Foster, knew all too well that a hint from Foster was actually a request; a request was an order; and an order was a command to be carried out instantly.

His conversation with Martin Weatherby of the Bank of North Virginia was circular, but the points he wanted made got across. BNV carried the paper on most of *Lamprey*'s electronic gear, which had been built and installed in the United States. Rather than finance the gear out of cash in hand, Saito Osha had opted to pay BNV's prime rate of 9 per cent, telling Paul Forsythe, "By putting my cash to work, I can earn fifteen to twenty per cent a year. If I pay nine per cent to the bank for operating money, I'm automatically eleven points ahead."

Under most circumstances, his assessment would have held up. But with the considerable pressure of the Department of Energy Resources applied against the moderately sized regional bank, the BNV's president found himself agreeing that if *Lamprey*'s contracts were canceled, there might be more risk than his directors would accept in allowing all that expensive equipment to be taken to sea.

Lawyers went to work, six deep, each drafting a single page of the long injunction. But by four-thirty on Thursday afternoon, it was ready, and had been telexed to Jacksonville, where one team of lawyers filed it at the courthouse while another, accompanied by federal marshals, served a writ of injunction on Paul Forsythe aboard the survey vessel.

Quietly, he asked one of the lawyers, "What exactly does this thing mean?"

"*Lamprey* is enjoined from leaving port until the bank is satisfied that its investment is protected," said the lawyer.

Forsythe nodded, a faint smile touching his lips. "You realize, of course, that Mr. Osha will merely pay off the loan as soon as he can transfer funds."

"If so, the injunction would naturally be voided," said the lawyer. "However, until then, the marshal here is under orders to impound the vessel."

"No," said Forsythe. "I will not attempt to leave port. But not you, nor the marshal, nor any of your staff, will come on board."

The lawyer looked at the marshal, who shrugged.

"Very well," said the lawyer. "Thank you, sir."

The legal force departed. The marshal remained.

"Would you like a deck chair?" asked Forsythe.

The marshal shook his head. "No, thanks. I'm not supposed to sit down on duty."

"Okay," said Forsythe. "But if your feet get tired, give a yell. Nobody's mad at you."

"Thanks," said the marshal. Then he added, "I'm only doing my job."

"Sure," said Forsythe. "Aren't we all?" He went back on board *Lamprey* and picked up the ship-to-shore telephone.

Saito Osha had boarded the supersonic Concorde jet in Tokyo, flown over the North Pole to London, where he connected with another Concorde bound to Dulles near Washington, D.C. When he embarked there for transfer to a private jet which would fly him to Jacksonville, he looked at his watch, which was still on Tokyo time.

He had flown nearly around the world in less than eight hours.

* * *

Gloria Mitchel sat in one corner of the small office, but there was no doubt that she was the center of attention.

"I don't buy it," she said. "Somebody's playing dirty pool. My guess, he lives at 1600 Pennsylvania Avenue."

Walter Wylie said, "What's new about that?"

"Nothing. Except we were right on top of the story, and we let it get away."

"We didn't let it do anything," Wylie said. "They took it, baby. Don't knock what you ended up with. First on the air, that's better than a sharp stick in the eye."

Pat Crosby, idly smearing the film gate of his Canon Scoopic with a little nose grease, said, "I agree with Glor. They cut us off at the knees. They've got their finks everywhere. That film I took down there, remember? I got some terrific stuff on the Prez. Only guess what."

Wylie sighed. "I know. There was an accident in the lab. Bad chemicals."

"Bad chemicals, my ass," said the cameraman. "Somebody flashed that footage. Come on, Walt. Do I really look as if I have dried egg on my tie? I've been around this business long enough to be able to tell the difference between bad soup and a deliberately light-struck piece of film. And besides, bad chemicals don't erase a magnetic sound track. Somebody put my stuff on a bulk eraser and wiped it all clean."

"What gives, Walter?" asked Gloria. "Are we in the news business, or are we in the government cover-up business?"

"You made an agreement," he said wearily.

"And I've stuck to it," she said. "I didn't mention a word about that farce down in Jacksonville. But I never said I wouldn't pursue the story further. Why all this resistance? You okayed a three-day trip last month for Woody to go down and, for God's sake, film a Cajun alligator-wrestling contest. Let's have it up front. Have they gotten to you?"

"I won't even answer that," he said.

"Then get off your ass and let's get something done."

"I'm getting flack from upstairs."

"Walt," she said grimly, "you can tell upstairs this. I've got my Fuck You money in a Mexican bank earning fourteen per cent. I can quit tomorrow and still get by. But if they force me to do it, I can also walk across the street to CBS and tell the whole lousy story on national TV. So who do I get the story for? Us, or the CBS Evening News?"

"I'll convey your message," he said.

When he'd left the room, Gloria turned to Pat Crosby and said, "Better start packing."

"Okay. Where are we going?"

"Your favorite hunting ground for the Wild Poontang."

"Out of sight," he said, clicking the film gate back into the camera.

That night, Jacksonville was chill and windblown. The Christmas lights swayed in the blustery gusts that came from the northeast, and threw red and blue and green shadows over the used car lots, the garish windows of the shopping center, the palm-lined residential streets.

Paul Forsythe had learned that Saito Osha was on his way. He and Beth decided to drive to the airport to meet the Japanese tycoon. Arthur Lovejoy and his daughter declined the invitation to join them. The Captain said, "I'm going to stay on board, in case those bank bastards get any idea about confiscating our equipment."

"Don't make waves," said Forsythe. "We'll get this straightened out in a few days."

"They're hassling us. Why?"

"I wish I knew."

"What about the press? We've been getting calls."

"They all know I'm going to make a statement tomorrow morning. Tell them to wait for that."

"What if they won't?"

"Then they can line up and stand in the cold with our friend the U.S. marshal."

Paul had asked one of the crewmen to exchange the balky Pinto for another car, and now he found himself driving a Toyota. He grinned. "It figures," he said. "Saito ought to feel right at home."

Beth laughed. "Not a chance. *He* drives a Lincoln."

Guiding the automobile onto the interstate highway, Forsythe said, "Is that a knock? Don't you like our old Dart?"

"I love it with passion," she said. "But are American cars really supposed to go two hundred thousand miles?"

"It's only nine years old," he protested. "And most of those miles were put on by you. Including two trips down the Pan American highway, which didn't do Irvina any good."

"I wish you wouldn't call it that. It's—"

"Piggy? Okay, Irving."

"That's worse."

He drove in silence for a while. Then: "Hon, are you shook?"

"A little," she admitted. "Oh, it's corny, but even after Watergate, I still believed in our system of government. And now, just look at what they're doing—"

"It'll blow over," he said. "Don't let it change anything you've felt. Our system stinks, but compared with the alternatives—"

Shortly, she said, "I know, I've made that same argument myself. But when they come after *you,* I find myself choking on the words. My God, Paul, if they can do this to you after all you've given your country, why nobody's safe."

"You got one thing wrong," he said quietly.

"Such as?"

"They haven't done anything to me yet. They're merely trying. What makes you think I intend to let them get away with it?"

She gripped his arm.

"Goddamn it," she said. "That's my guy. I'm sorry. I shouldn't have doubted."

"Sunny," he promised, "I don't know how this is going to turn out. But they'll know they've been in a fight.

"Paul—can they cancel the contracts?"

"Not legally."

"But they can anyway."

"Sure."

"Then what?"

"Maybe," he said, "we'll go in the Bermuda Triangle movie business."

CHAPTER 8

Thirty-six hours later, Forsythe's joking remark about going into the Bermuda Triangle film business had come true.

Saito Osha, who had arrived at Jacksonville with a stunningly beautiful Japanese girl on his arm, found his attempts to transfer two million dollars from his Tokyo bank to the Bank of Northern Virginia thwarted by obscure currency exchange regulations. A try at running around end with a blind transfer from a Swiss account met with the same obstruction.

Dourly, as he sipped a Suntory and water, he said, "Paul, your government is throwing up a wall around *Lamprey*. They do not want you to leave port."

"Too goddamned bad," said Forsythe. "Art, what can they do if we just cast off the lines and go?"

Lovejoy frowned. "At a minimum, send the Coast Guard after us. They might resort to force."

Paul laughed. "As if they haven't already? Remember the Marines?"

Beth Forsythe said, "There's something out there they don't want us to see. That's the only logical answer."

"How about it?" said Forsythe. "Do we take off?"

Osha shook his head. "No, Paul. We have too much to lose. How long can they delay us with their petty regulations? A day? A week? During that time, our lawyers will be attacking them through the courts."

"And in the same time," said Kenneth O'Keefe angrily, "all it'd take to sink us right here at dockside would be one magnetic mine attached to the right part of our hull."

Janet Lovejoy gasped. "They wouldn't. Not our own government."

"Don't bet on it," said the sub commander.

"Who knows?" said Forsythe. "The question is, what do we do now?"

"Wait," said Osha.

"Post a watch in the underwater view ports," said O'Keefe.

"Good idea," said Lovejoy. "I'll see to it."

"Who can we reach in Washington?" asked Beth. "I know Bernstein on the *Post*. Maybe——"

"Too slow," said her husband.. "Sunny, I had lunch with the President himself twice while we were planning the survey. If he'll go back on his word, anybody would. We're up shit creek without a paddle."

But he said that without knowing that, at that very moment, a rescue column was already on its way to the embattled gangway of the survey vessel *Lamprey*.

William Postiglion, apprehensive that any formal notice of his arrival might result in the cancellation of Forsythe's impulsive invitation, had chartered a Lear jet and pilot to fly himself and Anthony Dix from Hollywood to Jacksonville. The producer was trembling with excitement. Dix's idea of having Jack Begley fly his 1945 mission again as part of the film's research was dramatic and full of publicity opportunities. If only Forsythe would co-operate!

Without even checking into a hotel, he and Dix drove directly to the port, where they were confronted by a bewildered U.S. marshal who was not sure whether or not his orders included barring strangers from boarding the impounded *Lamprey*. Bluster won over civil service caution, and they were welcomed aboard the vessel with gloomy faces and alcoholic beverages.

It took only a few moments for Postiglion to realize that his worst fears had been realized.

"Osha-san," he suggested to the Japanese shipping magnate, "pay off the loan. Lose a little on your investments. It's worth it."

"Mr. Postiglion," said Osha, "I am trying to do so. But there are obstacles."

Forsythe said, "Obviously the Administration thinks there's some greater good to be obtained by canceling our project."

Posty said, "And you agree to this?"

"Hell no. But what can we do?"

The producer made his decision. "What price is this vessel worth for, say, a twenty-day cruise?"

Forsythe said, "Half a million. Anything less would lose money."

"So six hundred thousand would show you a profit?"

Forsythe turned his head. "Saito?"

The Japanese man lowered his eyes for a moment. "Mr. Postiglion, I do not appreciate being treated in this manner by the United States Government. If you were able to get this ship out of port by morning, I would gladly offer you the charter for nothing."

"Is that a deal?"

Forsythe said, "Hey, wait a minute."

Dix chimed in, "Posty, don't jump overboard."

They were both cut off by Osha, who said, "Yes, it is a deal. Set aside this injunction, and you have twenty days without charge. And I will, of course, reimburse you for any payments you may make."

"Done," said Postiglion. He got up. "Come on, Tony. We've got to raise some cash money."

Dix groaned. "Your bank or mine?"

In any war, in any battle, there are moments of calm, seconds of relative tranquillity. The struggle for custody of *Lamprey* was no exception.

Paul Forsythe had not taken possession of the main cabin, but when he had returned from the airport with his wife he discovered that he had been ousted from the smaller quarters he had occupied, and had been installed in the two-room suite which had been designed for owner's territory. Ice, glasses, and assorted bottles of hard liquor were in obvious display.

"We've got a brown-noser on board," he grumbled.

Beth hugged his arm. "Not so. Just somebody nice who wanted us to be happy."

"Are you?"

"Happy? No. I don't like to stand around and watch them screw you."

"That'll be the day," he said. "Sunny, I don't know what's going on, and until I do, I don't want to react the wrong way. But you can believe this, they aren't going to put this ship on the beach while they run their god-damned surveys. We had nothing to do with Apollo 19, and they all know it." He had poured them both healthy slugs of scotch. "What browns me off is that they didn't come out and openly ask for my help. I'm a company man. If it's so important that they have to do this, I'd have gone along."

"Maybe not," she said, sipping. "You're a rambling man now, Mr. Forsythe. The Company may not trust you any more."

"Then the Company's stupid."

"My point exactly. Baby, drink my love."

He touched her glass with his. "Mine too."

She drank. "Don't you ever fool around on the side?"

He choked. "What do you mean?"

"I mean, don't you have a condom in your wallet?"

"Shit no," he half exploded. "What the hell for?"

"Only that if you did, maybe we could still make out."

"Sorry. All my paramours take the pill."

She laughed. "Paramours? I'm afraid I have to believe in you. You're straight. Nobody's used the word paramour since Maurice Chevalier hung up his straw hat."

He caressed her breast. "So let's go it naked."

She shook her head. "No, sweetheart. I know how you feel about . . . mess. Either buy some rubbers or keep it packed in ice for the next three days."

He winced. "You're too clinical for me."

"It's the new Lib. God gave this problem to us female types, but the Supreme Court says we don't have to accept it."

"They're going to pass a ruling against the Almighty?"

"Why not? They already chased Him out of the public schools."

He pulled her close to him. She was warm and soft against his strained muscles. "Do you really mean any of that stuff, Sunny? Or is it just gallows humor?"

"Babe," she whispered, holding his swelling crotch gently, "don't ask that question, okay? Just play it by ear."

He groaned. "Okay, but you'd better play on some other flute. Or else."

She gave a gentle laugh and, as she leaned down, unzipping him, said, "What's so bad about 'or else'?"

Breakfast was at 8 A.M. Dix and Postiglion had spent the night at a nearby Holiday Inn, but when they reboarded *Lamprey* carrying suitcases, it was to the discomfort of a second-shift U.S. marshal, who took this invasion of new passengers as indication that the impounded ship was about to slip her moorings.

Osha had insisted that Forsythe retain the owner's quarters. He and the pretty Japanese girl, whom he had introduced as a former Takarazuka actress, Raiko Nakamura, took over the number two cabin.

Beth Forsythe sipped tea with the girl. "Is it true that there aren't any men in your opera company?" she asked.

"Regrettably," said the slim, dark-eyed Japanese girl. Her hair was cut short, and was jet black. "We are almost like—what you call them?—nuns. No man is ever permitted on the Takarazuka stage. I play most of the male leads."

"What sort of shows do you do?"

"Serious opera—but shortened to half an hour, or at the most, an hour. Musical comedy. Short comedy bits—what your comics call blackouts."

"And only with women?"

Raiko smiled. "That is true."

"Why?"

"It is the way of the Takarazuka. We are trained, and live in our dormitories, and perform only with women." She giggled. "Except for one time, when an American GI sneaked on stage."

"Oh?"

"It was in Tokyo, during the Korean war. This GI-Joe, he called himself Orson Welles, except of course he was not really Mr. Welles, but rather a sergeant who worked for the FEAF newspaper in the Old Kaijo Building."

"FEAF?"

"Far East Air Force," said the Japanese girl, as if surprised that anyone might not know what the acronym meant. "This GI, he wrote often for the Nippon *Times,* and the *Mainichi,* although it was forbidden by his commanders. He was always in trouble. At any rate, one time he was dating one of our star performers, which was strictly against Takarazuka rules. And it seems that he learned the words of one of her comedy blackouts in Japanese. So, one night, he locked her in her dressing room and went on stage and did the sketch. It was a major scandal. The girl almost lost her job. He was severely reprimanded by his superiors. As far as I know, that is the only time a man ever appeared on the Takarazuka stage."

"Who was this character? Somebody we might have seen on the stage or in films?"

"No," said Raiko. "No one has ever heard of him since. He was merely an unimportant GI. I believe his name was Corey. Or Korley. All we remember is 'Orson Welles.' Which was untrue."

"Are you on vacation now?"

"No," said the girl. "Osha-san and I, we intend to marry. It is not permitted for the Takarazuka girl to have a husband. So I have—retired? No, the word is resigned."

"I'm sorry," said Beth. "Why don't you get together

with the rest of the girls and raise hell? Make them change their stupid rules."

"But why?" asked Raiko. "I knew those rules before I became Takarazuka, and I accepted them. If I no longer agree, it is correct for me to leave, but what right do I have to demand that they change to please me?"

"Oh, wow," said Beth Forsythe.

"Here," said Kenneth O'Keefe, pouring more coffee for Janet Lovejoy. "Get your heart started."

"Thanks." The girl sipped. "How've you been?"

"Busy."

"Too busy to scribble a post card?"

He shrugged. "You know how it is."

"I thought I did. Maybe I was wrong."

O'Keefe, looking away, said, "I'm sorry. I didn't know you made that much of it."

"A girl's only got one cherry. Maybe it's old-fashioned, but, yes, I guess I made that much of it."

"Jan, you're a sweet kid—"

She stiffened. "But who can take a steady diet of 'sweet kids'?"

"That's not what I meant."

She tossed what was left of her coffee over the rail into Jacksonville Harbor.

"Oh, hell, forget it," she said. "It's my fault. You didn't make any promises."

"Sit down," he said, "and *settle* down. I don't know if you and me, we have a thing or not. But the truth is I've been busy as hell, so busy I didn't even write my mom."

"Et tu, Oedipus," she said.

"Are you coming along?" he asked. Then added, "If they let us drag anchor, that is?"

"I guess so," she said. "They're trying to screw my father. I intend to be on the scene and do a little eye-clawing, if they get too close."

"It may be interesting," said O'Keefe. "Jan, there's something weird out there. Something you wouldn't believe, unless you'd seen it yourself."

"And, dear heart, we can discover it *together?*"

"If you want."

She stood. "I don't know, Ken. Right now, I don't want. We'll see."

She strode away, stiffly, making her slight body jar the deck with its suppressed anger.

William Postiglion's entrance into the Bank of Northern Virginia was, to say the least, spectacular.

He was dressed in a gray flannel suit so severely cut that it seemed to be a parody of Brooks Brothers. Chained to his wrist was a leather valise.

Behind him, two cameramen followed. One operated a Sony Rover videotape camera and recorder. The other used a Kodak Super-8 sound camera, with the 200-foot magazine which gives more than thirteen minutes of sound-on-film capability.

"I am here," said Postiglion loudly, "to pay off the loan this bank holds with Saito Osha, the Osha Shipbuilders, and Paul Forsythe."

A dumbfounded junior vice-president said, "But—"

"No buts, young man," said Posty. "Take me to your senior officer."

"Pictures aren't allowed—" protested the vice-president.

"Under what law?" demanded Posty. "Sir, we are here to protect the interests of your depositors. You have expressed fears that your investment in the survey vessel *Lamprey* are endangered. Very well. I intend to remove those fears. Here"—and for emphasis, he patted the valise—"is the money, plus your rather handsome interest, which you apparently feel is in danger of default." He now patted his breast pocket. "I further bear a notarized authorization from Mr. Saito Osha to clear this obligation."

Still protesting, the vice-president let himself be shepherded to an interior office, where an even more surprised Martin Weatherby found himself confronting an immaculately tailored man with a briefcase handcuffed to his wrist and accompanied by two cameramen.

"This is most irregular," he protested.

"So," said Posty sternly, "is the injunction you slapped on the *Lamprey*. I am having this moment recorded so that you cannot stall me and later say that you misunderstood my purpose. In plain words, your actions indicate that you are afraid the electronic gear you financed may be a bad risk. Very well. We are paying off the loan. If you will have several of your cashiers come in, they can begin counting. The money is in new, serially numbered hundred-dollar bills, so it shouldn't take long."

"There are normal channels for these things," said Weatherby.

"And there are laws protecting not only your depositors, but also your customers," said Posty. "You are harassing *Lamprey,* for whatever motives we don't know. That is to stop at this moment, for here is your repayment. Decline it, or delay me, at your own risk."

Weatherby sat down. He had never really felt comfortable with the bargain he'd struck with the Department of Energy Resources anyway.

"Get three cashiers," he told the young vice-president.

"Will you instruct your attorney to lift the injunction?" asked Postiglion. "Or must you personally examine every hundred-dollar bill yourself first?"

Wearily, the bank president picked up his telephone.

"You know," Paul Forsythe said, standing on the bridge with his Captain, "we're getting ourselves surrounded by a pack of crazies."

"That," said Arthur Lovejoy, "is the understatement of the year."

In southern Wales, where the sun was setting against the cold gray of the sea, Diana Lean started up from a half daze. She had been working in the garden, and had sat down to rest, and the warmth of the sun had lulled her off. But now there was a chill to the air, and she felt her toes tingle as she stood and watched the blazing red of the sun dip into the far horizon.

"Oh, dear," she said to herself, "Roger, please be careful."

CHAPTER 9

Dimitri Ashkenazy had been at sea for most of his life. In those grim days after World War II, he had sailed aboard a series of small destroyers, in assignments that ranged from the Baltic to the North Pacific. His first command had been on a fishing factory, which operated in the shoals off Newfoundland, a post he found distasteful not only because of the smelly refuse left by the fish processing, but because he was never able to accept the deliberate destruction carried out by his crew against local fishermen's nets and buoys. Ashkenazy had, instilled when he was a cabin boy, a respect for the right of all men to sail the seas in freedom and without restraint. While he took orders, as did all masters in the Soviet fleet, he privately agreed with some and disagreed with others. There was no difference in his attention to duty, whichever position he held, but within his own mind, the distinction was clear.

His ship, *Akademik Knipovich,* had been built in 1968 as a Fishery Research Vessel. With a tonnage of 3,165 gross—1,666 tons net—the *Knipovich* looked rather like a small cruise ship, one which might be operated on short Caribbean tours. *Knipovich* sat high in the water, which made the vessel rather tender during rough weather; 278 feet long, with a fairly standard superstructure, *Knipovich* had been modified over the years until now the vessel carried sophisticated electronic gear, a submersible capable of depths down to 3,000 feet, and a low-frequency radio transmitter capable of reaching the nuclear submarines while they were submerged.

Knipovich led a dual life; fishery experts carried out their work, charting the ebb and flow of huge schools of fish, ignoring the casually dressed, but obviously military-trained, electronics men who disappeared into their off-limits enclaves and dimmed the ship's lights with their excessive power requirements.

Dimitri Ashkenazy studied his orders again. They seemed clear enough, yet somewhere under their language lurked a danger that sent sharp signals to him.

His instructions were to proceed to a point some hundred miles northeast of Bimini Island, where he was to observe any survey or suspicious activity by Western ships. He was, particularly, to observe any use by the Western powers of submersibles for possible salvage work.

Possibly, this assignment was merely another of the unlabeled training exercises constantly given to Soviet vessels. Admiral-of-the-Fleet S. Gorshkov often lectured, "Ocean cruises are a school of moral-political and psychological training for modern war." No matter what the mission, this background was never forgotten.

While, before the Second World War, ships of the Red Fleet were rarely seen beyond Russia's coastal limits, deployments from the Black Sea began shortly thereafter. NATO naval forces were never in danger of being overwhelmed with Soviet superiority, but a gradual increase went on, seemingly unnoticed by the Western powers. By the late sixties, the Russian breakout had progressed to the point where an actual tactical exercise could be carried out in the Caribbean with a "Kynda" class cruiser, "Kildin" and "Kashin" class destroyers, an "Ugra" support ship, a "November" class nuclear submarine, a tanker, and two "Foxtrot" conventional submarines visiting Martinique and Barbados, to the great embarrassment of the United States. Since that time, Soviet "trawlers" had been frequent visitors to the Windward Islands, and to the Bahamas.

Ashkenazy had been on post now for almost a year. In another three months, he would be relieved and, after a few weeks at home in Moscow, he would be reassigned to another command, one as different from his previous one as his superiors could find. Wryly, the Soviet commanders called the routine, "Punching out all the numbers." By the time one reached retirement, he could count on having served in every major area of the world.

His Navigation Officer, Aleksandr Tortsev, came into the Captain's cabin after a single knock, and presented Dimitri with an updated chart.

"We will be on position in approximately nine hours," said the young navigator. "The seas are calm, and our long-range weather forecasts are for another two days of this low-pressure area before a high moves in from Canada."

"Thank you," said Dimitri Ashkenazy. Privately, he wondered if the young officer ever lapsed from his formal speech. He could visualize Aleksandr in the act of love: "Assume the supine position, while my member approaches from the north, ten degrees above the target area."

He chuckled. Aleksandr stiffened. "Pardon me," he said. "I did not mean to——"

Slowly, Dimitri moved one finger in the air. "It is nothing," he said. "I remembered something humorous."

Tortsev, uneasily, smiled. "I will make another report on the hour," he said, and left.

Dimitri Ashkenazy watched him go, and wondered casually if he had ever been that callow.

Probably.

Joseph Horatio felt the wind against his right cheek. He frowned. This was not good. Sailing north, a sta'bod breeze might mean a cyclonic movement of the air. Hurricanes at this time of year were rare, but they had occurred.

But the air was warm; that bode well. Perhaps he was being too cautious. In these latitudes, the wind came around often and only a steady drop in the barometer meant real danger.

To Joseph Horatio, veteran of a hundred fierce storms, it meant nothing that weather satellites now photographed the entire hemisphere every twenty minutes, and that gathering storms were spotted long before they grew to maturity.

Television and radio were noise-making devices that entertained the tourists in Alice Town bars. No seafaring man took any notice of them.

He loosed the mainsail a trifle. The rough hemp rope made a pleasant scraping sensation against his worn fingers. Horatio had no patience with the new artificial rigs. Nylon ropes, bright yellow, were pretty, and very strong, but they rotted quickly in the sun, and you could not trust them. Better hemp; if it weakened, you could see the soft areas and splice them. The same was true of fiberglass bottoms. They gleamed brightly in the showroom, but how could a man put trust in them when within their shiny skin they might have hidden air bubbles or chemical-weakened pits invisible to the searching eye?

Wood, despite the dangers of dry rot and bore worm, was the only real material from which to form a hull. Wood needed no flotation chambers to keep it on top of the water. Wood was honest.

Joseph Horatio uncapped the metal water container and drank deeply. In his middle age, before the Spanish American War, he had often taken strong spirits. Those were the very bad years, those when he was in his fifties and sixties, when he thought final death was near at hand and had set himself to enjoying all the pleasures he had missed in his poverty-stricken youth and young manhood. Today, women were still pleasurable, although he suspected they now came to him out of some superstitious awe rather than from genuine passion. But his taste for rum and gin had almost vanished.

Death had come near to Joseph Horatio so often that he no longer feared it. Where, at first, he had seen it as a foul intruder into the house of man, sword in hand, taking blood and life in wanton abandon, he now saw the dark angel as a friend of those who lay, waiting, in pain and despair.

One day it would come for him, he knew. And he anticipated it with mild curiosity. What a voyage that would be, with no chart, no star, no compass to steer by.

Lamprey cleared the outer channel marker of the Jacksonville channel at 3 P.M. exactly.

Behind her, confusion reigned. Since the BNV's injunction had been lifted, the U.S. marshals had no further jurisdiction. Yet they had been advised, privately by their superiors, that the vessel was not to leave port.

The original marshal, who was back on duty when the ship cast off, shouted at his superior over the pay phone.

"What the hell was I supposed to do, take out my .38 pistol and fire a shot over her bow? The goddamned injunction was voided. I saw the papers. We had no right to hold her."

"This is trouble," said the shaken voice of his superior, over in Tallahassee. "Washington isn't going to like this."

"Tell Washington that if they want a boat held, they need papers, warrants, search and seizures, *something!* What do I do now?"

"Report to the Jacksonville office," said the voice. "We'll think of something."

"While you're doing that little thing," said the marshal, "do you know who's in command of that boat? Ever hear of a sub skipper named Paul Forsythe? Maybe you never served in the Navy, but I did, and if you ask me, you're fooling around with the wrong guy."

"Just report in," said the weary voice.

At the Jacksonville airport, a burly man had lugged his suitcase across the ramp to the civilian private sector, and presented himself at the offices of Southern Aircraft.

"I'm Jack Begley," he said. "I believe you've got a Hughes chopper on standby for me."

The clerk consulted his records, found a reservation slip. "Right," he said. "Thirty-day charter. Cleared for sea on-board landings. Can I see your rating?"

The pudgy man spread out his credentials. The clerk whistled. "Mister," he said, "you're what they call over-qualified."

"Boredom," said Begley. "I kept taking the tests."

"Sign here," said the clerk. "The bills are to be sent to North Atlantic Productions, Beverly Hills, right?"

"I guess so," said the pilot. "All I know is they told me I wouldn't have to pay cash."

"Not," chuckled the clerk, "unless you happen to have around twenty-five hundred bucks a day to plunk down."

"I do," said Begley. "But I won't."

"Oh," said the clerk. He stamped the rental agreement. "Do you want a check ride?"

"Why?"

The clerk considered for a moment and, smiling, said, "No reason, I guess. Have a good flight, Mr. Begley."

"Thanks," said the pilot. He stuffed the paperwork into his brain bag and, closing the well-worn briefcase, started for the helicopter.

The word reached the President's ears at three-twenty, Washington time.

"I see," he said calmly as Noah Henderson gave him the report. "Well, you did all you could."

"What now?"

"Nothing. We've stepped well over the line already. I'll have *Lamprey* put under observation, and if they find out anything, I'll just have to appeal to Forsythe's conscience as a good citizen."

"I hope you won't take this wrong, Mr. President," said Henderson, "but I think that might have been the best thing to do in the very beginning."

"Mr. Henderson," said the President, "I have a sinking feeling in my stomach that you're right."

* * *

As she throbbed through the slight swell off the east coast of Florida, *Lamprey* carried more personnel than she had ever held in her brief sea life.

As co-owners, Saito Osha and Paul Forsythe shared an overview of the ship's operation. But Arthur Lovejoy, as Captain, was in complete charge of the above-water portion of the vessel's mission.

Beth Forsythe was cleaning her cameras, and preparing their underwater housings. She had no intention of being supercargo.

Raiko Nakamura, pancake makeup from the Takarazuka Opera Company still caking some of her boyish shirts, unpacked Osha's small suitcase and set about making the cabin as comfortable as possible for both of them.

The Captain's daughter, Janet, was already settled into Cabin Three. She sat on the narrow bunk, her hands clasped, thinking about last night, and the goodnight kiss O'Keefe had given her when he returned after their argument. She had very nearly weakened and invited him in. Another kiss, and . . .

Anthony Dix studied his small stateroom carefully. Yes, he decided, there was just enough room to construct a small, perhaps three-foot, pyramid over his bunk. Like so many who profit from the mystic, Dix had come to believe in some of it himself in spite of his professional cynicism.

Kenneth O'Keefe, moved to the smallest officer's cabin, simply threw his duffel bag inside and went below to check out *Yellowtail*, and to make sure that nobody had planted a magnetic mine or a Claymore on the hull.

William Postiglion looked around his own cabin. It was so small, he thought. Like a railroad compartment. He sighed. A fortune in front money that he might never see again, and now he was expected to sleep in a telephone booth.

In the crew quarters, Henry Frazier stowed his gear silently. He did not appreciate being ousted from his private cabin. After all, he was an electronics expert, not a mere seaman. He'd been promised . . . well, not exactly promised, but there had certainly been hints, before he'd signed on, that he would be living in officer country. Now these Hollywood bastards had shoved him up forward.

As the early sunset darkened the shadows, Lovejoy switched on the surface radar, and reduced speed.

"Wind's coming around," he said.

O'Keefe, drinking coffee from a heavy mug, answered, "It always does. Go see any naval movie. Captain always said, 'Wind's coming around.' I'd miss hearing it if you didn't do the same."

Lovejoy chuckled. "Getting itchy?"

"I don't like what happened back there in Jacksonville."

"Neither do I. And Paul's got that look. But we'll get it resolved legally. This isn't the war of 1812."

"You mean, that producer paid the bastards off," said O'Keefe. "If that's legal resolution, give me a good old hijacking any time."

"Fifteen minutes to dinner," said Lovejoy. "I wouldn't be a bit surprised if they weren't mixing cocktails down there."

"Want one?"

"Later," said the Captain. "You go ahead."

"Okay," said O'Keefe. "I'll relieve you in half an hour."

"No bother. It's about time the crew started earning their pay. I've got watches set up beginning at seventeen hundred hours."

"Good for you," said O'Keefe, "because that's five P.M., and that was forty minutes ago."

Lovejoy looked at his watch and swore. "It's my fault. I told Sparky that I'd hit the bell when I wanted relief."

"So hit it," said O'Keefe, "and then let's go and drink some of that Hollywood booze."

Sir Roger Lean had had his gin and tonic, and then the second half, and a dividend besides, and because he was very tired, he had gone to bed early, setting the self-steering carefully and testing the wind before he went below.

Later in the night, as the wind came around abruptly, *Plymouth Hope* began hobbyhorsing, and slowly with each new excursion of her bow, she turned north.

CHAPTER 10

"Listen to this," said Anthony Dix, reading from an old issue of *Boating and Sailing*. "It's an editorial by Pete Smyth. Title: 'Braving the Jaws of the Bermuda Triangle.' Pete was taking a slam at the big hoopla about the movie *Jaws*. Then, obliquely, he takes a slam at *me*."

"What's new about that?" asked William Postiglion, seated near him in *Lamprey*'s comfortable "galley."
"Controversy sells books."

"Pete says, '. . . no one seems to be all that sure just where the Bermuda Triangle is.' Then blah, blah, various points of reference. 'Take your choice. They're all pretty much the same, and all composed of pretty much the same thing: ordinary ocean.' More facts. Then, 'It is in fact a dangerous place, but no more so than any other equivalent body of water. You can drown in the Bermuda Triangle just as surely as you can drown almost anywhere if you go to sea unprepared and unaware of the real dangers inherent in traversing an implacable ocean.'"

"What does 'implacable' mean?" asked Postiglion.

"Quiet, movie man," said Dix. He went on: "'Regrettably, the public press finds little appeal in the safe crossing, whereas braving Tierra de Fuego aboard a rubber duck would make a swell novel, a gigantic movie and maybe even turn into a long-run TV series.'" He put the magazine down. "Ah, good old Pete. He writes a tough editorial. And right on course."

Although William Postiglion was, in effect, paying the costs of the cruise, had agreed that the priorities should be (1) *Lamprey*'s scheduled exploration of the ocean bottom northeast of Bimini; (2) a return to the underwater "highway" found by O'Keefe; and, (3) a re-creation, by helicopter, of Fight 19.

Jack Begley had landed the Hughes helicopter aboard *Lamprey*. Now he suggested, "Why don't I take the chopper down to Lauderdale tonight? Give us a jump on tomorrow? Why wait? Weather might come in."

"I'm going with you," said Anthony Dix.

"Always figured you would," said the pilot. "I'll get started on the pre-flight."

"Give a yell when you're ready," said the writer.

"Tony," said Forsythe as the pilot left, "I read somewhere that your next book's about UFOs. The Triangle stuff is one thing, maybe there's something there, but flying saucers?"

Dix smiled. "Oh, they call me a nut. That's what they label anyone who dares to suggest that this planet may have been visited by voyagers from outer space. Somehow, in our colossal conceit, it's acceptable for our own astronauts to have walked on the moon, for our survey spaceships to have made soft landings on Mars, but we firmly deny that there might be some traffic coming down the other side of the street."

"I accept the possibility," said Forsythe. "But where's the evidence?"

"Ask the Air Force. They've bottled enough of it up in their Blue Book file."

"I mean physical evidence," answered Forsythe. "Listen, if there's anything our space travelers have been, it's litterbugs. We've strewn space garbage all over the lunar surface—everything from tin cans to abandoned LEMs. If they've been here—and particularly if they're still arriving, as you say—how come we never find an old bent second-stage rocket, or an empty kumquat container, or whatever they eat?"

"I don't know," said Dix. "But I'm convinced that if we are, indeed, being visited by intelligent entities who want to remain undetected, they would be very careful about *not* littering. And the best place to do that would be to set up their bases under the sea. That's why I was so excited about being invited to join your ship."

Osha said, "Underwater UFOs? Isn't that a bit fantastic?"

"Did you ever hear of Operation Deep Freeze?"

Osha shook his head.

"It was a U. S. Navy project at the South Pole. An icebreaker was stationed in Admiralty Bay. A Dr. R. J. Villela, a scientist from Brazil, was on deck when he heard a fantastic crashing sound from the surrounding ice. He saw great chunks of ice being thrown into the air. And the water, when it was revealed, was *boiling*."

"Volcano?" asked Forsythe.

"A silver-colored object which, after smashing through an estimated thirty feet of ice, took off into the sky like a rocket. The noise brought the officer of the deck and some sailors up, and they saw the rocket, if indeed that's what it was, shooting up through the clouds of steam."

"Naturally," Forsythe said, "nobody happened to have a camera."

"What if they'd had one? I've seen actual movies of a UFO. I spent nearly twenty thousand dollars having one sequence enhanced by the NASA computers. Result? I was accused of having hired some special effects expert to fake the whole thing. As for happening to have a camera, how often do you carry one around in your pocket?"

"You've made your point," admitted Forsythe.

Lovejoy said, "Mr. Dix, are you trying to tie UFOs in with this so-called Bermuda Triangle?"

"More specifically, with the Sargasso Sea," said Dix. He rubbed one hand nervously over his stubbled hair. "In 1963, the Navy held maneuvers out here. The mission was called Operation Detect, and its main purpose was to train sonar crewmen in advanced electronic tracking systems. There were specially equipped planes, too, aboard the flagship, the U.S.S. *Wasp,* and some submarines to act as decoys. The entire mission, remember, was to detect underwater objects."

"Don't tell me," said Forsythe. "They detected an underwater UFO."

"Exactly," said Dix. "First, the sonar operator aboard the *Wasp* got a readout that just couldn't be correct."

"Why not?" asked Lovejoy. "Maybe a sub out of position. Or a foreign intruder. The Russians love to bollix up our exercises."

"No sub, Russian or otherwise," said Dix, "shoots through the water at a speed of more than a hundred and fifty knots."

"Current shear?" suggested Forsythe. "I've had false readings caused by layering of the various currents."

"No," said Dix. "They tracked that object for two days. One thing all the operators agreed upon—and by now it wasn't just the *Wasp* involved, but fourteen other vessels, all getting the same readouts—was that the object had a single propeller. At one point, it submerged to nearly thirty thousand feet."

"What finally happened?"

"It disappeared toward the Azores. The Navy brass wrote reports for months. All were filed and forgotten."

"And that's what you're looking for now?" Forsythe asked. "A submersible that goes a hundred and fifty knots? Lots of luck. In a real bind, *Yellowtail* can get up to maybe twenty."

"I'm not interested in catching a UFO, or even chasing it. But with all the gear you've got on this vessel, if we should sight one, it seems likely that we might have a good chance of providing proof of its existence."

Saito Osha sipped the last of his Suntory and put down the empty glass. "And then what, Mr. Dix?"

Dix gave a little grin. "I write another best seller," he said.

Jack Begley came in. "The bird's ready."

"Good," said Dix. "See you guys later."

The Hughes made familiar bird-wing noises as it climbed from the small heli-pad, with its painted circle on *Lamprey*'s deck. The chopper slid westward, its lights going red-white-green, red-white-green, until a low cloud came between and blotted them out.

The low Florida coastline was just a murky blur on the horizon, but the sun sent bright bursts of orange and purple through the late afternoon clouds that had built up over the land mass. It was your classic tourist sunset.

Beth framed Paul against the bright burst of color and clicked off three exposures.

"Oh, Christ," he said. "If you're back to that kind of picture, let me go down and put on my medals."

"No heart," Beth said. "That's your problem."

The night had that special crystal clarity, like being at the bottom of a pool of absolutely clear water. The stars stared down with their cold orbs untwinkled by scattered clouds or haze. The Atlantic was calm, almost without a swell. No whitecaps broke the dark surface, which mirrored the stars like a million Christmas tree lights. The moon had not yet risen.

Bob Hart, Second Officer (O'Keefe was carried as First) had the duty. Hart at thirty-two wore a mild manner and a milder face, and had once killed a man in a barroom fight in Glasgow, when his name was not Bob Hart but Nathan Crane. Aware that his temper had its black side, Hart now forced it down to the bottom of his consciousness, and would go to wild extremes to avoid becoming angry. He had a vague resemblance to the comedian Bob Newhart, and capitalized on it. His speech, once fast and jumbled, had been trained to hesitate and underplay every scene, just like Newhart. Most often, Bob put the joke on himself, and had never had to fight again.

Now, as the wheelman called him over, he stared with disbelief at the radar readout.

"What the hell is *that?*" Hart said.

"Looks like the coastline," said the wheelman.

Hart checked the compasses. Their course was northeast by east. Florida was behind them.

"What range?"

"Fifty-mile circle," said the wheelman. That put the

apparent land mass some thirty miles ahead. Hart switched to the hundred-mile range. The "coastline" stretched, almost in a straight line, from one edge of the scope to the other.

"Take her down to one-third speed," Hart said. "I'd better get the Captain."

"One third," repeated the wheelman.

Hart hurried below and tapped on Lovejoy's door. He checked his watch and suppressed a groan. Nearly two in the morning. Lovejoy wasn't going to like being awakened.

Lovejoy didn't. He grumbled, and couldn't find one shoe, but in a very few minutes he was up on the bridge, studying the radar.

"I'm damned if I know what it is," he said. "Radar malfunction?"

"Let's make a turn," suggested Hart. "See how it reacts."

"Take her around in a circle," Lovejoy told the wheelman. "Right standard rudder."

They watched. The radar display showed them turning away from the hard edge of the mass, which was now some twenty-five miles due east.

"It's really out there," said Hart, pointing at the display. The mass was now to their left, as they had changed course to the south.

"Come on all the way around," said Lovejoy.

As the ship turned, so did the radar readout.

Paul Forsythe arrived. "What's up?" he asked. "Why are we circling?"

Lovejoy pointed to the radar. "This goddamned thing says there's a land mass up ahead."

"Impossible. There's nothing that way but open Atlantic."

"And *this*," said the Captain, tapping the cathode ray tube. "We made a three-sixty to check it out. It's not our radar, Paul. We've got something up ahead."

"Well," said Forsythe, "Let's find out what it is."

* * *

Two miles away from the dark mass that blacked out the sky as high as Paul could see, he ordered the engines slowed, and stopped *Lamprey* dead in the water. By now, almost everybody on board had awakened and, in various forms of nightdress, had gathered on deck. The barrier stretched in both directions as far as the horizons, and the radar showed an impenetrable object straight ahead.

"It's a fog bank," said Forsythe.

Lovejoy said, "I've never seen any goddamned fog bank like this. Radar goes right through fog. This thing's solid."

"Sure," Forsythe shot back. "It's Atlantis, risen from the deep."

"Cut it out, darling," said Beth, giving him a shot on the bicep with her fist. "How about some light on the subject? Maybe I can get some pictures."

O'Keefe unhooded the thirty-inch searchlight which, with its carbon arc, had a range of nearly ten miles.

Meanwhile, Lovejoy moved the ship in toward the mass, very carefully.

O'Keefe switched on the searchlight. Its lens was by now only half a mile or so from the mass. But it made a sharp, round circle on its side, fringed with rainbow shimmerings.

"Fog," Lovejoy admitted. "But not like any fog in the books." *Lamprey* moved in closer, until the vessel was only a hundred yards from the fog bank. It was a yellowish-brown, and even at this close range, the powerful light only penetrated a foot or so. The fog did not start at the waterline, but a few feet in the air, and beneath it the visibility seemed clear.

"Could it be volcanic dust?" asked Forsythe. "I heard that when Krakatoa blew, it sent dust around the world."

"I don't think it's dust," said Beth. "I remember, in one of Tony's books, he said that it was dangerous."

"Why?"

"Nobody knows. But a Coast Guard cutter, the *Yamacraw,* ran into the same stuff back in 1956."

Forsythe said, "They must have survived, or Dix wouldn't have known about it."

"They got out," Beth said. "But just barely. According to the Captain, it was pitch dark inside, like being surrounded by a dense cloud of dust, which is what her commander thought it was. But after a few minutes, the *Yamacraw* began losing steam pressure, and the men noticed that their eyes were irritated, and they began to cough. The crew reported later that it was just like sailing through a solid wall."

"Maybe it was dust, then," said Forsythe.

"There wasn't a trace of any sediment on the ship," said Beth.

"Put down the boat," called Forsythe. "I'm going to get a sample."

Lovejoy caught his wrist. "Don't," he said. "It's too dangerous."

"I'll tow a line. If anything goes wrong, you can pull me out."

Beth said, "I'm going too."

"In a pig's eye," Paul told her.

"Don't stop me," she said quietly. "I would never forgive you."

He looked into her eyes and saw the truth there.

"Okay, what the hell? It can't be that bad."

"Me too," said O'Keefe.

"Why?"

"Because I know how to run the motor and I bet you don't."

"True."

When the boat was ready, and they had passed several heavy plastic jugs with screw caps down into it, Beth boarded first, and took pictures while Paul and O'Keefe scrambled down the ladder. O'Keefe got the motor going, while Paul checked out the small CB transceiver.

"*Lamprey,* this is Forsythe. Do you copy?"

"Wall to wall," said *Lamprey*'s radio operator, Ray Barnstable.

Beth took two quick close-ups of Paul's face, the radio held up to his mouth, and the foul yellow-brown wall of fog just beyond the launch's bow.

"Okay," said Forsythe. "We're going in. I'll call you every five minutes. If I miss a call, have them pull us out."

"Ten-four," said Barnstable. *Lamprey* standing by."

"Ready?" Forsythe asked.

"Ready," said Beth, punctuating the word with a click of her shutter.

"Let's hit it, Keefer."

O'Keefe put the launch in gear and as they moved toward the yellowish mass, it loomed above them like a billowing cliff.

The light line they'd attached to the stern cleats was more than half a mile long, and had been intended for use in buoying markers to underwater locations. It spooled off a huge reel located on *Lamprey*'s bow. It was bright yellow nylon, and as the launch nosed into the fog bank, it lay behind them, floating on the still water, a garish link with reality.

Somehow, Forsythe had expected a temperature change as they entered the fog bank. But nothing occurred. The air was no cooler, no damper, than it had been outside. But the light from *Lamprey*'s searchlight suddenly dimmed, and now the fog around them glowed with a radiance that seemed to come from all sides. The launch had small running lights, but they seemed to penetrate the fog only a few inches.

"How the hell am I supposed to get pictures of *this?*" wailed Beth, clicking a wide-angle 23mm lens into her Pentax. "There's no light and nothing to focus on." But she kept making exposures anyway.

The air was deathly calm. Not a sound penetrated the fog's mass. There was not a breath of wind. Not a ripple stirred the ocean. Only the launch's wake broke its surface. The motors made a dull *thrumming* sound and the wake itself contributed urgent lapping noises against the launch's hull.

"Keep it slow," said Forsythe.

"Any slower," said O'Keefe, "and we'll be drifting."

"It feels like very fine dust," Beth said. "Lovely. If it gets down inside my cameras—"

"Shhh," said Forsythe.

He waved to O'Keefe, who cut the engines.

"Listen."

From ahead, how far they couldn't tell, a quiet ripple of music drifted through the fog.

"My God," said Beth. "It's one of the Beethoven string quartets."

"Shhh!"

The music became louder as the launch, still barely under way from its own momentum, moved ahead.

A shadow appeared in the fog.

The launch's bow nudged into the side of the sailboat before anyone could be sure what it was.

"Jesus Christ," said Ken O'Keefe. "It's the *Plymouth Hope*."

CHAPTER 11

The bridge of *Lamprey* was crowded.

Captain Arthur Lovejoy stood near the CB radio, which had been brought up from the electronics room. It was connected to the standby whip antenna outside the port hatch.

Lovejoy checked his watch. "Isn't it about time they made a report?"

"Two minutes more, Cap," said Ray Barnstable.

Posty said, nervously, "You shouldn't have let them go in there."

"Paul Forsythe's part-owner of this ship, Mr. Postiglion. How would you suggest that I could have stopped him?"

"Osha-san," said Posty, "use the radio. Recall them before it's too late."

"My friend," said Osha, "Paul knows his own mind and if he thought there were any genuine risk, he would never have allowed his wife to go with him."

"But—"

"The crew of the Coast Guard cutter survived," said Osha. "So will the crew of *Lamprey*'s launch. Please, do not be a doom-sayer. We are all worried, yes. So do not make it worse."

The CB chattered. Reception was very poor.

"Say again," asked Ray Barnstable.

". . . boat. We're . . . five minutes."

"Do you want us to pull you out? Repeat, do you want us to pull you out?"

Forsythe's voice was muffled, but audible. "Negative. Negative."

"Okay. I have 0340. We'll expect your next call at 0345. Do you copy?"

". . . four. Ten four."

Bob Hart came up from the electronics room. "Cap," he said, "we just picked up another radar target."

"More fog?"

"No. A ship. Approaching from the southeast, and closing at around thirteen knots."

"Passing course?"

"I'm afraid not. She's headed right for us."

"Put on the high-intensity blinkers. And start the foghorn."

"Right." The Second Officer hurried away.

Saito Osha said, "We are far off normal shipping lanes, are we not?"

"We're not within fifty miles of normal traffic," said Lovejoy. "I wonder what ship that is."

Osha added, "And *whose*."

"Slow to two thirds," commanded Dimitri Ashkenazy.

"Two thirds," repeated his Third Officer. He manipulated the telegraph to the engine room.

The steady thrum of the big diesel engine slowed, and the *Akademik Knipovich* took the gentle swells a little deeper, a little more ponderously.

"What do you make of it, Comrade?" asked the Third Officer.

"Except for the nearly straight edge of the target," said the Soviet Captain, "I would say it was a land mass. But we are more than a hundred miles east of the coastline."

"A mirage?"

Ashkenazy chuckled. "I have seen mirages in my time," he said, "but never on a radar screen."

"There is a smaller target just below the larger mass. It seems to be a ship."

"See if you can raise them on the radio," said the Captain.

"But that will alert them to our presence."

"Young man," said Ashkenazy, "this vessel is nearly three hundred feet long. Where do you expect me to hide it when daylight comes? Do as I say."

"Yes, Comrade," said the young officer.

Ken O'Keefe finished mooring the launch to the starboard side of *Plymouth Hope*.

While he was doing this, Forsythe had been calling, "Sir Roger? Are you aboard?"

His only answer was the gentle sound of the Beethoven quartet.

Beth said, uncertainty in her voice, "Maybe he's below, sleeping."

"All set," said O'Keefe.

"Okay," said Forsythe. "You stay here. Don't miss that radio report at 0345."

As he reached up for *Plymouth Hope*'s railing, Beth said, "Me, too." She had clipped a small electronic flash to her Pentax, and as Forsythe scrambled aboard the yacht, fired off a shot. The flash made a bright circle of light in the heavy fog mass that surrounded them, and nearly blinded all three.

"Knock it off, Sunny," Paul called. "You'll put our eyes out."

O'Keefe, who was rubbing his, noticed that they were smarting. "I think some of this crap is getting in mine," he called.

Beth said, "I've noticed what feels like dust going down my neck. I don't care what Dix said, maybe that's what it is."

Forsythe, on board the yacht now, looked around. The small flashlight he carried barely penetrated a yard into the "fog."

"Sir Roger?" he called again.

Carefully, he felt his way around the deck. All seemed in order. The lines were coiled and tied. Although he could only see part of them in the gloom, he could tell that the sails, although limp now in the still air, were set. Both life rings were in their brackets, and the tiny dinghy was still lashed to the cabin roof.

"I'm going below," Forsythe said. Beth, in the cockpit, said, "Be careful." She took a series of pictures without flash, and without hope of capturing anything on the high-speed Ektachrome.

She waited for what seemed an hour.

Forsythe reappeared.

"He's not there," he said. "Just this."

He held up a cassette recorder, which was playing the Beethoven.

Beth gasped. "That's a C-90 cassette. If it's still playing, that means he was on board less than forty-five minutes ago."

"Well, he's not here now," said Forsythe, shutting off the music. He coughed. "This stuff tastes like dust. Maybe you're right. We'd better get the hell out of here."

When they climbed back aboard the launch, O'Keefe was just getting ready to make his radio report.

Forsythe took the transceiver, pressed the transmit button. "This is Forsythe. We're coming out. Repeat, coming out."

To O'Keefe, he said, "Put her in reverse. But slow. We don't want to swamp the transom."

The rope linking them with *Lamprey* tightened.

"Oh, shit," said the sub commander. "They thought you said to pull us out."

"Help them along," said Forsythe. "Back this tub up."

Beth said, "We're shipping water."

"Want me to cut the rope?" asked O'Keefe.

"Not yet. We're tied to *Plymouth Hope*. We won't sink."

"I wouldn't bet on that," said Beth, standing ankle-deep in water that had spilled over the launch's low transom. But she kept taking pictures. The sailboat loomed over them like a ghostly shadow, and she used it as a background for some misty shots of O'Keefe at the wheel of the launch.

Suddenly, without a transition, they were clear of the

fog bank and the stars were so bright that they seemed to blaze in the night sky.

"*Lamprey,* we're out. Give us rope."

"Roger," said Ray Barnstable's voice, now clear and distinct. In a moment, the rope loosened, and O'Keefe freed it from the launch's cleats.

"Hook it up to the yacht," said Forsythe, meanwhile freeing the launch from its own mooring to *Plymouth Hope.*

"Got it!" called O'Keefe. "There's a tow-ring just below her bowsprit."

"Okay," said Forsythe. "Let's get on board. We've got a missing man somewhere in the water."

His voice was drowned out for a second by a blast from *Lamprey*'s foghorn.

"Bring her alongside," Forsythe shouted to O'Keefe.

As soon as the launch bumped against the side of the survey vessel, he scrambled up the ladder and hurried to the bridge.

"Art," he said, breathless, "that's Sir Roger Lean's sailboat. He's not on board. He went into the water sometime within the last hour. What are our chances?"

"If he didn't stay afloat, none. If he had on a life jacket, maybe one out of fifty."

"Get some men in the launch and start a circular pattern," said Forsythe.

"In the fog bank too?"

Forsythe hesitated. "No. You wouldn't have a chance of seeing him in there. *Plymouth Hope* was headed into the bank, so the chances are good that he went overboard behind us somewhere." He looked at his watch. "What time is first light?"

"Not for another two hours or so," said Lovejoy.

"Well, do the best you can. Once the launch is under way, we'll take *Lamprey* on a series of runs five miles or so down from the fog bank, sweeping the water with our lights."

"Okay," said the Captain. "Give me five minutes to get the launch organized."

Ray Barnstable came onto the bridge. "Cap, we've

got a Russian trawler on the blower. They say they saw us on their radar, and wonder if we need any help."

"We sure as hell do," said Forsythe.

"Hold on," said Lovejoy. "You know as well as I do what a Russian 'trawler' really is. That's a spy ship."

"Good," said Forsythe. "Maybe they'll have some sophisticated gear on board that'll help. Get that launch moving. I'll talk to the Russians."

He bobbled a little over Dimitri Ashkenazy's name, but managed to get it fairly correct.

"We have reason to believe that Sir Roger Lean has gone into the water within the last hour," he told the Russian skipper.

"The around-the-world navigator?"

"The same. We'd appreciate your help. Do you have small boats you can put out in a search pattern?"

"Yes, we do," said Ashkenazy. "Do you know if Sir Roger is a good swimmer?"

"Negative," said Forsythe. "But if we're to have any hope of finding him, he'd better be."

Lamprey, her launch, and two boats from the *Knipovich,* searched an area of ten square miles working until well into the morning, but no trace was found of Sir Roger Lean.

The survey vessel happened to be near the fog bank when the sun came up.

One moment, in the pink haze of dawn, the yellow-brown mass stretched from horizon to horizon and up as far as the eye could see. Then, as the sun appeared, it seemed to tremble, like some greasy, solid thing, and in seconds, vanished.

The sea lay calm, almost mirrorlike, and the barrier that had baffled the radar screens disappeared.

Wearily, the small boats returned to their mother ships.

It was Saturday morning.

CHAPTER 12

The fog over Jacksonville harbor was lifting.

"What do you mean, they've sailed?" demanded Gloria Mitchel.

The Port Superintendent shrugged. "Why not, miss? That's what ships do."

"Where to?"

"Who knows, miss? It's my understanding that they're doing survey work in the North Atlantic. That could put them anywhere by now."

She softened her voice. "Please, this is very important. I'm Gloria Mitchel from the *Morning* program, and I—"

"I know who you are, Miss Mitchel," he said. "Sometimes I catch your show when I'm on the late shift."

His voice grated her ears with the repeated "miss" and by calling the program a "show." One fact that John Francis had drilled into her without mercy was that *Morning* was most definitely *not* a "show." He put it this way: "Sonny and Cher do a show. *We* do a program."

But she kept any affront or impatience out of her voice. Gloria had long since learned that it was one thing to get someone in a chair before the cameras and proceed to let out his air; it was quite another to try it on his own home grounds.

"Is there any way we can contact them by radio?"

"Probably."

She put a deliberate gush into her voice. "You see, we're doing this perfectly *wonderful* documentary about men of the sea, and since Paul Forsythe is so representative of the finest traditions of sailing—"

Wearily, he said, "I don't know anything about Mr. Forsythe, but if you'll go down to the first floor, to the communications room, I'll call ahead, and we'll see if Sparks can raise the *Lamprey*."

" '*Sparks*'?" she said. "Do they still call radiomen that?"

"Only when their names happen to be Herbert Sparks," he said.

"Thank you, you've been very helpful," she said.

"It's my job."

On the stairwell, she muttered, "Prick."

In his office, he sipped his now cold coffee and growled, "Bitch."

Getting ready to go on board the *Knipovich* for a luncheon invitation which had been formally delivered in a sealed envelope by the Russian vessel's launch, Paul Forsythe spoke briefly with Gloria Mitchel on the radio.

"No," he said shortly.

"I don't think you understand. We can present your side of the Apollo 19 story."

"I don't have a side," he said. "We were in the area, and that's all. Miss Mitchel, we're out here to work, not posture for your TV cameras."

"You're news, friend," she said harshly. "If you cooperate, it can be good news. If you don't, it might be bad."

"Good," he said. "We record all radio traffic on board this ship. What you just said will be used when we petition the FCC to lift your station's license."

"Why are you being so hostile?" she said. Her voice almost cracked.

"Because you came flying at me like some kind of vulture, clawing at the flesh of those poor guys who died out here. Frankly, I don't give a damn if you get your story or not. I don't care if you take pot shots at *me* or not. We've got a lot to do out here and I don't have time for what you want."

"I'm sorry," she said. "I know, after what's happened, that you must be sensitive. Believe me, all I want is to find the truth."

"I don't know the truth," he said. "When you find it, send me a copy."

He handed the microphone back to Ray Barnstable, who said, "This is *Lamprey*, ending transmission."

Gloria yelled, "Hey, wait a—"

But the radio loudspeaker in Herbert Sparks's shack had gone dead.

The Coast Guard air search for any trace of Sir Roger Lean found nothing except some floating debris from another wreck which had gone unreported.

The Coast Guard commander radioed his report to the station at West Palm Beach.

"Search negative. Returning to base."

"More caviar?" asked Captain Ashkenazy.

"None for me," said Lovejoy. He sipped the ice-cold vodka and nibbled at a bit of celery.

"I'll take some," said Beth. "It's delicious."

"Iranian, I'm afraid," said Ashkenazy. "We haven't seen a home port in almost a year."

"How's the spying business?" asked Forsythe, accepting some of the black caviar with its chopped onion and boiled eggs.

"Poor," said the Soviet Captain. "Détente is wonderful for world peace, but it reduces the appropriations for patriots like you and me."

"Not me," said Forsythe. "I'm strictly a money-grabbing businessman. In fact, I'm fighting with my own government right now."

Ashkenazy chuckled. "Of course." He lifted his glass. "To President Foster."

Forsythe and Lovejoy raised theirs. "To Premier Nabov."

They all drank.

"I am distressed about Sir Roger," said Ashkenazy. "He was an inspiration to all seamen. How could he have been so careless?"

"I don't think he could possibly have been washed overboard," said Lovejoy. "There simply wasn't any sea last night."

"He was an old man," said Beth. "Maybe he fainted."

"Or," said Paul Forsythe, "he may simply have stepped over the side."

Ashkenazy said, "Suicide? But why?"

"I may be wrong, but he had a sadness about him, and this voyage he was undertaking was obviously meant to be his last. He was saying good-by to all that he loved."

"The poor man," said Beth. "Paul, you liked him, didn't you?"

"Sure. You would have too."

Ashkenazy poured more vodka. "I'm sorry Mr. Osha couldn't join us."

"He has jet lag," lied Forsythe. In truth, Osha had curtly refused to have any social contact with the Russian vessel. He carried old memories and hatreds.

"If you aren't spying," said Ashkenazy, "what brings you to the Sargasso Sea?"

"Originally," said Forsythe, "we intended to search for underwater energy resources. But now, believe it or not, we're investigating the legends of the Bermuda Triangle."

Ashkenazy raised his bushy black eyebrows. "With government support?"

"No way. They tried to beach me. No, Hollywood's paying the tab in the long run. They want to make a movie out here."

Lovejoy said, "While we're trading confidences, Captain, what brings *you* here?"

"Research," said Ashkenazy.

"You're inside the two-hundred-mile limit."

"But I am not catching fish, I am merely studying them."

"Tell that to the Coast Guard."

"I will be glad to do so," said the Russian.

"Damn it," shrilled Gloria Mitchel. "Who cares about money? We *need* that boat!"

Walter Wylie said, "Baby, it took blasting powder to get us down here for the week. How the hell do you think we're going to be able to get the network to pay for a chartered boat?"

"A lousy three thousand dollars for the week. A one-minute commercial will pay for that ten times over."

"One commercial," he reminded, "gets cut up fifty different ways. Most of the dough goes into payments to the local stations. Some goes into overhead. More into salary. How much do you think is left to pay for boat charters?"

"Walter," she warned, "let's not go on like this. Just, please, get that boat. All right?"

He stared at her. This was the crunch. If he gave in now, he would always do so.

"Well, Walter?"

He sighed. The fifty-one thousand, the virtually unlimited expense account, the company car, and that goddamned alimony around his neck for the rest of his life or until that bitch living it up in Acapulco with her Mexican stud died, made his answer almost automatic.

"I'll see what I can do," said Walter Wylie.

At exactly 2 P.M., just as the leader of Flight 19 had done more than thirty years before, Jack Begley took off from Fort Lauderdale.

"Jack, has this bird got the range?" Anthony Dix asked, peering nervously at the heli-pad, dwindling below the Hughes chopper.

"And then some," said Begley. "Those TBMs were safe up to a thousand miles. We've got at least five hundred miles more than that in our tanks."

"I thought choppers were short-range birds."

"Not this one. It carries extra fuel instead of cargo."

"I forget, although I've used it in half a dozen books: What does TBM stand for?"

"Torpedo Bomber Medium."

As the Hughes lifted off, the wind seemed to rise, and for a moment there were gusts of thirty knots or so.

"Funny," said Begley. "There wasn't even a breeze five minutes ago."

He pressed the transmit button and said, "This is Bogey, calling Shortstop."

From *Lamprey,* designated Shortstop, Ray Barnstable's voice answered, "We copy, Bogey. Over."

"Takeoff at fourteen hundred hours, per flight plan. Proceeding east to Hen-Chicken Shoal target area. Over."

"Roger. We'll be listening. Shortstop out."

"Bogey on the side and listening."

On *Lamprey*'s bridge, Ray Barnstable reported to Forsythe, "We just got another call from Begley. He buzzed the old target area, and now he's a hundred and sixty miles east of Fort Lauderdale and just turning on the northward leg."

"Then he's supposed to jump Flight 19 in just a minute or so," said Postiglion, excited.

"Keep us posted," said Forsythe.

"What the hell's wrong with this radio?" said Jack Begley. "Shortstop, do you copy?"

No answer. Only the sound of frying eggs.

"Okay," said Begley. "Shortstop, I don't know if you hear me. But I'm going in for Flight 19, out of the sun."

There was no answer, except for Tony Dix, who shouted, "Tally-ho!"

The chopper had no wings. Yet . . . for an odd moment, it was as if it wore the folding stubby wings of the TBM Begley had flown so long ago. And while there was a scudding mass of small clouds below him, wasn't there something more? A cluster of five dark objects, winging north at three hundred miles an hour?

Jack Begley shook his head. Such daydreams were crap. "Bang, bang, you're dead," he shouted into the radio microphone.

Did he hear, in return, "Begley, you prick!"?

"Hell no," he muttered. All he heard was the biggest omelette in the world frying.

Into the radio, he said, "Got three of you, by God! Three for sure, and two probables."

Worried, Dix said, "Hey, Jack, are you still on this planet with us?"

To the radio, Begley said, "I'm on my way home. Bogey clear."

He switched off the microphone.

Then—and he was sure this was not a memory or delusion—he heard someone key a far-off mike.

BEEP-BEEP.

Fuck you.

"Now what?" asked Dix.

"We'll get right down on the deck," said Begley. "Gives you the feeling of really flying."

"I've already had that feeling, Jack," said Dix. "Honestly, I can do without it."

Begley stiffened as he heard something in his earphones. He answered, "I hear you. What do you mean, you're lost?"

"Who's lost?" asked Dix.

"Give me a long count," said Begley, ignoring him. "We'll try the RDF. Just keep talking. We'll come to you."

Dix grabbed the earphones and, pressing them against his own ears, listened for a moment. Then he said, "Jack, there *is* somebody on this frequency, and they're yelling for help. They say they're lost!"

CHAPTER 13

Something was wrong about the ocean. It had turned to a whitish green and seemed, dishlike, to curve up toward the horizon.

Dix said, "What's going on down there? It looks like the inside of a washing machine with too much detergent."

"Surface winds," said Jack Begley. Or had he actually said it? Was it just an echo, a memory of another December afternoon, long ago?

"I'm going up to thirty-five hundred," he said.

He had put on the earphones again, but did not hear any distress signals. "Nothing," he said.

Begley looked at his watch. A little after four. It was time to turn to a course of twelve degrees.

Dix said, "I heard them, Jack. They said, 'We're off course. We cannot see land. Repeat, we cannot see land.' That's just what Flight 19 radioed."

Begley turned up the RF gain and frowned. The static had turned everything to hash. He heard brief bursts of what might have been human voices, but they were so garbled that there was no way of knowing what the message was.

"Bogey calling Shortstop," he said.

No answer.

Dix said, "My God, look at that!"

Begley glanced up and, as he had expected, saw the silvery-gray lens cloud.

"Right on time," he said softly.

The compass rose had started swinging, and the eggs were frying in his earphones, and the instrument panel began to give impossible readings.

"Tony," he said softly, "hang on."

At that moment, the engine shut down.

"The radio's all screwed up," Ray Barnstable reported.

Posty asked, excited, "What about Tony?"

"Haven't heard anything since Jack reported he was turning north."

"Flight 19 is repeating itself," said Posty. "Tony was right."

"Sunspots," said Paul Forsythe. "I've gone for days without radio communications."

"But our radio was perfect an hour ago," said Posty.

"Art," said Forsythe, "how far are we from Jack's last position?"

"Four, maybe five hours."

"Let's steam that way."

"Give me five minutes. We're putting two men aboard *Plymouth Hope* to sail her back to the mainland."

"Okay. But hurry it up."

Beth, still photographing everything in sight, lowered her camera. "Does that mean you've given up hope of finding Sir Roger?"

"I'm afraid so," said Forsythe. "There wasn't much chance to begin with, but every hour cuts it down."

She touched his arm. "Paul . . . I'm sorry."

"It's set," said Walter Wylie. "The brass are screaming like banshees, but we've got one week. John and Woody'll carry the program. Management realizes that if we're at sea, we won't be able to send daily film packages, but they want us to keep them posted, so they can run promos. At the very least, Glor, we've got to come back with enough footage for a half-hour special report, plus outtakes for use on *Morning.*"

"Easy," she said. "See? I told you that you could get us a boat."

"Yeah," he said, remembering how keenly she had divined his weaknesses. "You told me."

"When do we sail?"

"Maybe an hour. They're still taking on supplies."

"What about Pat? Do they have everything he needs?"

"Power sources, refrigeration for his film, everything except one of his dumb blondes."

She gave Wylie a gentle poke on the shoulder, and said—the words sharpened by a hard glint in her eyes—"Sexist, Walt."

"Okay. Wildly intelligent blondes."

"Poor Pat," she said. "He may have to turn to self-abuse."

"Give the kid a break," Wylie said, trying to laugh.

"No way. You've heard the expression the Mafia uses? Never make dirty on your own doorstep?"

He looked away. He wanted to ask, "Is that what you think sex is, dirty?"

But he did not have the courage.

Young Steven Gaines was so happy that he spent half the day calling friends around the world.

He did not use his blue box to bypass the telephone company's billing system. He did not have to.

Steven Gaines was now an employee of the Bell System, with a special code number that allowed unlimited free communications.

He sipped a Doctor Pepper and smiled at the jumbled mass of equipment on his workbench. He was well along on the decoder for the RCA satellite. And Bel Tel had promised to provide him with the dish antenna.

He switched on his new UFH/FM receiver and set the automatic scanner to blinking.

He was just opening the latest issue of *Electronics Journal* when he saw the scanner lock into channel three, and then he heard a man's voice calling, "Mayday. Mayday. We're going down. Position—"

He had grabbed for a pencil, but the voice faded, and there was no position to write.

* * *

Raiko Nakamura sat near *Lamprey*'s stern rail and watched the sun, low on the horizon, make hypnotic reflections in the smooth waters of the Atlantic.

Kenneth O'Keefe arrived with two drinks. He had been looking for Janet, but even on this small vessel, one could remain unfound if that was her intention.

"Scotch, Miss Nakamura?" he said.

She accepted the sweating glass. "Thank you."

"That stuff Mr. Osha drinks, Suntory? What is it? Some kind of rice wine?"

She laughed. It was a tinkle of many bells in the quiet afternoon. "No, Mr. O'Keefe. Suntory is a Japanese copy of scotch. Rice wine is saki."

"Shows my ignorance," he said.

"Not so," she said. "Suntory is not scotch, although it is very good."

"Is this your first trip to America?" he asked.

She laughed again. "I have not seen anything of America but airports, and ocean. Yes, it is my first, and I have already informed my *corbito* that I have no intention of returning to Japan without spending some time looking at your country."

"There's lots of it to look at," he said. "I guess I haven't seen all that much myself."

"You love the water?"

"I guess so. I seem to spend an awful lot of time on it. And under it."

"And Janet? Does she like the water?"

"I don't know," he said.

"Shouldn't you?" she asked.

"Why?"

"Mr. O'Keefe," said the Japanese girl, "you are not a stupid man, but I believe you are a stubborn one."

"What's that supposed to mean?"

"Janet is in love with you."

"Oh, hell, she's just a kid."

"And you are her grandfather?"

"Nearly old enough, if you want to know."

"Then you should be wise enough not to start fires you cannot extinguish."

"Holy Christ," he said. "What have I ended up with, the Tokyo Ann Landers?"

"Ann who?"

"The expert on romance. So she divorced her husband after twenty-some years of marriage. She and you ought to get together."

"You are throwing up smoke, O'Keefe-san. Why? You must face this problem some time."

"Good. That's when I will. Some time. But not now."

"Sir," reported *Knipovich*'s communications officer, "a target."

"Air or sea?"

"Sea. It is approaching from the southeast, at approximately twenty knots. The radar return indicates that it is a small vessel, perhaps forty or fifty meters."

"Any transponder marker?"

"None. Merely a blip."

"Keep watch," said Ashkenazy. "It may be one of the American Coast Guard vessels."

"Very well, sir," said the communications officer. He left, closing the door behind him.

Ashkenazy sipped a glass of tea.

His position was delicate. There had been no reason in trying to hide from *Lamprey*. Even if he had made it a point to stay over the horizon, their radar would have picked him up. He felt that his display of panache to Paul Forsythe might have disarmed the American. It had been his experience that Westerners approved of openness. By joking about spying on them, they might conclude that he really wasn't. Even if they did not, he had lost nothing.

But the appearance of more vessels clouded the situation. He sipped more tea, thought for a moment, and rose to put on his tunic.

It was time to go to his secondary plan.

Beth Forsythe sat quietly in the "galley" of *Lamprey*, as Saito Osha spoke at length about his plans for the survey vessel.

"At one time, not too long ago, we regarded the resources of the sea as our—what do the card players call it?—our ace in the hole. They were apparently limitless, and great plans for 'harvesting' the oceans were part of our lexicon. Now we know all too well that the sea's resources are as finite as those on our lands, and that we must maximize their potential while limiting their destruction. Mrs. Forsythe, I am very wealthy, and not all of that wealth has come to me without causing human misery somewhere. I deplore that misery, and would like to stop it. But between me and the poor worker in Osaka, there are so many links, so many intermediates, such a long chain of command, that as good as my intentions may be, I am helpless. At one time I seriously considered distributing my entire wealth to the poor of Japan. But it took only a few moments to see that such a distribution would leave me destitute, while only putting a few hundred yen into each pocket. And once that gift was gone, what? I would no longer have jobs to pay their wages, I would no longer build ships that would catch their fish. Then I heard of Paul Forsythe, and we spoke at length of his dream of underwater energy research, and I realized that if we could make such a project successful for the United States, it would soon be feasible for the world."

"Yet, apparently, you're running into roadblocks."

He made a wry face. "For some reason, your government is attempting to go back on their agreements concerning our project. But that will not stop us. It would have been very handy to have their financial backing, but we can exist without it."

"It's not merely withholding the backing, they're actively setting up deterrents to your work."

"All too true."

"Why?"

"I wish I knew. Mrs. Forsythe, perhaps you can find out. After all, it's *your* government."

She laughed gently. "Don't remind me."

Now *Lamprey* picked up the new vessel. Bob Hart reported its location to Arthur Lovejoy.

"Can we raise them on the blower?" asked the Captain.

"Not so far."

"Could it be another Russian trawler?"

"I don't think so. It's coming from the wrong direction."

"Okay," said Lovejoy. "Keep me posted."

When Hart had gone, he examined his charts. It was time to start southwest to see if he could locate Jack Begley's helicopter. Yet, although he was mildly worried about the lack of communications, he had a strange unwillingness to leave his present location. He hesitated, made a decision, and pressed the intercom button.

"This is Captain Lovejoy. Would Mr. Forsythe join me on the bridge?"

"We're going in," warned Jack Begley. "Hang on. I'm going to try to put her down easy. The minute we hit, throw out that big yellow bag. It's the life raft."

"Got you," said Dix.

"Five hundred feet," said Begley. "No winds, no waves. We're in fat city."

The Hughes struck the water gently. It had come down like a slow elevator. There was no cross wind, no high waves. If the chopper had been equipped with the optional floats, it might have remained on top of the water until rescued. But with only skids, it quickly began to fill with water.

Dix heaved the life raft into the ocean, holding onto the lanyard. There was a popping noise and, like a giant balloon, the raft began to inflate.

Dix had already fallen out the open hatch and into the raft, legs sprawling, when he shouted, "Hey, don't forget the booze! We may be out here a while."

"Too late," said Jack Begley, stepping neatly into the raft just as the helicopter sank behind him.

But Dix had the last word. The polystyrene ice chest floated to the surface, still cradling its cargo of vodka, brandy, beer, and two soggy sandwiches.

CHAPTER 14

As *Lamprey* cruised south, Bob Hart reported, "That new ship has changed course. She's apparently planning to intercept us."

"Coast Guard?" wondered Forsythe.

Lovejoy said, "I don't think so. They'd be coming from the west."

"What about the Russians?"

Hart said, "They're staying where they were."

"Okay," said Forsythe. "Keep an eye on our visitor. See if Ray can raise him on the radio."

"We've been trying, but that interference is still screwing up all the frequencies."

"Okay," Forsythe repeated. "Do what you can. Let us know when he's four or five miles out."

"Got you," said the Second Officer.

Lovejoy said, quietly, "I'm worried about that chopper."

"Me too," said Forsythe. "But no use in broadcasting it all over the ship."

"It'll be dark soon," said Hart.

"Think we should put out a Mayday?" asked Forsythe.

"It's not justified," said Lovejoy. "They'd fry our asses for Maydaying just because we'd lost radio communications. The chopper wasn't supposed to rendezvous with us, their flight plan called for them to return to Lauderdale."

Forsythe said grimly, "And we can't raise Lauderdale, or anybody else. I thought radio had improved in the past thirty years."

"Apparently not in the Triangle," said Lovejoy.

Forsythe frowned. "Art, I wish you wouldn't perpetuate that garbage. We've got enough genuine problems without having to cope with myths too."

"Sorry," said the Captain. "I say what I think, and I guess when push comes to shove, I have to admit that I believe in some of that stuff you call garbage."

"Okay," said Forsythe sharply. "But you don't have to talk it up, do you?"

"Simmer down, Paul. I know you're worried about Begley and that writer. It's okay. They'll be all right."

Forsythe laughed. "Yeah, that's what I told Beth. And she said just what I'm saying now. How do you *know?*"

"I don't," said Lovejoy. "But the water's calm as a millpond. Even if they went down, for which I can find no reason, they have rafts and an emergency SOS radio."

"If ours aren't working, what chance would that peanut transmitter have?"

"Paul," said the Captain of *Lamprey,* "you're my boss, but I'm Captain of this vessel, and in my official capacity, I'm ordering you to go below and have yourself a good slug of booze."

Forsythe let himself chuckle and said, "Aye, aye, sir."

It would be hard to find a proper designation for the vessel *Tiger Shark.* At one time it had been a plywood PT boat, of World War II vintage. But her owner, Dan Gregory, better known as "Moose," had bought the hull at a Naval surplus auction for only eight hundred dollars, without engines. That was four years ago. Now *Tiger Shark* had been mated with a pair of diesels which had begun their own lives in long-distance eighteen-wheeler trucks. Mounted in the fifty-seven-foot hull of the PT boat, they had to be force-fed ventilation, and every time Moose Gregory pressed the starter button, he waited in expectation of being blown sky-high by gas fumes in the bilge. So far, the ventilation system and the vapor sniffer he had built up from a Heath kit had warded off catastrophe. Two years ago, he had fiberglassed the hull, and in so doing, and because of an unfortunate accident in mixing the coloring agents for the fiberglass, had given the vessel a color that matched, approximately, that of a long-dead crocodile. A strange greenish-purple, *Tiger Shark* could make the susceptible seasick while lying at anchor.

But once on the water, she could *move!* She had been built well in Bayonne, New Jersey, had not been launched soon enough to see action in the war, but had served well in naval training schools before her retirement in Key West.

Moose had built a flying bridge on her, and between it and the twin booms he had coupled to powerful electric winches, the former PT boat now resembled a miniature ocean-going dredge.

As she pulled up alongside *Lamprey,* Moose activated the high-powered loud-hailer and called, "Ahoy, the *Lamprey!*"

"Shear off!" bellowed Lovejoy. "You're too close."

"Permission to come aboard!" blasted Moose Gregory.

"We're looking for a downed aircraft," called Lovejoy.

"I'll help you. But first let me come on board."

"Let him," said Forsythe. "That baby's got enough speed to run circles around us. We can use his help."

It took half a mile of sea room to slow and stop the *Lamprey*'s forward speed. The boarding ladder was lowered, and the commander of the *Tiger Shark* scrambled up it. He was followed by a chunky, blonde-haired man who wore only cut-off blue jeans, and behind him came a dark-haired woman who overflowed her bathing suit in all directions.

"I'm Arthur Lovejoy," said *Lamprey*'s Captain. "This is Paul Forsythe, one of the owners."

"Moose—sorry, Dan Gregory," said the tall man who had boarded first. His face, fiery red from many suns, was lined with squint marks, and a millennium of laughter. His bright blue Hawaiian sports shirt was cut off at the shoulders, sleeveless. Khaki trousers had suffered the same fate just below the knees. He indicated the man behind him. "David Lester. He writes books. And this is my girl friend, Lucia de la Renata. She cooks and is generally useful around the boat." He chuckled. "Very useful."

"And you?" asked Forsythe. "What do you do?"

"Me? I raise treasure, partner."

"Successfully?"

"Enough to stay afloat. Which is why I wanted to talk to you birds. What the hell were you doing on top of my wreck?"

"Your what?" Lovejoy asked.

"My goddamned certified treasure wreck, bought and paid for with my salvage license from the state of Florida. Do you want to see the certificates?"

"No," Forsythe said shortly. "We're not interested in treasure."

"That's your story. One look at this tub and anybody can see that you're rigged for underwater work. Put two and two together, and I say you've been poaching my claim. Now, what did you bring up?"

"Nothing," said Forsythe. "Listen, we're in a hurry. A helicopter attached to us has been missing for more than an hour, and we're afraid they may be down."

"When was your last report?" asked the man who had been introduced as a "book writer" named David Lester.

"Around four P.M."

Lester frowned. "Moose, I heard a Mayday just around four-twenty."

"Is your radio working?" Forsythe asked.

"Why not?"

"We're in some kind of blackout here," said Lovejoy. "Nothing but sunspot noise."

"So that's why you didn't answer our calls. Well, it was weak, and off frequency, and I couldn't get a fix, but I'm sure it was a Mayday. I relayed it to the Coast Guard, but it could have come from anywhere. With skip, it might have bounced halfway around the world before I heard it."

The girl, Lucia, asked—in a heavy Italian accent—politely, "Is it permissible for me to go below for a while?"

"She needs a head," said Moose Gregory. "Ours has been broken for two days, and she's sensitive about such things."

"Of course," said Lovejoy. He indicated the companionway and the entrance to officer country. "Help yourself."

The girl nodded her thanks and went below.

"Now," said Moose, "with the lady gone, let's not fuck around. How much of my treasure did you pirates glom?"

"Not an ounce," said Forsythe. He tried to fight down a grin, lost. "Two days? How did you manage those calls of Nature?"

"Hanging over the transom, how the hell do you think? Can I trust you, bud?"

"We're in the business of scouting underwater energy resources," said Forsythe. "I guess I wouldn't pass up a chunk of gold if I stumbled over it, but we're not looking for treasure, and we're certainly not stealing it from someone else's wreck."

"As a matter of fact," said Lovejoy, "we never even saw your marker buoys."

"And you wouldn't. They're ten feet underwater. Put floaters up so anybody and his brother could head right for my wreck? Like hell!" Moose looked at David Lester. "What do you think, Dave? Are these birds straight?"

"If this is the Paul Forsythe I think he is," said Lester, "not only are they straight, but you're lucky you haven't had your head handed to you."

"Were you Navy?" asked Forsythe.

"Somewhat. Got in just in time for Midway, and then I did most of the grand tour of the islands."

"I'll be damned," said Forsythe. "*That* David Lester? You wrote *Force Ten*."

"For my sins," admitted Lester. "Sometimes I wish I hadn't."

"Good book," said Forsythe. "Not many were able to catch the way things really happened. Herman Wouk. Monsarrat. And you."

"Thanks," said the writer. "Moose, we're wasting time. If that chopper's down, we ought to be looking." He motioned below. "Leave Lucia here. She'll probably take a shower." He grinned at Forsythe. "Didn't mention, the shower's gone too. We've been doing the sponge bit."

"How long have you been out?" asked Lovejoy.

"Nearly a month," said Moose. "Okay, tell you what. We'll take it in grids. An hour south, ten minutes east, an hour north, and start over. You go in a diagonal course, southeast. That way we'll cover more area together than both of us could separately. If your radios still don't work, I'll give you a shout on the loud-hailer when we get within range."

"Thanks," said Lovejoy. "Need anything?"

"Later," said Moose. "Come on, Dave, let's haul ass."

But by then, the life raft had already been found.

The battered wooden scow came out of the setting sun like some giant bit of floating driftwood.

The tall black man threw a rope to the raft.

"Please come aboard," he said. "I am Joseph Horatio of Alice Town, Bimini Island."

"I'll be a son of a bitch," said Jack Begley. "Joe Horatio! Don't tell me you're still alive!"

"Lieutenant Begley," said the old man. "You are welcome to my boat."

LIMBO LEGENDS
JOSHUA SLOCUM AND THE SPRAY:
Joseph Horatio's Story

In my day, I have known many great sailing men, some of whom history has passed over. But if you were to ask me who was the greatest sailor of them all, I would be forced to answer, Joshua Slocum. Although Master Slocum had houses in Boston and West Tisbury on Martha's Vineyard, so far as we of the Caribbean were concerned, he was an islander like ourselves.

I first met Captain Slocum in Boston in 1894. He had been thrown on the beach at the age of fifty, because with the coming of steam, the tall sailing ships had become unprofitable. It was a sin, the way the proud vessels were stripped of their masts to be towed as coal barges to fuel the arrogant newcomers who spurned the pride and the knowledge of the sailing masters.

It was because of just such a fate to my own ship that I found myself laid up in Boston; the Island Trader, on which I had shipped as an able seaman, hauled a load of bananas to that port and, unable to find cargo for another voyage, had been sold as salvage by her owners, and her crew was cast ashore like so much ballast.

It has often been said that the Irish were the niggers of America; luckily, they had even more deprived niggers to kick—those of us with black skins. Boston in that year of the nineteenth century's last decade was as hostile to blacks as any Georgia township. We were not permitted to frequent the better lodgings or cafes—as if we would have had the wherewithal to pay for the privilege anyway—and nearly every man's hand was turned against us. The Irish feared that we would take away the low-paying menial work they themselves hated, and the good folk of Anglo and Germanic descent feared our baser inclinations and so hid away their daughters and their wealth in terror that we might purloin both.

I said "nearly." For some hands were outstretched in friendship. One such hand belonged to Joshua Slocum, who came to my rescue after I had been "short-changed" in a harbor alehouse. I had given the barkeep a silver dollar, and he returned change for a two-bit piece. When I protested, he brought up his bung starter and threatened to apply it to my head.

A short, white-haired sailor in a ragged coat and a West Indies straw hat who had been sitting at a nearby table, rose and said, "Now, we'll have none of that, Sean. I saw the man give you a dollar, so admit your mistake."

The barkeep whirled on the intruder, but when he saw whose face it was, he lowered the club.

"Aye, Cap'n," he said. "Perhaps it was me own mistake after all."

For all that, he threw the change on the bar so carelessly that I had to grub for part of it in the spit-dampened sawdust.

"Have a glass with me, lad," said the white-haired "Cap'n."

"Only if I may repay," I replied. My pride, not yet destroyed by that evil and cold city, had risen.

"Feel free to do so," he said. "The night is young."

We sipped rich dark beer, and although the conversation seemed casual, I soon became aware that he was sounding me out.

"You are an American," he said, "yet you choose to live in the islands? Why?"

"In the islands," I replied, "a black man is practically ignored by the white leaders. To them we are invisible, not a constant burr under the saddle, as we are in the United States, where I am constantly admonished for having caused the Civil War. By remaining an invisible man, I am able to better my lot without being forced to fight for every step toward actual freedom."

To my surprise, Captain Slocum (for by now we had exchanged names) nodded. "It is a horrid situation," he agreed. "And I do not think we shall see the right of it in our lifetimes." He raised his hand and signaled for two more tankards.

Chagrined by his previous bad behavior, the barkeep surprised me by standing us for this round. He did not even slop my brew onto the table as he put it down.

"I presume you're on the beach, lad," said Captain Slocum. To my surprise, his use of "lad" did not anger me, although at that time I was some four years his senior. He had been born in 1844, and I in 1840. In fairness, I must say that my slim physique and hairless face shaved years off my actual age. At that time, I had no inkling that my allotted span would be so great, so I was in the habit of thinking of myself, as, if not an old man, at least one on the edge of that last twilight of life. You must remember that in those years, a man of fifty-four was an ancient. Few achieved that biblical three score and ten, because of constant exposure to accident and disease.

"Yes, sir," I admitted. "I shipped from Trinidad aboard the Island Trader, and when we landed here, she was sold out from beneath us. I have no influence at the hiring hall, and although I have looked for work on shore, there is none to be had."

"I understand," he said. "May I put a proposition to you? I like the cut of your sail, lad. If you would care to sign on with me, share and share alike, there is a chance that we might carry off a venture with great profit at its end. If not, I will use all my influence, of which I immodestly must admit I have considerable, to procure you a berth aboard one of the steamers, although I myself would never set foot on one of those stinkpots."

"I feel much the same," I said. "What is the nature of your venture?"

"One of my old friends, a whaling captain who has now retired, has offered to give me a ship that wants some repairs. Sign on with me for ten dollars a month and find, and you and I will put her in shape. Then, my friend, it's the seven seas open to our sails again, and no fence around the horizon!"

"I like that, sir," I said. "You have shipped yourself a hand."

As we found, when we went to see the ship Captain Slocum had accepted, sight unseen, we had both been shanghaied.

The **Spray** was not a ship, she was a wreck, bottled up in a farmer's field five miles from the beach, and she had been there so long that nobody could remember when she had been dragged there by mules.

Captain Slocum pulled a sad face, but he was not discouraged.

"I knew she needed some repairs," he said. "First, we must get her closer to the water. No point to repairing the hull only to rip it away on the crown of the road."

I myself would have given up on the spot. But in the face of his courage, I could do no less than put up a good front of my own.

We labored for a full eighteen months rebuilding **Spray.** I was vaguely aware that the Captain had a family, for he often brought his son, Victor, to watch our work. But he spent so little time with them that it must have seemed to them, at least, that he was still at sea. Perhaps that is what makes a man turn to the sailing life —an inability to tie himself down with ordinary cares and duties. Certainly, when it came to work or to his seafaring purposes, Captain Slocum always gave to the fullest. But I am sure that his family felt deprived of his full attention.

We had accepted the **Spray** at Fairhaven, across the water from New Bedford, and in fairness to Captain Slocum's old shipmate, he never asked for a penny from my Cap'n, only indulging in frequent laughter and glee at having gulled him. To everyone's surprise, Slocum announced his intention of putting the ancient vessel into shipshape condition.

And so we did. Captain Slocum spent $553.62 in materials, which was a huge sum of money in those days.

Many of his seafaring cronies, most of whom were on the beach themselves, came to help, and not a one of them expressed the slightest hope that we would ever float her again. One swore that he could not be sure if **Spray** was a new ship with some bad planking, or an old one being rebuilt, so extensive were our changes to her hull.

My own records indicate that, in addition to the bill for materials and my ten dollars a month, which added up to $733.62, Captain Slocum must have spent another two or three hundred dollars in minor expenses. My room cost nothing, for I slept aboard the hull, and oftentimes, so did he. But there was food, and an occasional barrel of beer, and twice during those long months, trips into Boston, where we gorged ourselves on huge lobsters and drank not beer but wine.

Still, one day **Spray** was finished.

We launched her with a bottle of the finest wine, supplied by Mrs. Stella Wright, the New Bedford school-marm, and **Spray** took to the water like a spry little mallard duck, bobbing in the quick waters of the bay with a healthy delight.

Our test runs proved that **Spray** could outsail most ships anywhere near her size. We could gain nearly a full day down the coast to New York. Three to Norfolk. Time and again, we proved this to the shippers. On several occasions, we beat the times of the steamers, whose freight rates were nearly twice those of ours.

But no consignments came our way. We were reduced to leasing **Spray** for commercial fishing voyages, and they paid little for considerable aggravation and smell.

Reluctantly, the Captain and I parted ways.

"I shall sail **Spray** around the world," he told me. "But to be meaningful, I must do it alone. I am sorry."

"There is no reason. We have enjoyed these two years."

"Let me get you a berth on a clipper leaving on the nineteenth," he said. "It is going down around the Horn, to explore the islands off the west coast of South America. The duration is for two years, and since the master is an honest man, and a friend of mine, you will not be shorted on the pay-off."

I thanked him, but declined. "I think I will go back to Bimini Island, Cap'n. I have friends there, and perhaps I will do a little fishing—which, I may add, is far easier there than in these cold waters."

"All right," he said. He did some figuring on the back of an old newspaper, opened his grouch bag and fumbled with some gold certificates. "I estimate that I owe you the sum of forty-one dollars."

"I disagree," I said. "You owe me nothing. If anything, I owe you for your friendship and your teaching."

"Bah," he said. "There is no charge for either. Here"— and he pushed some money at me—"this will pay your passage to the Bahamas and leave a mite to buy yourself a small boat. I am only sorry that it isn't more."

My honor bade me to push the money back to him, but my good sense told me that I needed it, so I accepted it with great thanks.

He did not stop there; by asking around the town, he found me a one-way berth aboard a schooner bound for Nassau, which left me within a few days of Bimini. I had signed aboard, but we had not yet slipped anchor when he departed on his famous voyage, on April 24, 1895. His goal, the same port, forty-six thousand miles in reach. You must remember that **Spray** was only thirty-six feet and nine inches in length, and her beam was barely over fourteen feet. It took the Captain three years, but he became the first man to circumnavigate the globe single-handed, and this without a self-steerer, which had not even been imagined in those days. I am a great admirer of Sir Francis Chichester, and even more of Sir Roger Lean, but both of those great sailors have had the advantages of self-steering, and, more important, of "kicker" motors which, when they found themselves in a bad harbor or a lee shore, could be cranked up to push them to better winds. Captain Slocum had none of these.

I read of his exploits in a copy of the Kingston, Jamaica, **Gleaner,** which came up my way on a banana boat. Intending to write to Captain Slocum, I never did, and for years we lost contact.

You can imagine my surprise when he pulled up at the

very end of my dock in **Spray.** She was older, and beaten by the seas and the sun had bleached her decks. But I recognized every peg, every beam, that I had helped install.

He was alone. I suppose, thinking back, that the Captain was always alone. Some said that he and his wife did not get along, and that this trouble was one reason he was happier at sea. I cannot shed light on the matter. He never spoke of it.

We shared rum, and a fine meal, and he told me what had been happening in the more than fourteen years since we had last seen each other.

"I was lucky enough to sail around the globe," he told me. "But in so doing, I fell under an experience so odd that it has changed my life."

It was near the Azores, where he had fallen ill, during a wild gale that demanded his attention on deck. With full sails, **Spray** was in great danger. But the Captain was in such pain that he could not move from where he had fallen to the deck of the cabin.

It was critical that sail should be shortened. But, in his pain, the Captain was unable to do so. He remembered fainting several times.

Once, when he came to his senses, instead of being tossed about on the deck of a ship out of control, he saw, through the hatch, a sailor wearing wet-weather gear that looked centuries out of date.

The helmsman introduced himself as a crewman of the **Pinta,** one of Columbus' vessels which had weathered a storm like this more than four hundred years earlier.

"Rest, Cap'n," he said. "I will guide your ship tonight."

The gale worsened, and still **Spray** held her course. With the dawn, the wind abated and when the Captain's pain lessened, he dragged himself to the deck.

It had been swept clean by the wind and the raging waters. Any object not secured had been washed away.

The sails he should have furled for the night were still set, and when he cast his log and took a reading he found that he had covered a distance of more than ninety-five during the night. Such a reach was impossible without a helmsman, and without one the sails would have been torn to ribbons.

"God sailed with you," I said.

"Perhaps," he said. "But, Joe, I do not deny it, when the gale was at its highest, before my strange visitor appeared, I wished mightily that you were there."

In the morning, we drank coffee together, and he sailed away from my pier, and away from the entire world, for from that moment on, nobody ever saw or heard of Captain Joshua Slocum and the **Spray** again.

PART THREE
SARGASSO

CHAPTER 15

Aside, Dix said, "Is he really a hundred and some odd years old?"

"I believe him," said Begley.

Dix said, "Why not? There's an area in Russia where people live to a hundred and twenty without causing any fuss."

Joseph Horatio returned to the wheelhouse. "Come forward," he said. "It is time to eat."

"Maybe later," said Dix, uneasily. Begley, who had enjoyed the old man's cooking more than thirty years ago, just smiled.

The cabin smelled musty, but overriding that odor was the aroma of something delicious which was boiling atop the small alcohol stove.

"I took a large sea turtle yesterday," said Horatio. "Do not mention it, for it is now illegal."

"Not a word," said Dix, sniffing.

Begley noticed the number of bowls on the rude table. "Four?" he asked.

"Oh, boy," said Dix. "He's set a place for the Ancient Mariner."

Joseph Horatio had gone to the darkened forward end of the cabin, where the bow of the vessel squeezed together with two bunks clinging to the bulkheads. He bent over one of the bunks, shook a corner of it.

"Sir," he said. "Come eat. You need your strength."

An object stirred, sat up.

"What?" said a voice in strong English accents. "I'm sorry. I was dreaming. I thought I was swimming the Atlantic."

Horatio laughed heartily. "Sir, you very nearly were. Come, we have more guests."

The man he helped from the bunk looked older than Horatio. He was thin, and the shirt he wore had obviously been lent to him by the much taller black man. His eyes blinked at the lamplight.

He stood unsteadily at the end of the table and extended his hand to Jack Begley.

"How'ja do," he said. "My name is Roger Lean."

"Sir," reported *Knipovich*'s first officer, "the Americans have joined with the smaller boat. Now they seem to be conducting a search pattern."

"For the Englishman, perhaps."

"Radio reports that there have been calls for a code name, Bogey. We believe it is a helicopter."

"Hold station," said Dimitri Ashkenazy. "Our orders are to observe any underwater activity. Since we assisted in the rescue attempt for the Englishman, this may be an attempt to enlist our aid again and draw us off position."

"Shall we prepare *Vanya?*" This was the small submersible which could be launched over the side by winches. The sub was stored in a breakaway structure aft.

"Not yet," said the Soviet Captain. "Continue monitoring the American transmissions."

Radio communications had resumed normally, and it was soon learned that the helicopter was overdue at Fort Lauderdale.

"One more hour," Forsythe decided. "Then we put out a general Mayday. The Coast Guard'll love us. We've given them more business today than they normally get in a week."

"Why are you waiting an hour?" Beth asked. "Why not call for help now?"

"Because," he said gloomily, "my figures show that they've got another hour of fuel. Then they're either home, or they're down."

Raiko Nakamura lay quietly, cradled in Saito Osha's arms. Their cabin was dimly lit by a single lamp, with a towel thrown over its shade.

"I am afraid," she told him. "This is not a good place."

"The ship?"

"No, the ship is all you promised. This ocean, this Sargasso Sea."

He chuckled. "You do not really believe in the fantasies of the storytellers."

"I know," she said. "For every strange occurrence, there is a natural explanation. But what good do those explanations do to those who vanished? We are beset by odd happenings. The mysterious fog. The Englishman's empty boat, with the tape recorder still playing Beethoven. And now a vanished helicopter. You may call it coincidence, my *corbito*, but I am still afraid."

"Is that why you were so anxious to make love? To push fear aside?"

"To have it while we can," she said.

William Postiglion was half drunk.

Beth said, "Let me get you a sandwich."

"I'll never eat again," said Posty. "This project was doomed from the start. Charlton Heston put a curse on us."

Janet Lovejoy handed him a cup of coffee. "Drink this," she ordered.

"Or?"

"Or I will punch you in your tummy."

Her tiny figure, poised with such determination, her half-angry face, her intense stare—all combined to drive the demons of gloom from the producer.

"You're wonderful!" he choked, reaching for the cup. "Thank you. Beth! Where is my sandwich?"

"On the way, C.B.," she said.

He stared down into the dark brown of the coffee. Softly, he said, "I hope they're all right."

*   *   *

The chartered boat swerved again.

"We're lost!" declared Gloria Mitchel.

"No, we're not," said Walter Wylie.

"If we're not lost, why are we going in circles?"

"We're searching for *Lamprey*. They aren't at their last reported position."

"Fancy talk," she said. "I suppose you go out on the island every weekend and *sail*." Her tone turned "sail" into a dirty word.

"Not every weekend. But whenever I can."

"Nice fun, huh?"

"For some. Those who like it."

"But not for little girls from the Bronx, who have to spend their weekends dealing dishes off the arm at the Blue Plate Seafood House."

He met her eyes. "Is that what you did?"

"You bet your tuti."

He smiled. "Me, I unloaded fresh vegetables at the Fulton Street Market."

"Hah! You never did an honest day's work in your life."

"Wrong, Glor. Most of us, we had hard times. I'm sorry you don't seem able to leave yours behind. Me, I've forgotten every lousy day of them. Live for now and tomorrow, Gloria. You've paid your dues. We all have. What's the point in dragging up the bad times to spoil the good ones?"

"Is that what you think we've got now? The good times?"

"Well, don't we?" he challenged. "I'm doing all right, and if that piece in *New York* last month is anywhere near correct, you're doing around three times better. You want to sail? You've got enough money to make my little twenty-footer look sick. Or travel. Or anything you damned well want, because you've earned it."

"No, I haven't," she said. "We haven't broken a hundred stations yet."

"So what? That's the network's problem, not yours. Do you think *Morning* can single-handedly go out and round up those missing four stations? What about the rest of our daytime programming? It's what they call, for lack of a nastier word, 'weak.' And as good as John Francis is, where's our Walter Cronkite? Where's our 'MASH,' where's our 'All in the Family'? Where's our first-run premiere of *Gone With the Wind?*"

"We're going to get those four stations after this trip," she said grimly.

"Honey," he said, "for your sake, I hope so."

Posty sat near Bob Hart, at the sonar.

"Anything unusual?" he asked.

"Not really. I think we passed a school of porpoises a while back. I heard them chattering."

"Do they really talk?"

"Who knows? My guess is, they do. There's too much regularity, too much of a pattern, to what they do."

"But birds sing. Is that talking?"

"A little. They have one call for danger, another for breakfast. But porpoises go further. They're curious, and you can tell that when you hear them."

"Ever hear anything else that didn't fit in?"

"You mean UFOs? Sorry, Mr. Postiglion, but I haven't. When I was a kid, I read all that stuff, and it was exciting to think that it might be true. Hell, that may be why it's so successful. I don't think we're all that happy believing that down here under our fourteen pounds of atmosphere, at the bottom of the well, if you see it that way, that we're the only intelligent beings in the whole universe. But so far, there hasn't been any evidence to the contrary."

"Dix says they're out there."

"Could be, sir," said the young Second Officer. "But if so, why haven't they made their presence known?"

"Maybe," said Postiglion, "they're afraid of us.

Less than ten minutes before Paul Forsythe had determined to put out a missing-aircraft report, Ray Barnstable came rushing up to the bridge.

"They're safe!" he gasped. "*Tiger Shark* just radioed in."

"Safe? Where?"

"They crashed, or anyway ditched. A native sailboat picked them up. *Tiger*'s alongside right now. But that's not all."

"What else?"

"It's a grand slam. The native rescued Sir Roger, too!"

CHAPTER 16

Showered, wearing a jump suit provided by Dix, who was the nearest to his size, Sir Roger Lean sipped hot tea and fascinated his audience.

"I had been warned not to go to the north until midnight, GMT, but it was a long day, and I turned in early. *Plymouth Hope* is a dear craft, but on self-steering she tends to come about if the wind conditions are wrong."

"But how did you go overboard?" asked Forsythe.

"That's the mystery of it. I remember awakening and realizing at once that I was off course. It was nearly dawn, and I had no idea how long I had been sailing north, or indeed what my position was. Obviously, the first order of business was to get back on my intended track, and with that intention in mind I started for the helm."

The old sailor paused. "What happened next is puzzling. One moment, I was in the center of the vessel, and there was no noticeable pitch or yaw. The next, I found myself in the water, and *Plymouth Hope* was sailing away from me. I swam after her, but as you must know, a man in the water has no chance to catch even the slowest sailboat. It soon became obvious that I had no hope whatsoever of overtaking her, so I stripped down to my shorts and concentrated on staying afloat. It was a miserably tiny chance of survival, but since it was all I had, I did my best."

"How long were you in the water?" asked Forsythe.

"Perhaps five hours, maybe longer," said Sir Roger.

Lucia de la Renata gasped. "But that is not possible, to swim that long."

"My dear," said Lean, "I did not attempt to swim. I merely floated."

Paul Forsythe said, "But you've no idea how you got into the water?"

"None. There are no bumps on my head, as if I might have been struck by the boom coming around. That might have produced temporary amnesia, but frankly there was almost no wind, so that's a long bet. All I know is that it is as if I were instantly transported from the deck of *Plymouth Hope* into the ocean, which incidentally is not all that warm right now. Cold was my greatest fear, other than not being sighted at all. I moved rather more than I really should have, just to keep warm. Luckily, there were no sharks in the area."

"Did you see any trace of a fog bank?"

"None. I understand that's where you found the yacht, becalmed."

"Right," said Forsythe. "She's probably back in Florida by now. We put two men aboard to sail her in."

"Rightly done," said the old sailor. "You could hardly have towed her about."

"What about this native?" asked Forsythe. "He seems to have done a good day's work."

"And not for the first time," said Jack Begley. "He fished me out of the drink back in 1945. Mr. Forsythe, he's the one I told you about."

Forsythe said, stunned, "And still alive?"

"Fit as a fiddle," said Begley. "You ought to talk with him. He spins a good story."

Beth Forsythe, who had been taking photographs with her quiet Leica, asked, "Where is he?"

"Heading this way. He should fetch up with us by morning," said Moose Gregory. "We offered him a tow, but he was afraid his old hull wouldn't take the strain."

"What's he doing out here in open water?" asked Forsythe.

"Looking for something," Begley said. "He didn't say

what it was, and we were too busy eating turtle stew to ask."

Sir Roger Lean said, "I got the impression, from some things he said when the two of us were alone, before we picked up your airmen, that he has spent most of his life cruising these waters. He said, as if in jest, that back on his island of Bimini, he is regarded as something of a witch-man. Incidentally, he is not a native of the Caribbean, but a natural-born American, from Charleston, South Carolina. But he left the United States for good when he was fifty-five years old, which, according to him, was back in 1895."

"I suppose it's possible," said Forsythe. "But it's hard to take. Anyway, we all owe him our thanks. Will he accept money?"

"I don't think so," said the old sailor. "But he could use supplies. He seems to be living off the sea."

"He's got them," said Forsythe.

Ray Barnstable came in. "Paul, we've got another visitor. A charter out of Jacksonville."

"What for?"

"There's a TV crew on board, and some woman named Mitchel. She says she's from the *Morning* program."

"Yeah, she is," said Forsythe. "What do they want?"

"To come on board and film some interviews. Cap said to ask you."

"You can't refuse them, Paul," Beth said. "Not if they've come all this way."

"Why not?" he said. "I didn't invite her. In fact, I told her not to come, that I didn't have time."

"But it's her job," Beth said. "Please, Paul."

"Oh, hell, why not?" he said. "Okay, Ray, tell them they can come on board."

Kenneth O'Keefe sat, sipping beer, with Dan "Moose" Gregory. He asked, "How deep is your wreck, anyway?"

"Two hundred and thirty feet," said the treasure hunter.

"That's a long way down," said O'Keefe. "Are you free diving?"

"No. We did at first. But with the decompression schedule, we only had a few minutes on the wreck. So now we go down with one SCUBA tank for emergency, and breathe an air mixture forced down hoses from the *Shark*."

"We? There's only two of you."

"Right. Dave and me. Lucia runs the air compressor and breather mixer."

"Jesus," said O'Keefe.

"It's not that bad," said Gregory. "She knows how to do two things very well. One of them is running the compressor."

"I didn't realize that Dave was so famous. Paul told me. What the hell is he doing diving for treasure?"

"Researching his next novel. He only writes one every ten years or so, and he lives every page of it first. It ought to be a barn-burner. He's made dives that turned *my* hair white."

"Is it worth it? Is there that much stuff down there to be recovered?"

"It's there all right. The trouble is in finding it, and in getting it up, and in making the right kind of deal with the state or the feds, so we can hang onto what we've found, at least a part of it." He gave an evil chuckle. "Those pricks. They let us do all the work, take all the risk, put up all the front money—and then if we luck in, they show up with both hands spread wide."

"What kind of wreck are you working now?"

"Spanish galleon. Back around 1700, the privateers were running wild around here."

"Pirates?"

"Legal pirates. They hold commissions, usually from England, which gave them man-of-war status. They could pull anybody over to the curb, steal everything of value, hang the crew, and sink the vessel. All in the name of patriotism. Anyway, the Spanish built huge galleons, faster than most of the ships on the seas then, and once a year they'd send an armada to South Amer-

ica and Mexico. They'd load up with slaves and treasure. Those Spaniards were hell on wheels when it came
to treasure. In 1600, most of the gold in the world was
in the Western Hemisphere. A hundred years later,
thanks to the Spanish armadas, most of it was either in
Europe or on the bottom of the sea."

"How come so much went to the bottom? I'd figure
the privateers would have carried it off."

"They weren't the biggest enemy the galleons had.
Those babies were top-heavy, and when they ran into a
storm, they had a bad habit of going down like a bucket
full of rocks. In the two centuries or so that the Spanish
had real power in Latin and South America, they lost
more than a hundred galleons, and every one a treasure
trove."

"How about yours?"

"We think so. Of course, we've only started nibbling
at her. It'll take a couple of months of work to get down
inside. The hull's hard to get through, and dangerous.
The fishing boats have got her all wrapped up in old
nets, and it's damned easy to get an arm or a flipper
through that mesh, and then it's Good-by, Charlie."

"Would a little muscle help?"

"What kind?"

"*Yellowtail*. Working in close, without all the drag of
a long chain, she could yank the sides right off a
wreck."

"Sounds good. How big a cut?"

"I hadn't even thought of one. I don't think Forsythe
or Osha would accept it. We're out here for energy resources—"

"*And*," added the treasure hunter, "a movie."

O'Keefe grinned. "That too."

"Well, if you want to look around down there, be my
guest. You won't go away empty-handed, if we find anything at all. Forsythe and Osha may be rich, but I don't
think you are."

O'Keefe lifted his can of beer. "Truer words were
never spoken."

* * *

Captain Dimitri Ashkenazy had not remained unknowing of the traffic gathering around *Lamprey*. Although the American survey vessel was now some forty miles away, *Knipovich*'s radar was easily able to separate the various ships as they drew together.

"*Lamprey*," he said, studying the radar charts. "And the unidentified vessel from the southwest. A third, out from Florida. And"—here he studied a dim return—"what seems to be a sailing ship approaching from the south."

He turned to the officer in charge of the small submersible. "Are the holding rings in place beneath?"

"Yes, comrade."

"How much speed can we safely assume, with the submersible hanging from our bottom?"

"No more than seven knots."

"Very well. See that *Vanya* is fueled, provisioned, and launched within the next hour. Attach to the bottom. I presume your crew can exit with the self-breathers."

"There is no problem," said the officer. "Do you think we will see action?"

"Action?" smiled the Captain. "We are not at war, we are merely observing. Scrub your head of words like 'action.' See to your duty."

"Yes, Comrade."

Gloria Mitchel said, "This is the Ramada Inn, all over."

"Not really," Paul Forsythe replied. "We were all in the area before the splashdown. By accident. We're still here."

"I know you don't want me aboard," she said. "I'll stay out of your way."

"No, you don't have to," he said. "Earlier, we had problems. They've been cleared up. At least, most of them."

"Those that haven't? Are they politely referred to as Big F?"

He laughed. "Sometimes."

"Why your ship? I don't think you actually had anything to do with what happened."

"I don't either; certainly, not knowingly."

"So you've opted for the movie business instead of energy?"

"No. We're still planning to continue our survey. But other options have arisen. The movie thing, yes. And something else."

"What?"

"I'm not at liberty to say. But it might be important."

"How about an interview? It'll only take a minute."

"About what?"

"More or less what we've been saying."

"If you really want it," he said. "But I insist that you either run it without cuts, or not at all. I don't want to be taken out of context."

"Agreed," she said.

"I think I'd like to bounce a light," said Pat Crosby. "Do you mind?"

"Be my guest," said Forsythe.

The cameraman took a small Lowell spotlight from his gadget bag, plastered it to one of the bulkheads with a gray strip of gaffer tape, and plugged it into a small leather case which contained a battery.

"All set," he said, cradling the Canon camera. He flickered on the light, which was aimed at the ceiling, and Gloria Mitchel held a pencil microphone close to her lips.

"We're aboard the survey vessel *Lamprey,* cruising the mysterious body of water known as the Sargasso Sea. It was just a few miles from here, earlier this week, that the crew of Apollo 19 met tragedy. Some sources in Washington have hinted that the complicated electronic gear aboard *Lamprey* might have interfered with Apollo's splashdown. With me today is Paul Forsythe, former nuclear submarine commander and part owner of this unique vessel. Mr. Forsythe, do you have a comment on those allegations?"

"Sure," he said. "Pure nonsense."

"Yet you were well within the splashdown footprint."

"With specific permission from the same authorities who are now pointing the finger at us," Forsythe said. "According to the best information we've received so far, Apollo's heat shield failed. There's no way any kind of known electronics could have caused that."

"Perhaps laser beams?"

He smiled. "Or death rays? Miss Mitchel, I'm afraid you've read too much science fiction. Apollo was a tragic loss. But I don't see what's to be gained by pointing accusing fingers. I hope that NASA is examining the capsule carefully, to find out what really happened."

"Yet," said Gloria, "I understand that you were flown personally to a secret meeting with the President—"

"You ought to know," he interrupted. "You were there too."

"Cut," she said to Pat. "Mr. Forsythe, I've given my word not to report on that meeting—"

"Then don't try to get out of your promise by pulling an end run dragging me into talking about it," he said sharply. "You promised, incidentally, that this interview would run in its entirety, and now you've already begun cutting." He pointed to a small microphone on a nearby table. "However, *my* tape is still rolling. Keep that in mind when you get back to your editing room."

She flared, "The people have a right to know—"

"To know what *you* want them to know? Miss Mitchel, I've been there before. Maybe it's true that the only news is bad news, but with the power of your visual medium, you distort the real world. A thousand kids can gather at a rock concert, three smoke pot, and it's those three the world sees on the six o'clock news, and all the others wear the brand. Franklin Roosevelt practically lived in a wheelchair, but the press aimed their cameras somewhere else. Thirty years later, when George Wallace was campaigning, I saw more shots of *his* wheelchair than of his face."

"His health was an important issue."

"And FDR's wasn't in 1944? Like hell, lady. You've

got a new word for it—adversary journalism. There's nothing new about your methods—Hearst did it in 1899. Only the name has changed. Smear the opposition, and anybody who doesn't fit snugly into your eastern liberal establishment is the opposition." He waved at Pat Crosby. "Come on, friend, why aren't you filming this?"

Pat shrugged. "Why bother?" he said. "They wouldn't put it on the air."

Gloria said tightly, "If this is all you wanted to say, why did you let us come on board in the first place?"

"You'd traveled a long way," he said, "and I was trying to be courteous. Also, my wife asked me to."

"So you threw a bone to the little homemaker," Gloria said bitterly.

"Say that to Beth," said Paul Forsythe, "and she'll probably find that bone and shove it down your throat."

"Come on," said Gloria. "Unplug your lights, Pat. We aren't getting anything here that we can use."

"I could have told you that," Pat said.

Trying to make a joke, she said, "You can be replaced."

He threw back his head and cried, "Please, boss, do that little thing!"

"Oh, hurry up," said Gloria Mitchel. She stalked out of the "galley" without looking back at Paul Forsythe.

CHAPTER 17

Moose Gregory said, flicking the hazy photograph with his thumbnail, "She went down in 1747. *La Isobel de Guadalupe.* She was part of a fleet of six galleons, and they were loaded to the gills with gold and gems the Spaniards had ripped off from the Indians of South America and Mexico. *Isobel* had a high deck, too high, but she was as fast as a round-heeled senorita in Tijuana. The galleons had made their standard rendezvous at Havana, then they came up through the Florida straits and into the Bahama Channel, taking advantage of the northward flow of the Gulf Stream. If the privateers had been equipped with radar, they could have laid an intercepting course, but standing on watch and relying on visual sightings, by the time they saw the galleons, they didn't have a chance in hell of bisecting their course unless by bad luck the Spanish were approaching from directly downwind. Which was unlikely at that time of year. In the fall, the winds are usually from the southwest."

"What happened?" asked Ken O'Keefe.

"Nobody knows. All six went down in this same general area. But none of the reports that have survived from other ships—fishermen, merchant vessels, even the privateers—mention any really foul weather. Certainly there wasn't a hurricane. Yet all six of the galleons just vanished."

"How did you find *Isobel?*"

"Pure luck. Some time back, I signed on with the film company that was shooting the movie of Peter Benchley's *The Deep.* Scouting underwater locations for

them. Benchley himself had mapped out all the good
stuff up around Bermuda, so I sort of roamed around.
I've got a new metal detector that bounces up and down
a variable focus laser. When it hit the iron mass in *Isobel*'s cannons, the return was so strong that it blew out
the power transistors. I marked the location for future
reference."

"Without telling the producers?"

"It's unsuitable for filming. Too deep."

O'Keefe grinned. "A little shady," he said, "but not
actually dishonest."

"That's the way I see it," said Moose. "Anyway, I
registered her in Florida. She's inside the two-hundred-
mile limit."

"I thought that limit was just for fish."

"And anything taxable," grumbled Moose. "Do I
have to tell you about our busy tax collectors?"

"If the wreck's as valuable as you think, I don't see
why you're doing this on the el cheapo," said O'Keefe.
"Just you and that writer."

"Don't forget Lucia," said Moose Gregory. "Listen,
Dave's putting up the front money, and whatever we
recover, we split down the middle. We can do the job.
Why bring in more shareholders?"

"You invited me in."

"Hell, you were sitting right on top of her. I didn't
have much choice. And you're right, that sub of yours
might save us a lot of work. I never liked working that
deep with explosives."

"Is that how you were going to do it? Blow her hull
apart?"

"If we had to."

"When can I take a look at her?"

"What's wrong with right now?"

"Now? It'll be dark soon."

"That doesn't matter," said the treasure hunter.
"Down that deep, it's always dark."

William Postiglion and Sir Roger Lean had just finished an interview with Gloria Mitchel.

"Thank you," she said as Pat Crosby switched off his portable light. "It's good to see you again, Sir Roger. I'm glad you're safe."

"Sheer luck," he said. "Without that wonderful black man, I'd be shark bait by now."

"Is he aboard?" she asked.

"No, he's out there somewhere on his own sailboat."

"I plan to use him in my movie," said Posty, always alert for publicity.

"Oh?" Gloria said, aware of what he was doing, but willing to go along if it meant a good story. "As a sort of old man of the sea?"

He waggled a finger. "Ah, that's part of the mystery," he said. "You wouldn't want to give it away and spoil the film for everybody, would you?"

"Is the movie definite?" she asked.

"Oh, yes," he said.

"Do you have a script?"

"Here," he said, tapping his forehead. "As for putting the words on paper, Tony Dix will see to that."

"Aren't you afraid the Charlton Heston film will take most of the market?"

"Of course not. There's always room for good entertainment. And without wanting to disparage Chuck's film, it is, after all, merely fiction, whereas ours will reveal many of the true mysteries of the Triangle."

"And you think you'll unravel those mysteries on board *Lamprey?*"

"Without doubt."

"Good luck," she said. "It's my impression that Forsythe isn't interested in anything but exploring the ocean bottom."

"And who's to say that the answer to the mystery doesn't lie there?" asked the producer.

"No," said Paul Forsythe. "We're not in the treasure business. You can't risk the sub fooling around with Gregory's wreck."

"There's no risk," said O'Keefe. "I want to run some

more checkouts on *Yellowtail* anyway, and I've got room for three passengers."

"Keefer," said Forsythe, "let it alone. You were out of line with this film business, although I'll admit that it worked out all right. But we've got a job out here, and damned little of it has gotten done yet."

Hurt, O'Keefe said, "I'm not feathering my own nest, Paul. Any treasure share we might get would go to *Lamprey*, not me."

"I appreciate that," said Forsythe. "But we can't spare the time, and we can't risk *Yellowtail*. I thought you were anxious to take her back to that underwater highway you found."

"It's probably been there a million years," O'Keefe said. "It can wait a couple more days."

"Have you mentioned this to Osha?"

"Hell, no. I wouldn't try to sneak around you like that."

"Thanks," said Forsythe. "It's a good thing you didn't. Not because I'd have gotten mad, but I don't think he's any too happy with this whole operation right now, and I'd hate to have him get the idea that we've been going in business for ourselves."

"Okay, we'll forget the sub. Any objections to me diving down with Gregory just to take a look?"

"Yes. Same reason. Without you, the sub's not much good to us."

"Paul, you're leaning too hard."

"I'm sorry. I guess that's just the way it has to be."

"Don't bet on it. I could quit."

Forsythe looked at him for a while. Then he said, "If that's what you want, Ken. But let me know now, so I can get a replacement."

O'Keefe hesitated. "Oh, shit," he said. "*Yellowtail*'s my baby. I can't let anybody else teach her to swim."

"Thanks," said Forsythe.

O'Keefe left.

Beth, who had come onto the bridge during the conversation, kissed Paul Forsythe's cheek. "What was that all about?" she asked.

"Keefer got the treasure itch. But I think I scratched it off."

"Are you planning to eat any time this week?"

He glanced at his watch. "Is it that time already?"

"You missed lunch. Yes, it's that time."

Looking down at *Lamprey*'s bow, he saw O'Keefe talking earnestly with Moose Gregory. The treasure hunter raised a hand, spoke for a moment, then gave a shrug and walked away. O'Keefe stood there for a brief time, jammed both hands in his pockets, and went below.

"Poor Keefer," said Forsythe. "He could just about taste that treasure."

"He'll survive," said Beth. "It's you I'm worried about. This voyage isn't exactly what you had in mind, is it?"

"No," he admitted. "But you don't just quit."

"Not even when the White House tells you to?"

"Especially not then," he said. "Come on, Sunny. Let's eat."

Henry Frazier adjusted the submersible's television camera lenses with rough motions that bordered on violence. He was steaming mad. His crew quarters were crowded and uncomfortable. And while he was grabbing forty winks, he'd heard a click and looked up to see that Forsythe broad photographing him.

"Hi," she'd said, as if it was standard operating procedure for a woman to be in crew's quarters. "Don't let me bother you."

"You oughta knock," he'd mumbled as he turned his back on her.

The starboard TV camera did not fit well into its recessed port, because of the new lens hood.

Frazier should have taken it out and trimmed down the hood a fraction of an inch.

Instead, still angry, he forced the camera into its mount and slammed the covering hatch shut.

Within, unseen, a sharp metal edge nicked a power

cable. A spark arced from the cable to the nearby bare metal hull of the sub, then died as Frazier tightened the hatch securely, moving the cable a few tiny centimeters away from the hull.

Saito Osha had taken Raiko Nakamura to *Lamprey*'s bridge. Bob Hart was at the helm. He showed the Japanese girl how to steer the vessel, and let her do it for a few moments, retiring to the port wing for a smoke and to give them privacy.

"Oh, my," said Raiko. "I am driving a ship."

"It isn't hard," said Osha. "When we are married, we will have our own little ship, and you may command her."

"I wish I might command this one to take us back to Tokyo," said the girl.

"You have now said the same thing twice," said Osha. "If you really wish it, I will call a helicopter, and we will leave."

She touched his arm. "No, you must not do that for me. I know this work of yours is very important. I will not say such things again."

"You must say what you think," he said. "Our life cannot be built on lies."

"But I am only a stupid girl," she said. "I know nothing of the sea or of this Bermuda Triangle."

"Nor do I," he said. "And you are not stupid."

Happily, she said, pointing at the yellow path the moon painted toward the horizon, "Look! It is the yellow brick road."

He smiled, puzzled.

Saito Osha had never seen *The Wizard of Oz*.

Moose Gregory thanked Arthur Lovejoy for the hospitality shown by *Lamprey*. "Especially," he said, "thank your guy who fixed our head."

"Where is he?" demanded Lucia de la Renata. "I will kiss him. I will make love to him!"

"He's on duty below somewhere," said Lovejoy, not wanting to admit that it had been he himself who had unjammed the balking valves of the toilet's water system. "But I'll give him your message."

She caught both his ears and gave him a burning kiss. "I do not expect you to give him this, but you may describe it."

David Lester said, "I hope you guys don't run into trouble out there. I don't like the way this feels."

"Are you going to dive on the wreck?" asked the Captain.

"Maybe," said the burly writer. "Moose and I have to talk about that."

"Give our regards to Paul and to Sir David," said Moose Gregory. "Come on, let's get our tails moving. We're getting further and further away from the wreck every minute."

"Have a safe trip," said Lovejoy.

"I'm always careful," said Moose. "It'd be easier if your boy O'Keefe hadn't changed his mind about using the sub, but we'll still hack it."

Casually, Lovejoy asked, "How did you plan on using the sub?"

"Keefer said we could chain *Yellowtail* to the hulk and just yank out a chunk of timbers. It would have saved me and Dave a week's diving."

"Too bad," said the Captain. To Lucia, he said, "I think you'll find that your shower's working again, too."

"Bellisimo!" she cried. "This crewman, he must be a genius."

"Just a guy who knows something about water fittings," said Lovejoy. Pointedly, to Moose Gregory, he added, "If you plan any more extended sea voyages, you ought to learn a little about them yourself."

"Sure, Skipper," said Moose. He helped Lucia over to the rope ladder, which led down to the *Tiger Shark,* which had been pulled up from its towing position. "Take it easy, baby. You don't want to slip and sprain that nice tail."

Quietly, in a voice heard only by Lovejoy, David Lester said, "I'm going to see if I can persuade him to go in and get a trained crew."

"Not a bad idea," said Lovejoy. "Good luck, Mr. Lester."

"Same to you," said the writer. "Keep your eyes open. I'm not so sure that all of this Triangle stuff is only myth."

He followed Moose down into the converted PT boat and as its engines roared, waved up at the small group who had gathered to see the treasure hunters off.

Sir Roger Lean said, "Nice chap, that. I must read his book some time."

Joseph Horatio, sailing through the dark night, saw the lights of *Lamprey* far ahead, near the horizon. A great distance to the east were more lights—the Soviet vessel *Knipovich*. Horatio put the battered Royal Navy night glasses to his eyes, and saw a spray of fluorescent water as a smaller craft separated from *Lamprey* and set course to the southwest.

Horatio had not made any definite commitment to rendezvous with the American survey vessel, although when his passengers had gone aboard the PT boat, it had been assumed by them that he would. He knew what such a meeting would involve. They would try to pay him, and then, uncomfortably, press unwanted stores on him.

Horatio preferred to live simply from the sea. He carried enough fresh water for a month, and dried fruits and canned meats in case he was unable to catch a turtle, or a red-blooded fish. White fish were all right once or twice a day, but a man needed blood to stay alive. He had three cans of lard aboard for the necessary fat to sustain him, and a gallon jug of island rum. He needed no more.

He shifted course slightly. He would pass to the west of the American ship, he decided, and leave it at that. If she saw him and signaled, he would join her. If not, he would continue toward the heart of the Sargasso, where something waited.

CHAPTER 18

Later, Arthur Lovejoy was sure he had knocked at the door of Kenneth O'Keefe's cabin. He could remember it positively. He had tapped, and a voice within had answered.

But when he opened the door, the small room was darkened. Only a light behind him, high on the starboard rigging, cast some small pool of illumination inside.

But it was enough. He saw the odd jumble of bodies on O'Keefe's bunk. Not one body, but two. And they were moving, and the voice he had heard was a woman's, and it had spoken not with words, but with the urgent cries of passion.

Lovejoy froze. He could have backed out onto the companionway and closed the door. He should have. But he was petrified, because even in its orgasmic distortion, he recognized the voice of his daughter.

Then O'Keefe said, "What the hell? Who's that?"

Without thinking, with an almost involuntary motion that he could have cut his hand off for having made, Lovejoy flicked on the light.

Janet sat astride the sub commander, who lay on the narrow bunk. Her hands were gripping his naked shoulders. She herself was nude. Her back was toward her father, and as he watched, her hands left O'Keefe's shoulders and balled into fists.

"Turn off the light," she said quietly.

"I—" he said.

"Damn you, turn it off!" she cried.

He threw the cabin into darkness.

Her voice trembled. "Leave. Now."

He tried to say her name. "Jan—"

"Now! Daddy, get out. I mean it. Don't say anything, just *go!*"

Trembling, he backed out and shut the door.

As he almost staggered up the metal stairs that led to the bridge, the radioman, Ray Barnstable, called after him, "Cap'n, I—"

"Not now, damn it!" Lovejoy shouted.

Barnstable stared after him.

Captain Dimitri Ashkenazy listened quietly to the report from his radar officer.

"It is a wooden sailing vessel?" he repeated.

"Yes, Comrade. She is moving very slow, and the return indicates that she is quite small and carries almost no metal."

"And she is passing the American vessel?"

"To their west."

"Could it be a cruising yacht or racer?"

"Perhaps."

"I think it is of no importance," Ashkenazy decided. "Advise me if there is any change of course."

The radar officer nodded. "Good night, Comrade. I am sorry to have disturbed you."

"It is no matter. I do not sleep much at sea." The Russian Captain reached for his pipe. "I do not have my matches."

"Allow me," said the radar officer. He held a wooden match for Ashkenazy's pipe bowl.

"Thank you," puffed Ashkenazy. "Well, Pytor, are you looking forward to the home voyage?"

"Very much. My mother is getting very old. I think perhaps this may be my last leave with her."

The Captain frowned. "That is unfortunate. Would you like me to have you assigned to shore duty for a while?"

The radar officer shook his head. "No. My sisters are there."

"Your father?"

"He was on board the *Rimsky,* in the Baltic."

"Ah," said the Captain. He did not need to say more. The sub tender *Rimsky* had gone down in a winter storm with all hands.

"Will that be all, Comrade?"

Ashkenazy converted a sigh into a puff on his pipe. "Yes," he said. "Thank you."

The young officer left. The Captain peered up at the blue-white pipe smoke rising toward the tiny ventilating hatch. It would have been nice to talk for a while, but he realized that the young officer was uneasy in his presence. One was young and one was old, one was junior in rank and one was senior, one was still bound to the land by family ties and one was not. The gulf between them was too great.

Ray Barnstable found Forsythe on the fantail, staring out at the starlit ocean.

"There's a small vessel passing just about half a mile off our port beam," said the radioman. "It might be that guy, Horatio."

"Did you tell the Captain?"

"I tried. He was upset about something."

"Okay," said Forsythe.

"Should we signal? Maybe he's looking for us."

Forsythe thought for a moment. "No. We've got enough lights on. If he wanted to join us, he could. It must be that he wants to go his own course."

"The Russian's still off to the east," said Barnstable. "I think he's shadowing us."

"That's his privilege," said Forsythe. "Anything else?"

"Only that I'm getting a CB skip all the way from Kansas City. Some ratchet-jaw yelling at the Smokey Bears."

"Translate," said Forsythe, who had somehow missed the huge boom in Citizens Band radio.

"Ratchet-jaw's a guy who hogs the channel and won't shut up. Smokey Bears are state cops. The truck drivers started calling them that, and when everybody got ears—radios—the civilians just picked it up."

"I thought CB range was four or five miles."

"It is, except when the signal gets bounced off some disturbance in the ionosphere caused by sunspots. Then the broadcast can go five hundred, a thousand miles. Or more."

"Can you bounce back at him?" asked Forsythe, a tight smile pulling at his lips.

"Maybe."

"Then tell old ratchet-jaw to button his lip or we'll send the Bermuda Triangle Monster out there to eat his antenna."

Captain Arthur Lovejoy sat in his cabin, a straight Bourbon in his shaking hand. He sipped at it without tasting the liquor.

The door opened.

"Come in, Janet," he said.

She came straight to him and sat down beside him on the small couch. She took the glass of Bourbon from his fingers, and put it down on the deck, then held both of his hands in her own.

"Daddy, I'm sorry. I really am. I wouldn't have had that happen for anything in the world."

He started to answer, and she put one hand over his mouth.

"No, let me finish. I know what you're thinking, and I know how upset you are, and that's why I'm sorry, not because Ken and I were making love. Daddy, I'm grown up, and even before I was, I'd had what you'd call 'experiences.' But they were always private, personal things, which hurt no one else. And now I've hurt you, and I am very, very sorry about it. But it was an accident, and you must think of it that way. I don't know how sex was between you and Mom, but I know you wouldn't have wanted to be observed doing it, and I'm afraid that I'm just as old-fashioned as you are. There's nothing shameful about the act of love, yet we behave as if there were. That's what's wrong, not *doing* it, but being somehow ashamed of it. I want to say all this now, because I know you're going to make a big scene, and if you do then I'm going to have to leave this boat and go someplace else, and I don't want to. Because there isn't anything dirty or shameful about Ken and me. Can you understand that?"

He nodded, not trusting his voice.

"Daddy, you have to promise me that you're not going to make a big thing out of this, or start taking it out on Ken. I can't assure you that it won't happen again. I love Ken, and I think he's starting to love me. But I'll try. This ship is your home, and I don't want to do anything in it that upsets you. So please promise me not to do anything mean. Do you promise?"

Again, Lovejoy nodded.

She kissed his cheek. "I love you, Daddy."

Janet slipped out of the cabin.

Behind her, Lovejoy stared at his hands. He knew he was wrong, that each person has a right to private decision and happiness, and yet there was a chill anger at Ken O'Keefe, like a tight band, squeezing around his heart.

Shortly before dawn, he was awakened from a troubled sleep by Second Officer Bob Hart.

"Sorry," said the young officer. "You'd better come on deck. Something funny's happening."

Lovejoy slipped into his light robe and followed Hart up to the bridge. Except for the legal running lights, *Lamprey* was blacked out. The bridge light, for compass and engine gauges, was an eye-saving red, to preserve night vision.

Yet, he saw at once, the deck was almost as brightly lit as if by daylight.

Green, flickering bands of light seemed to rotate around the railings of the ship. Flaring and waning with a purposeful rhythm, they made no sound.

"It started about five minutes ago," said Hart. "What do you make of it?"

"St. Elmo's fire?" said the Captain, more as a question than as an answer.

"I don't know," said Hart. "If I remember, St. Elmo's fire is an electrical discharge from a projecting object into the atmosphere. It's like a ball of fire, or a flaming bush. This stuff isn't discharging anywhere. It's just glowing around our railings."

"Radio Frequency sometimes makes metal objects glow," said the Captain. "Are our transmitters operating?"

"Shut down for the night. No RF from there."

The two men watched.

Hart asked, "Should I turn out the crew?"

"No," said Lovejoy. "I can't think of anything they could do."

"They could stand by the launch in case we need to lower it in a hurry."

Lovejoy glanced at the younger man. No, he did not appear to be panicking. He was merely doing what any sensible ship's officer should do, suggesting alternatives to his commander.

"It doesn't seem to be throwing any heat," said Lovejoy. "I don't know what the hell it is, but it apparently isn't dangerous."

"Not," said Hart dryly, "unless it's some kind of radioactivity."

"In that case," said the Captain, "we've already been zapped. I left my lead underwear back on the mainland."

The mysterious glow had now turned into a bluish-green, and the outlines of the railings appeared fuzzy, badly defined. The pulsing had slowed, and the glow was steadier.

"Let's see if our course has any effect on this stuff," said Lovejoy. "Right standard rudder."

"Right standard rudder," repeated Hart. He had put the ship on autopilot when he'd hurried below to awaken Lovejoy. He disconnected the automatic steering and put *Lamprey* in a slow turn to the east.

"Aha," said Lovejoy, as their course approached ninety degrees. "Look."

The blue-green glow flickered in patches, and began

to die. In less than five minutes, it had completely disappeared. By then, *Lamprey* had made an almost complete circle.

"Resume course," said Lovejoy.

He waited, to see if the glow would reappear. It did not. In the east, the sky was turning rosy. It would be dawn soon.

"I guess maybe I should have woke up Mr. Dix, too," Hart said, suddenly remembering the writer.

Lovejoy laughed. "You can give him an interview. I'll back your story. Maybe he'll give you a free copy of his next book."

"More likely, he'll give me a punch in the eye," said Hart. "Do you think our turn is what made it vanish?"

"Either that or it may have just been a short-lived effect and its fading coincided with the turn. I had an idea that the magnetic lines, north and south, might have been involved. But maybe they weren't. Who knows?"

He went down on deck and examined a section of the railing. It was unmarked. No burns, no evidence of any abnormality.

Lovejoy glanced at his watch. He could still get another hour of sleep before going on duty again. If he could only put Janet out of his mind for that long.

Hart had been correct in his assessment of Anthony Dix's reaction to being left out of the mysterious happenings before dawn. The writer was furious.

"What the hell do you think we came all the way out here for?" he demanded. "I've heard about this kind of glowing, but never saw it. You should have called me."

"Don't blame Bob," said Lovejoy. "He asked me if he should get you, but I didn't want either of us leaving the bridge when there might have been danger to the ship."

"Damn it," Dix persisted, "you could have blown a whistle, or set off General Quarters, or whatever it is that you do."

"Everybody knock off the squabbling," said Lovejoy.

"I'm sorry, Tony. Yes, I should have called you. Now that you're here, do you have any idea what it was?"

The writer shrugged. "I'd be better qualified to speak if I'd seen it first-hand."

Lovejoy said, "One apology per day is my limit."

Dix said, "Ionization, maybe. If the air through which we were passing were positively ionized, and the electrical charges within our own hull were negative, the interaction might have caused some slow discharge, perhaps visible as a glow."

"We made a three-sixty turn," said Hart. "Halfway around, the flow flickered and went out."

"The turn may have taken you out of the patch of ionized air," said Dix. "Or the changing magnetic field might have had something to do with it."

"That's what the Captain said," Hart told him.

Dix studied Lovejoy. "Ah? You're starting to become a believer?"

"Not in the whole Triangle legend," said Lovejoy. "But I'll agree that some odd things have been happening."

"With luck"—the writer smiled—"they'll get odder still."

Forsythe, Osha, Dix, and O'Keefe were seated around *Lamprey*'s plotting table, studying a chart. Forsythe had just bisected three lines to form a tiny triangle.

"Right about there," he said. "Does that match your figures, Keefer?"

"In the ball park," said the sub commander. "We ought to be within a mile. But I've had the inertial guidance system cooking anyway, ever since I spotted the highway."

Osha frowned, tapping the chart. "Paul, I understand that you lost power. Wouldn't that have tumbled the inertia's gyros and glitched all the memory recall?"

Dix said, "Shit, sure it would."

"But," O'Keefe said, "*Yellowtail* didn't lose power. *Lamprey* did. *Yellowtail*'s been on standby power ever since we retrieved her, and that includes our stay in Jacksonville."

"Are you sure?" asked Forsythe.

"I checked this morning. There's a fail-safe indicator with its own separate nicad battery that shows red whenever there's been a power outage, even one as brief as a microsecond. We're in fat city. I'll put us right down on that underwater road, take my word."

Forsythe measured distances with a divider. "Say four this afternoon. That'll put us on site."

"I'll start powering up," said O'Keefe.

"Beth wants to go with you," said Forsythe. "Pictures. Is that all right?"

"No problem," said O'Keefe. "I'd planned to take Janet anyway. If *that*'s all right with you."

Mousetrapped, Forsythe said, "As long as you have the room."

"Plenty. I can carry three passengers, as I think I mentioned to you yesterday."

"You did that," Forsythe agreed. "All right, let's get to work."

Jack Begley confronted William Postiglion and Anthony Dix.

"I'm a pilot," he said. "How's chances of me getting back to the valley and my crop-dusting?"

"Won't you be needed for the crash investigation?" asked Dix.

"What crash? We had engine failure and ditched. I can make a deposition when I get ashore, and if they need me for an inquiry, I'll fly back. Meanwhile, I can be doing something more useful than floating around the Sargasso Sea."

"It's all right with me," decided the producer. "You served the purpose, although it may prove expensive to us."

"Look," said the pilot, "I signed on to fly on my old course. I did *not* plan on going in the drink again, or I'd have charged you five times as much. What happened to that chopper wasn't my fault. The engine just quit, and that isn't supposed to happen with a Hughes. They've got a terrific safety record. If it's anybody's fault, look at him—" His finger was pointed straight at Anthony Dix. "He's the guy who seems to be masterminding this whole thing. He wasn't even surprised that we went down."

Quietly, Dix said, "I did *not* sabotage your helicopter, if that's what you're implying."

"I didn't say you did. But you sure in hell knew something. Maybe the weather conditions were the same as back in '45, maybe you can read the future. I don't know, and right now, I don't care. All I want is to go home. You can mail me my check. *If* you birds get out of this alive."

"How do you figure on getting ashore?" asked Dix. "It's a long swim."

"I'll hitch a ride back on that TV charter boat," said Begley. He looked around, at the empty horizons. "Hey, where the hell *is* that charter boat?"

"It was with us until midnight," said Dix. "I saw its lights about half a mile back."

"Well, it sure as hell isn't there now," said Begley. He swore. "That's my luck. Stranded on the *Flying Dutchman*."

The thirty-six-foot Chris-Craft Walter Wylie had leased for Gloria Mitchel's exploration of this part of the Bermuda Triangle was, by then, thirty miles from *Lamprey*.

Her name was *Little Judy,* for the skipper's nine-year-old. His name was Ellard Wiggins, and he had been chartering boats out of Jacksonville for twenty-three years. He invested in the best equipment, gave it first-class maintenance, had never had an accident.

When the three TV people had come back aboard, down the shaky Jacob's ladder from the survey vessel, it was nearly midnight.

"Head in?" asked Wiggins.

"No," said the woman. She seemed to be the boss.

"Just keep them in sight. We'll be going on board again in the morning."

Wiggins did some mental computing of fuel usage.

"Ma'am," he said finally, "if I keep her going all night, you're going to lose six or seven hours of range that we might need later on. I'll burn more gas poking along following her than I would if we just hove to, and caught up with her in the morning."

"Can you anchor out here?" asked Wylie. "I thought it was too deep."

"Do it all the time," said Wiggins. "I've got three special-made sea anchors. We're off shipping lanes, so there's no danger. We keep the lights on anyway. Everybody get a good night's sleep and we can put her up on the step, run flat out, and catch that baby in three hours easy.

"Just so we're on board at nine A.M.," said the woman. He had seen her on TV, he remembered. Kind of snippy in person. Well, it had been a long day. Good thing it wouldn't be a longer night. With only Johnny to relieve him at the wheel, it would have been a real mess, running all night. Now everybody could get some sack time.

Although there was plenty of room below, he and Johnny would sleep on deck. The sleeping bags and air mattresses would keep them warm, and if a rain came up, they could go into the wheelhouse. That would leave the forward cabin free for the woman, and the two men could take the convertible sofa-bunks in the salon.

When he explained this arrangement, the woman merely nodded, taking it as her due. The young one, with the camera, said, "Thanks. You sure you won't be cold up here?"

"Makes for better sleeping," said Wiggins. "You folks go below, get comfortable. I'll call you for breakfast."

The quarters aboard *Little Judy* were paneled and carefully laid out, giving the impression of more space than there actually was. The dinette, which converted into a bunk, had some glasses, ice, and bottles of liquor and mixers on it.

"How about a drink?" said Wylie. "I'll do the honors."

"If it's a quick one," said Gloria. "Wow. Look at my hair. I should have brought a hairdresser."

"You look fine," said Wylie. "Gin and tonic?"

"Light on the gin. Do they have showers on these boats?"

"Sure," said Pat Crosby. "All the comforts of home."

"Well," Gloria said, taking the glistening glass from Wylie, "if any of you characters need the john, you'd better grab it now, because I'm going to stand under that hot water for about half an hour."

"Half a minute's more like it," said Wylie. "The skipper won't want you using up all his fresh water."

"Screw him," she said. "We're paying the tab. That includes the water."

"It's not that," he said. "Except that once you've used up what he has in the tanks, it's a hundred miles or so for us to get some more."

"Oh," she said, sipping her drink. Then, to Pat: "Did we get any good stuff?"

"Photographically, yes."

"What's that supposed to mean?"

The cameraman shrugged. "Only that everything we shot could just as well have been done in Jacksonville. Or even in the studio."

"Damn it," she said tightly, "we aren't *in* Jacksonville, or the studio. We're out here. I expect you to get as many production values as you can."

"Gloria—" began Wylie.

Pat cut him off. "Yes, ma'am, boss lady! I'll fill that old TV screen with bodacious waterspouts tearing huge ships from the sea and scattering them over the Bahamas. And big close-ups on flying saucers, and ghost ships sliding out of the fog. All I ask that you do, Great One, is lead me to them, because I sure as shit can't photograph something that isn't there."

"Oh, go screw," she said.

Flicking an imaginary cigar, Pat put on a Groucho Marx voice and asked, "Is that an invitation?"

"Both of you, shut up," said Wylie. "What did you have in mind for tomorrow, Glor?"

"I want a decent interview with Superman, that loud-mouth Forsythe."

"Lots of luck," said Pat Crosby, downing his scotch.

"Damn it," she said softly. "I've *got* to. If we don't come back with something hot, maybe something on Apollo 19, we might as well sail this lousy boat to the Azores and take up goat herding."

"You'll do fine, baby," said Wylie. "Just settle down and relax, get some rest. We're both on your side." He shot a glance at Pat.

The cameraman responded, "You bet your sweet pa-tootie, Glor. Now, about that invitation—"

In spite of herself, she laughed. "You're all mouth, Pat. If I really asked you in, you'd turn bright green."

"My favorite color," he said. "Try me."

"Not tonight, baby. I'm too tired. Walt, can I have another one of those delicious gin and tonics? I think I'll skip that shower."

Pat said, "The skipper will be pleased. Now the crew will be able to go back on water rations."

Wylie said, "Fifteen minutes more. Then everybody turns in."

"I don't know if I'll make it that long," sighed Gloria.

Pat had a double entendre ready to shoot back, but the warning look in Wylie's eye gave him second thoughts. Instead, he said, "Want Old Pat to tuck you in?"

"Some other time," she said drowsily. She put down her second drink, untasted. "Nighty night, kids. Call me if we're sinking."

The door to the forward cabin clicked behind her.

"She's beat," said Pat. "I'll give her that, she works her ass off."

"Yeah," said Wylie. "And she's right about one thing."

"What's that?"

"If we don't bring home some strong footage, we'll be lucky if even the goats will talk to us."

On deck, Ellard Wiggins and his nineteen-year-old son, John, drank hot coffee from a thermos. They had put out the three sea anchors, placing them to keep *Little Judy*'s bow into the waves.

Lamprey's running lights were merely colored stars near the horizon. Just as sailors for centuries have done, the two men stared out over the water, letting hazy thoughts drift through their minds.

"All this Bermuda Triangle stuff, Pa," said the boy. "You think there's anything in it?"

"I've been coming out here twenty-three years," said his father. "You can't prove it by me."

"But there's sure been a lot of disappearances."

"There's a lot of boats out here, most of them run by amateurs who don't know anything about the sea. It surprises me that we don't lose more of them."

"But that doesn't explain those lights in the sky, and all."

"Have you ever seen any of those lights, Johnny?"

"Not that I remember."

"Neither have I. When I do, then I'll try to figure it. Until then, the ocean is a bad place for people who don't bother to learn its rules. That's enough explanation for me."

"You want me to take the first watch, Pa?"

"Aren't you sleepy?"

"Not a bit."

"Fine. But call me if anything unusual happens." The man chuckled. "Like funny lights in the sky."

What happened was not accompanied by lights. And it came without warning. Johnny Wiggins did not have time to wake his father.

The night was clear, and very calm. The stars filled the sky. Johnny was playing the AM radio in the wheelhouse very softly, listening to station WWL out of New Orleans. He liked the all-night show which was aimed toward truckers. Unknown to his father, Johnny Wiggins planned to abandon the sea as soon as he was twenty-one, and become a long-haul trucker.

Lately, a lot of the records the station played dealt not only with trucking, but with Citizens Band radio. There was "Convoy," which told the incredible tale of a thousand eighteen-wheelers, linked together by CB transmissions, all headed en masse for New Jersey. And another depicted the adventures of a highway patrolman who, using the nickname "White Knight" lured sleepy truckers into breaking the speed limit by telling them they had a green light all the way to the state line—and then pulling them over for a ticket.

Little Judy had standard maritime radios, but no CB. Ellard Wiggins disparaged CB as "kiddie radio."

When he became a trucker, Johnny Wiggins fully intended to have a CB radio in his cab.

"Ten-four, back door," he hummed along with the song. "Hammer down, good buddy. Put the pedal to the metal, and let 'er roar!"

He was lounging on the padded stool behind the controls, at the right of the wheelhouse. One foot was up on the console, tapping in time with the music.

Then, abruptly, without any warning, he was flying through the air. He crashed against the padded bench that doubled as a tool chest and, as he struggled to get up, felt *Little Judy* lurching forward through the water. It was moving so fast that he was forced back against the bench twice before he could stagger to his feet.

The boat had her bow down, almost dipping into the light waves. Two of the sea anchors now trailed behind them, their lines taut and vibrating.

But the third, the one fastened to the center cleat, stretched ahead, and it was pulling the Chris-Craft along at more than twenty knots. It vibrated and thrummed. The wake the boat left behind was huge.

Ellard Wiggins fought his way up from sleep. He lurched to the wheelhouse. "What the hell's going on?" he yelled.

Johnny pointed. "I don't know. Something's pulling us."

The sea anchor line made a twist to the right, and as *Little Judy* followed, she almost capsized. Tons of water spilled over the sides, and the boat sank deeper into the water. The sound of the violin-string-tight rope increased.

"It'll pull our bow off!" shouted Wiggins. "Cut the rope!"

Johnny scrambled forward, one hand clutching the chromed railings, the other pulling out his fisherman's knife. He released the railing for a second, to open the blade, and just then the boat swerved again and he tumbled over the side into the plunging water. One second he was there, the next he was gone.

"Jesus!" cried his father. He let go of the wheel, which he had been using to try to keep the Chris-Craft on an even keel, and pulling a bait knife from its sheath, fastened to the bulkhead, rushed forward.

He had to saw at the rope to part it, but then it gave way with a twanging sound and, held back by the other two sea anchors, the boat came to a sudden stop and dove its bow under the waves, and more water cascaded aboard. The cockpit was knee deep, and Wiggins heard the water pouring down into the cabin and the engine compartment. A sharp snapping noise came up from the battery locker, and all the lights went out.

Into the darkness, Wiggins called, "Johnny?" No answer. He called again, and again, until his voice was hoarse.

But he heard no answer.

CHAPTER 19

Gloria Mitchel had still been asleep when she was thrown from her bunk. The forward cabin was dark, and scrambling on the vibrating deck, she could not remember where the light switch was, or have any hope of finding it. Instead, she crawled toward the rear, and managed to push open the door that separated her cabin from the salon.

Walter Wylie and Pat Crosby had both been jerked from sleep, although neither had been thrown to the deck. One overhead light was on. Wylie had gone to bed in pastel blue pajamas; Pat wore only boxer shorts, and their fly gaped.

"Gloria!" said Wylie. "Are you hurt?" He helped her up. Pat was scrambling into his trousers.

"I don't think so. What happened?"

Pat said, "I think we hit an iceberg."

"Knock it off, clown," said Wylie. "Let's find out."

Just then, a cascade of frothing water poured down into the salon from above.

Gloria screamed, "My God, we're sinking!"

They scrambled for the hatchway. The boat made a diving motion and they fell against the bulkheads and furniture. Pat Crosby made a grab for his camera, which had been on top of the galley stove, missed it, and saw it smash against the small refrigerator. He caught it before it fell into the sloshing water.

More water came down from above, there was a sizzling, snapping sound beneath their feet, and the lights went out.

But the boat had stopped moving. It settled in the

gurgling water, and tiny waves washed around their ankles.

Wylie lit his cigarette lighter. He rummaged in the galley and found a candle, lighted it. He melted some wax, and affixed the candle in a saucer. "Pat, go up there and find out what happened." He grabbed two saucepans. "Gloria, you and I had better start bailing." He slid open one of the windows, and began throwing pans of water out through it.

Distantly, he heard a man's anguished voice calling, "Johnny?" Johnny?"

Twice during the morning, Ray Barnstable, at Jack Begley's request, tried to raise *Little Judy* on his radio. There was no answer.

"They must have gone in," he said.

"Shit," said the pilot. "Listen, get me Jacksonville, and—" He paused. No, that would not be a good idea, he decided. One does not call up the flying service whose helicopter you have ditched in the ocean, and ask them to come out and give you a lift. The accident had already been reported, and so far the response had been one of deep silence. He suspected teams of lawyers were consulting, and wondered why his ears were not burning.

While he powered up *Yellowtail*, Kenneth O'Keefe posed self-consciously for pictures taken by Beth Forsythe, and briefed both her and Janet Lovejoy on the submersible.

"Her depth range is six thousand feet," he said. "We could go deeper, but you run into limits of air supply."

"Can't you add more air tanks?" asked Janet.

"It isn't just the amount of air we carry," said O'Keefe. "The critical factor in diving is the amount of carbon dioxide you build up in the cabin. All the air in the world won't help you if the CO_2 gets above two per cent of the atmosphere."

"Where does it come from?"

Beth, clicking off several frames, answered, "It's

what people breathe out, honey. Paul told me all about it. But, Ken, he said that on board his submarine, he never let it get above half of one per cent."

"That's regulation," agreed O'Keefe. "Above that, the crew can get headaches and nausea. But you have to remember, they're on board for weeks or months at a time. We can tolerate a higher level in *Yellowtail*, because we're only down for a few hours."

Janet said, "It's a funny-looking boat. I thought it would be long like a cigar. It looks more like that lunar module they sent into space."

"Essentially, it's not a boat, but rather a sphere, surrounded by housing for lights, motors, and all the rest."

Taking a close-up of what appeared to be claws projecting from the front of *Yellowtail*, Beth asked, "What's this for?"

"It's the manipulator assembly," said O'Keefe. "We can fasten various tools to it, and operate them from inside. I can cut through steel cables, or dig a trench or drill down through the seabed. It all depends on the mission."

"What will we be doing today?" Janet asked.

"Trying to find that strip of hard-top road I saw before."

"Can you?"

He grinned. "Sure."

"How? There aren't any road signs down there."

"We've got what they call an inertial guidance system on board. All nuke subs use them, and now some airliners do too. You set it at a known point, and from then on, it can take you to any square foot on earth, above or below the water, as long as you know the coordinates."

Beth said, "That control console looks pretty complicated in there. Can one man really operate it?"

"Mostly. The pilot's console controls the vehicle itself. We've got three electric motors mounted outside. One main engine, at the center of gravity, for principal thrust, and two smaller ones on each side. Instead of a rudder, you just give one or the other more power to make a turn."

"How do you go up and down?"

"By venting the sea into the aft sphere. Well, not actually into it. The seawater forces its way into a container filled with bags of oil. Oil is lighter than water, so when this happens we can trim the sub heavier or lighter, depending on which way we want to go."

"I'm lost," said Janet. "All I want to know is what I'm going to see down there."

O'Keefe indicated three heavy floodlights mounted below, and to the front, of the pilot sphere. "Without these, you wouldn't see anything. Below two hundred feet, it's pitch dark. But these give us plenty of light, and one of the TV cameras combines the Star-light lens, which can take pictures in absolute darkness, with an infrared tube, so even if our main lights fail, we can still bring back videotapes."

"I don't believe all this," said the girl. "It's right out of science fiction."

"Wait until you get below. The most disconcerting thing is the effect of scale. Or, the lack of it. You see, in the water, you can't tell how far away anything is, or how big it may be. Say I'm trying to find a sunken barge. I'll see something that looks like it, maybe two hundred yards away. But it turns out to be an orange crate only ten feet ahead. Or vice versa. I might think it's the crate, close enough to reach out and touch, except it'll turn out to be the barge."

Beth asked, "How will *Lamprey* know where we are?"

"Basic search procedures call for me letting out a line with a blaze orange marker attached to it. It follows me around like a kite. I've got 15,000 feet of thin nylon line on a reel aft. They'll keep touch with sonar, and I've got a submarine telephone which can transmit through the water, unless we run into a school of dolphins. Their cries play hell with our phone."

Clicking off some more shots, Beth asked, "Back to that carbon dioxide. How do you get rid of it?"

"We scrub it out of the air every thirty minutes or so, by drawing it through a canister of lithium hydroxide. A little fan pulls the sub's atmosphere through the canister. When the scrub is completed, the sphere's pressure will have dropped, which lets us add some more oxygen from the cylinders."

Janet said, "Now to the important question. Where do you go to the bathroom?"

O'Keefe chuckled. "On *Lamprey* before you board the sub."

Captain Arthur Lovejoy conferred with Paul Forsythe about the submersible's mission. He had been avoiding O'Keefe; he did not know how he would react when he saw the sub commander. The cold lump of anger still gnawed at his guts.

"I don't like the idea of Janet going along," he said.

Forsythe said, "Beth's going too. There's no danger, Art."

Lovejoy started to say, "That's not the point," but he chewed his lip instead.

"If that road's really there," said Anthony Dix, "it's worth the whole voyage."

"I saw tapes," said Forsythe. "They weren't conclusive, but they proved that something's down there."

"What time do we reach the point of departure?" asked Dix.

"Four P.M.," said Lovejoy. "It's a hell of a note. We started out to find new energy reserves, and now we're chasing flying saucers."

"Blame that on President Foster," said Dix. "He tried to cut your balls off, didn't he? He's a disgrace to the office."

"Hold it down," said Forsythe. "All the facts aren't in yet. He's reacting to what happened to the crew of Apollo 19. There's no way we could have been involved, but give him fair due, maybe he's not convinced of that."

Dix, changing the subject, said, "There's room for one more on board that sub, right?"

"So?"

"I want to go along."

Forsythe hesitated. "Why?"

"Videotapes and pictures are fine, but there's nothing like eyeballing it yourself. I'm not throwing my weight around, Paul, but this is what Posty's paying for. I'd like the chance to see it first-hand."

Forsythe looked at Lovejoy. "Art?"

"It's all right with me," said the Captain, realizing with a pang of self-loathing that he would secretly be glad to have another man aboard the sub with his daughter and O'Keefe.

Dix looked at his watch. "I'd better get into some coveralls," he said.

Little Judy was foundering, but the flotation kept her from going down.

It had been daylight for some hours now. They had stopped bailing. Apparently the boat had been holed somewhere below the waterline, because no matter how much water was thrown over the side, it never diminished the level within the cabin and bilges.

Ellard Wiggins had stopped calling his son's name. The boy had not been seen since he went over the side. Wiggins had spent more than an hour on the flying bridge, searching the ocean with his field glasses. The sea was not rough, and if the boy was anywhere within a mile, he should have seen him.

Pat Crosby had managed to save his battered camera and most of his film. Now he and Wiggins were busily engaged in trying to rig up a lead from the camera battery belt to power one of the maritime radios. The job was harder than it seemed. The radios drew twelve volts, and the camera belt delivered six. But through some mysterious paralleling of the nicad D cells, Pat thought he could produce what the radio needed.

Gloria Mitchel was willing to let him try, but only after he had shot a four-minute sequence in which, her hair stringy with seawater, she did a by-line on what had happened. This was done out of sight and without the knowledge of Ellard Wiggins, or he might have thrown her overboard.

Meanwhile, Walter Wylie was calmly diving beneath the water in the salon, retrieving as many canned supplies as he could. It was anybody's guess how long they would be adrift. He had already cut the inflatable raft free, and was ready to blow the CO_2 capsules if *Little Judy* decided to head for the bottom.

"When we get it fired up," warned Pat Crosby, "you won't have much time. These D cells don't have the punch your wet batteries do. Five, maybe eight minutes, and we'll drain them."

"Just get it working," said Wiggins. "I'll raise somebody."

Gloria said, thoughtlessly, "Do you know our position?"

He glared at her. "Sure, lady. Adrift and in danger of sinking. Is that accurate enough for you?"

She flushed. "I'm sorry," she said.

Oddly enough, she meant it.

In *Lamprey*'s spacious "galley," William Postiglion and his associates were holding a meeting.

The producer said, "What about it? Are we wasting our time?"

"I say no," Anthony Dix answered. "We've already experienced a number of unusual events."

"But what exactly have we seen so far? The fog bank? Easily explainable. Dust from some volcanic upheaval far away. Or perhaps an inversion of pollution from one of the coastal cities."

"And the mysterious glowing all over the ship?" asked Dix.

The producer shrugged. "Who understands electricity? We all use it, but nobody understands it. To this day, it's unexplained. This was just another of its weird manifestations."

"I suppose my chopper going down was another weird manifestation," said Jack Begley.

"Well? Have you never had engine failure before?"

"Not in the same goddamned place, at the same time, under the same lens cloud that I did more than thirty years ago," the pilot flared.

"But if you hadn't been conditioned by Mr. Dix to regard it as something supernatural, it would have been merely another unfortunate forced landing, wouldn't it?"

"I guess so," he sulked.

"Power and radio failures?" asked Dix.

"It's a known fact that there are dead areas out here, where radio communications are impossible."

The writer jumped in: "But what about batteries and power generators failing at the same time?"

Postiglion spread his hands. "Electricity," he said. "The completely mysterious beast of burden we've tamed, but have never understood. Why does a compass needle point to the north? Why are there thunderstorms? Why do magnets attract metal? Oh, we have piles of theory. But, my friends, nobody really *knows*. And in my humble opinion, electricity is behind everything we've found so incomprehensible out here."

"I gather," said Dix, "that you want to go home."

"Wrong," said Posty. "That means I want to see more, learn more. It'll make a hell of a movie."

Fifty miles away, aboard *Tiger Shark,* another meeting was going on, between Dan "Moose" Gregory and his partner, David Lester. The girl, Lucia, was forward, cooking.

"I think we ought to dive down for a survey, and that's all," said Lester. "Moose, we aren't set up to pull this off. We're stretched out to the thin raw edge. Absolutely anything wrong will be enough to ruin the salvage, and probably kill us both in the bargain."

Moose scowled. "I never thought I'd see you run scared, Dave. Where's all that *macho* you used to have?"

"Down where it belongs," said the writer. "Mixed up with some common sense, which you seem to have lost.

Don't get greedy, Dan. We can afford to pay out another couple of shares, to do it right and do it safe."

"Sure," said the treasure hunter. "That's easy enough for you. With your million-dollar book contracts."

Lester said, "Those contracts are mostly press agent flack. I get paid what I'm worth, and that happens to be a hell of a lot less than a million bucks. I'm not swimming in gelt, my friend. I have my taxes, and my living expenses, and my risk investment, which happens, at this moment, to be tied up in this venture."

"I knew you'd bring that up," said Moose. "Do you think your crummy money buys a man?"

"I know it buys his fuel and chow and salvage license," said Lester. "So that gives me a vote in this operation, and I vote that we play it a little safer. I don't think that's unreasonable."

Lucia came back with three plates of fried eggs and sausages. "Lunch," she said.

"I'm not hungry," said Moose Gregory.

She put the plate before him. "Eat," she said. "Why are you both fighting?"

Moose, picking at a sausage with his fork, said, "Dave thinks we ought to bring in some more help. Experienced salvage men."

Lucia beamed at him. "Good," she said.

He looked up at her.

"Why did you say that?"

"Because Dave is right, and he has kept me from having to tell you the same thing. David, I owe you one kiss."

"After lunch," he said, smiling. "Anything sweet spoils my appetite."

Aboard *Little Judy,* Pat Crosby said, "I think I've got it. Twelve volts, Skipper."

"Give me the hot lead," said Wiggins. "Clamp the ground to the radio chassis."

"Ground is clamped already," said Pat. He handed a red alligator clip to Wiggins, who attached it to a bare wire coming out of the marine radio.

"Here goes," he said. He switched the unit on.

A red light glowed above the S-meter.

"Mayday," said Ellard Wiggins. "Mayday. This is *Little Judy,* out of Jacksonville, Florida. We are swamped, and have lost one crewman." His voice broke, then strengthened. "We need immediate assistance. Three passengers and myself still on board. Over."

He waited. Static ripped at the speaker. Not wanting to leave this emergency frequency, he flicked in the delta tune, and heard, "Repeat, *Little Judy.* This is trawler *Knipovich.* In your area. Do you have exact location? Over."

As nearly as he knew, Wiggins gave his position. He waited for the other vessel to acknowledge.

"*Knipovich,*" said Gloria. "That's the Russian trawler that's been shadowing *Lamprey.*"

"Be glad they were," said Walter Wylie.

The Russian radio operator came back. "We are some forty miles northeast of you. We are on the way."

"Many thanks," said Wiggins.

"Do you want us to notify your Coast Guard?"

"Yes," said Wiggins. He paused. "You always have to notify them when you lose a man overboard."

"Say again?" asked the Russian.

"Never mind," Wiggins replied. "I think we can stay afloat until you get here."

"Good luck," said the Russina. "*Knipovich,* signing off."

Wiggins yanked the red alligator clip to save power. Into the dead microphone, he whispered, "*Little Judy,* signing off."

CHAPTER 20

Yellowtail separated from *Lamprey* at three minutes after 4 P.M. There was no ceremony; indeed from on deck no one would have known of the sub's departure. The submersible had been cradled in a nest within the survey vessel's bottom, and the launch was merely a slow settling away from *Lamprey*'s belly.

To Beth Forsythe, who had never been in a submersible, the silent running of the craft was weird. It was as if the sub was hanging dead in the water, and *Lamprey* was moving away from it. It was unlike her voyages aboard nuclear submarines.

But while her mind struggled with the new sensations of being a creature underwater, ones she had never felt while aboard the larger submarines, her eye and her fingers kept winding high-speed color film through her two 35mm cameras.

Anthony Dix, peering out through one of the ports, was not so preoccupied. He said, "Jesus, this is scary."

Janet Lovejoy said nothing. Seated beside Kenneth O'Keefe, she squeezed his arm.

O'Keefe said, "We're at fifty feet. On course." He indicated a small dial in the center of the pilot's console. A needle was centered, and digital numerals flashed beneath it. "I've punched in our target's co-ordinates and now the autopilot will guide us there hands off."

"What about the effects of currents and drift?" asked Dix.

"Compensated for. It's this gadget that makes the Polaris missile possible. No sub commander, caught in the first minutes of a one-day war, could ever surface, find his position, crank in the co-ordinates of his targets, and fire in time to do any good. Inertial guidance was invented to do it for him. And now it's slopping over into airline and private use."

Beth said dryly, "Another example of the good things that come from war."

O'Keefe gave her a hard look. "Beth, it was you who married a nuke sub commander, remember?"

"Because I loved him," she agreed. "That doesn't mean I have to love everything he ever did."

"No," he said. "I guess it doesn't. Excuse me. I have to test the phone." He lifted a small handset. "*Yellowtail,* calling *Lamprey.* Come in, please."

Ray Barnstable's voice said, "*Lamprey.* We read you five by five, *Yellowtail.* How's it going?"

"Very smooth," said O'Keefe. "We're right on course. Can you see my marker?"

"Affirmative," said the radioman. "We're pacing you, about two hundred yards back."

"Roger," said O'Keefe. "Give me a check on bottom depth, will you?"

"Hold on," said Barnstable. "Checking." A pause. "Sonar reports nearly eighteen thousand feet, but the upward slope is beginning. You ought to be in operating depth soon."

"Roger on that operating depth," said O'Keefe. "I'll call again in five minutes. *Yellowtail* out."

Dix said, "What would happen if we went all the way to the bottom right now?"

O'Keefe winced. "I don't even like to think about it," he said.

Pytor Bedovy, *Knipovich*'s radar officer, let himself into the radio shack with his secret key. Duty impelled him to do so, yet he felt guilt at betraying his Captain. Ashkenazy had always been very good to him.

But Bedovy was under strict orders to report any deviation from the assigned mission. He had not done so during the search for the Englishman, because during that operation, *Knipovich* had always kept the American survey vessel in view. But this new rescue mission was different. *Knipovich* was leaving her station, responding to a distress call that might well be a deliberate diversion.

He switched on the shortwave CW transmitter, uncaged the Morse code paddle, and after checking to see that he was on the right frequency, sent a rapid string of numbers which identified him to the Naval Office in the Kremlin.

A burst of dots and dashes gave him the simple message: "?"

"K leaving station for distress call," he transmitted. "What are my instructions?"

A long pause.

Then: "Be prepared to assume command, but take no action. Report situation in two hours."

Bedovy transmitted, "Understood."

Silently, he closed down the transmitter and, leaving the radio shack, locked the door behind him.

The first Navy search plane flew over *Little Judy* at ten minutes past four, Eastern standard time. Its pilot was unable to reach the foundering boat, but the Russian radio operator picked up his call.

"We are about four miles away," said *Knipovich*'s radioman. "We will effect the rescue."

"Will they want a tug to bring the boat in?" asked the pilot.

"Just a minute," said the Russian. He spoke with Wiggins on another frequency. Then, back to the Navy plane, he said, "We will handle all of that from this ship. The Captain thinks his boat may well sink before any assistance could arrive. Can you orbit him until we are within view? We can see you, but we do not see the boat."

"Roger," said the Navy pilot. "Orbiting."

"What do you think it was?" Gloria asked.

Wiggins, coming out of his shock, said, "Who knows?

A whale, maybe. Whatever it was, it either took the sea anchor like a bait, or got tangled up in it."

"We were really moving," said Walter Wylie. "Can a whale go that fast?"

"I don't know," said Wiggins.

The producer had rescued one bottle of Bourbon. He poured a stiff shot of it into a plastic cup and gave it to Wiggins. "I'm sorry about your son," he said. "I feel responsible."

"It's none of your doing," said Wiggins. "If it wasn't on your charter, it'd have been on somebody else's. Nothing like this ever happened to me. No way we could have figured on it."

Gloria said, "Maybe we'll still find him."

Wiggins tightened his lips. "No. Johnny never could swim too good. Funny, a lot of sailing men can't." He choked down some of the whiskey. "You know, Johnny never wanted to be a sailor anyway. He was going to cut out on me in a couple of years and take up truck driving." He choked again, but not on the Bourbon. "I wish he'd done it sooner."

Kenneth O'Keefe indicated the sonar display on his console. "The bottom's shoaling now," he said. "Less than nine thousand feet, and uphill all the way."

"How deep are we?" asked Dix.

"Around two hundred feet." O'Keefe checked the inertial guidance readouts. "Right on course. About two thousand yards from target."

"Why didn't you release directly over it and go down?" asked Beth.

"The guidance doesn't work like that. I'm retracing my original course. It's easier this way."

His Sub-to-Mother-Ship phone made a quiet beeping noise. He picked it up. *"Yellowtail."*

"Keefer, this is Forsythe. How much longer to target?"

"Maybe ten minutes. Why?"

"There may be some weather brewing up here. The sky looks funny. Hurry it along, will you?"

"Don't be a worrywart," said Beth, into the telephone. She heard Paul laugh.

He said, "I'm not worrying, but I can't guarantee that I won't get seasick. I'd rather be down there where it's nice and calm than up here where it looks like it's getting ready to blow."

"We'll pedal faster," she said.

O'Keefe retrieved the instrument. "Paul, is it really bad?"

"Negative. I'm just covering the bases. I'd hate to get us in a situation where we couldn't retrieve you."

"Got you. We'll make haste. *Yellowtail* out."

Janet said, carefully, "If the weather's bad enough to worry Paul, it must be pretty lousy."

O'Keefe said, "But it was fine just a few moments ago. Not even a squall line could move in that fast."

"Forsythe doesn't get himself flapped," said Dix. "Something's happening up there. Like you said, let's make haste."

Actually, Ellard Wiggins had noticed it first. The long, slender, snakelike gray lens cloud was forming from horizon to horizon. He was always sensitive to weather changes, particularly now that his beloved *Little Judy* was foundering in the rolling swells. He said nothing to alarm his passengers; they had been through enough already.

As for Johnny, he blotted the boy out of his mind. There would be time enough to face that when he had gotten his charges safely aboard the rescue ship, which was now only a couple of miles away. He did not even try to imagine what he was going to tell his wife. She had never completely agreed with the boy going to sea anyway; she had always supported him in his drive to become a trucker. Now he would have to face her with this ultimate, final conclusion to all the dreams and hopes they had both held for their son.

His attempt to shelter his passengers failed, because Walter Wylie had a sailor's eye and the odd behavior of the sky had attracted his attention too. He had already spotted the Russian vessel heading for them, and knew that the Chris-Craft would remain afloat long enough for their rescue. But that odd cloud in the sky, and the complete calmness of the air, these troubled him. Like Wiggins, he remained silent, but even non-sailors can sense when another person is worried, and Gloria broke the silence.

"Come on, damn it," she said. "What's bothering you two? Are we sinking?"

"No," said Wiggins. "There's the Russian ship. Another fifteen minutes, and we'll be aboard."

"Then what?" she persisted. The cloud had caught her attention. "I see, you bastards. We're in for a tornado, right?"

Wylie chuckled. "No, Glor, not out here in the ocean. It's just that the skipper and I, we've both got a feeling that the weather is going to change, and not for the better."

"So bad that our big Russian boat would be in trouble too?"

"No," he said. "She looks pretty seaworthy."

"Then screw the weather," said Gloria. "We've got other problems. Like how the hell are we going to get our film back to the station? And was any of it ruined by that unexpected bath?"

Pat Crosby said, "Frankly, sweetheart, I think the world can survive without your precious film."

In Wales, Lady Diana Lean reached for the telephone. Her thin hand was trembling.

"Please, overseas operator," she said. Waiting for a few moments, she leaned back and closed her eyes. "Oh, please," she said. "Not *now*." A voice somewhere in the mysterious depths of the Postal Service answered her, and she said, "Dear me, no, I was only talking with myself. Overseas? I want to connect through the American Ship-to-Shore telephone system to the U.S.S *Lamprey,* off the coast of Florida. Person to person for Sir Roger Lean." A pause. "Yes, of course I'll wait. But please hurry."

She heard tiny tones that sounded like modern music. Her call, she realized, was probably being routed around the world, bounced from one communications satellite to another, all efficient and mechanical. Please, God, she thought, let it function perfectly tonight.

CHAPTER 21

"Paul," said Saito Osha, "I think you should recall *Yellowtail,* and we should make for harbor."

"Weather bothering you?"

"Not merely that. This is an ill-fated voyage. Let us not risk anything worse than losing some money." The Japanese shipbuilder paused. "I am concerned for Raiko. She is very frightened."

"You built this ship, Saito. She'll hold up in any kind of storm."

"Normally I would agree. But this is not a happy ship. Our guests from Hollywood are worried. Your own Captain is under some private strain. It is too much, Paul. In such a condition, errors magnify. A small mistake becomes larger, and breeds another, worse, mistake. You know that. There will be another day. We have gone as far on this path as we should."

Paul Forsythe thought for a moment. He had been increasingly disturbed with this voyage, beset as it was by unusual occurrences. Now his partner was expressing even greater concern. Perhaps it was time to accept temporary defeat.

"Okay," he said to Osha. "I'll call them back, and we'll head in."

"Thank you, Paul," said the Japanese man. "I know how difficult this choice was for you."

Forsythe picked up the intercom handset and said, "Ray, patch me through to *Yellowtail* again."

"Right," said Barnstable.

There was a long pause. Then the radioman's voice

said, "Paul, something's wrong. I can't get through to them."

"Interference?"

"No, they've gone completely dead. There's no carrier wave at all. It's as if they've lost all power."

"That's impossible," said Forsythe. But then, remembering what had happened to *Lamprey* the day of the Apollo 19 splashdown, he said, "Does sonar have them on the screen?"

"Yes. Just a minute."

"Make it quick," Forsythe said.

Barnstable replied, "They're off course, and around fifty feet deeper than the mission plan."

"Try to raise them again."

Barnstable said, "We've been doing that all along. Negative contact."

"Keep trying," said Forsythe. "I'll stand by. He put down the handset.

"I am sorry," said Osha. "I think now that I waited too long."

Gloria crawled up the rope ladder first, feeling it sway against the side of the Russian ship. She was barefooted, and her slacks, which had been rescued, soggily, by Walter Wylie, slipped down on her hips, leaving a fleshy gap between them and the tank top she wore.

"Let's move," said Ellard Wiggins. He had been taping some red cylinders together while they were approached cautiously by the Russian vessel. Now he jammed them into his hip pocket. "I don't like the looks of that sky."

Wylie went up the ladder next, followed by Pat Crosby. The skipper of *Little Judy* came last.

He paused at the railing, looking down at the half-sunken boat. "I'm sorry, baby," he said softly.

Then, before anyone knew what he was about to do, he took the lump of red cylinders from his pocket, lit a fuse with his cigarette lighter, and tossed the bundle down into the flying bridge of the Chris-Craft.

A few seconds later, a bright flame burst out, and

began to consume what remained above water of the hull.

To a surprised Captain Dimitri Ashkenazy, he said, "You'd better get some water between us. There's a spare gas drum on my deck, and it'll probably go up."

Ashkenazy shouted orders, and *Knipovich* pulled away from *Little Judy,* which was now completely ablaze.

Wylie said, bewildered, "Are you crazy?"

"Not a bit," said Wiggins. "I tossed those flares down there because my boat's a floating hazard."

Ashkenazy said, "But, sir, we could have taken her in tow until the tugs arrived."

Wiggins said, "I don't want her salvaged. I hate the sight of that piece of crap." He turned away.

Ashkenazy looked to Wylie, who said quietly, "His son was lost overboard."

Ashkenazy nodded. "I see," he said.

The Chris-Craft's gas drum exploded then, and for a moment the boat was a ball of bright orange flame. When the black smoke lifted, there was nothing left.

"Something's wrong," Ken O'Keefe said quietly. He indicated the console. A red light blinked there. "We've lost guidance."

"I think the lights flickered a minute or so back," said Anthony Dix.

"We may have lost power," said O'Keefe. "That'd glitch the guidance system but good."

In fact, that is what had happened. The bare cable in the television camera port had touched ground against the sub's hull, and in the subsequent surge, a secondary circuit breaker had thrown. A slight movement of the sub had broken the cable's contact, and the circuit breaker had made a power connection again, but the brief loss of electricity had disabled the inertial guidance mechanism. It would be useless until reset and reprogrammed. It was as if the two thousand-plus transistors and integrated circuits had undergone a nervous breakdown.

"Now what?" asked Dix.

"We eyeball it," said O'Keefe, flicking on the outside lights. They stabbed bright beams through the darkness of the ocean. "We're close enough to the target, so I may be able to find it anyway."

Yellowtail glided through the Sargasso without apparent motion. Curious fish, attracted by the bright lights, came right up to the view ports and stared with bulging eyes at the strange creatures within this odd intruder to their world.

Clicking off some shots, Beth Forsythe said, "Don't forget what Paul said about the weather up there, Ken."

"I'm not. Ten minutes on the search pattern, and we surface. We wouldn't feel the effects of a storm this deep, but it might be pretty hard to link up with *Lamprey* topside."

Janet Lovejoy said, "I never realized it was so quiet down here. It's as if we were suspended in time, with nothing moving, nothing happening."

"Plenty is happening," said O'Keefe. "The bottom's now only around a thousand feet below us, and it's rising fast. With any luck, we're still more or less on course."

"What about when we find it?" asked Janet. "Or, *if* we find it."

"It's there," said O'Keefe. "This time we'll try to take some samples. I've got tools hooked up on the waldoes that'll let us cut off a little chunk. We can find out what it's made of and, by carbon dating, how old."

"Waldoes?" asked Beth.

"Those gadgets outside the sub that I control from in here. The name comes from atomic research, when they used to handle radioactive material with artificial 'hands.' Some science fiction writer used the name 'waldo' in *Astounding Science Fiction,* and it stuck."

From a small speaker on the console, a strident "BEEP!" sounded.

"Bottom's coming up fast," said O'Keefe. "We're only two hundred feet above it now."

Yellowtail slid through the quiet water, leaving, as

the only reminder of its passing, a wake of gentle eddies behind the sleek hull.

Now the endless scope of the water gave way to a darker mass, like a distant range of mountains.

"Bottom," said O'Keefe. "Keep your eyes open. We could be off course a hundred yards either way."

Beth took a sequence of photographs. With the camera still at her eye, through its reflex viewer, she saw an object looming ahead of them. She started to say something, but then Dix cried, "Jesus Christ, look at that!"

"What is it?" asked Janet.

"I don't know," O'Keefe began, but Dix's excitement could not be controlled.

He said, loudly, "It's a flying saucer!"

CHAPTER 22

Forsythe asked, "Where does sonar show them now?"

Ray Barnstable said, "Right on the bottom."

"Moving?"

"Slowly."

"Is there any other way we can signal them?"

Barnstable said, "Pressure waves, set off by light changes detonated in the water."

"Can we communicate a message that way?"

"Barely. One blast calls attention to us. Then after a ten-second interval, we can signal 'Recall' by setting off four blasts in a string."

"Let's get set up for it," said Forsythe. "Hold it until I give the word, but let's be ready." He turned to Lovejoy. "Is that all right with you?"

Distracted, the Captain said, "Sure, why not?"

"Are you all right?"

"I'm fine. It's this weather that's got my attention. I never saw a sky like this."

He was right. It had a greenish cast, with flickers of yellow, and few sailors had ever viewed such a display.

Ray Barnstable, listening to his handset, turned and said, "Sir, there's a Ship-to-Shore for Sir Roger. Is it all right if he takes the call?"

Lovejoy said, "Of course it is. Tell him to go ahead."

"Roger from the Captain," Barnstable said into his handset.

Forsythe said, "Have there been any weather reports to account for this?"

"None," said Lovejoy. "Rather than falling, the barometer is actually holding steady. This morning's satellite photos don't show any circular patterns."

"Well," Forsythe said, "something's happening."

"Paul," Lovejoy said suddenly, lowering his voice so Barnstable could not hear, "Janet's screwing O'Keefe."

"What?" said Forsythe, not accepting what he had just heard.

"I said Janet and O'Keefe are sleeping together. What the hell am I going to do?"

Forsythe hesitated. Then he said, "Janet's twenty-two, isn't she?"

"So?"

"I'm sorry, Art. She's of age. It's her life. I don't know that there's anything you could do. Or should."

"He's a diving bum."

"When you and I were that age, we were sort of bums too, Art."

"Yes, but O'Keefe's not twenty-two. He's a hell of a lot older than she is."

"He's a pretty good man."

"Not in my book."

"Art, this is a hell of a time to go into something like this. Can't it wait until we've gotten ourselves safely back into harbor?"

Lovejoy stared down at the deck. "Yeah," he said. "I guess so. I'm sorry, Paul. It's just that I—"

"I know. Don't worry about it. Let's just put *Yellowtail* back in the slot and get the hell out of here."

He turned to Barnstable, ready to order the explosion of the recall signals, but was interrupted by the sudden arrival of Sir Roger Lean.

"Captain," said the old sailor. "We've got to leave this area at once."

"What?" asked Lovejoy, bewildered.

"I've just heard from Diana. She was most upset." Lean mopped his sweating forehead. "She told me she had never had such a vivid impression of danger."

"What the hell are you talking about?" Lovejoy said impatiently.

Forsythe waved him into silence. "Go on," he said.

"We are in extreme danger," said Sir Roger. "Paul, I spoke of this before. You do believe me, don't you? Diana's not balmy, and neither am I."

"Nobody said you were," said Forsythe. "We've already decided that we don't like the looks of things, and we're heading for port."

"When?"

"As soon as we retrieve the submersible."

"We don't have much time," warned the old sailor. "Diana was very insistent about that."

Forsythe consulted his watch. "Ray, get the signal charges set. We'll use them in five minutes."

"Just a minute," said the radioman. "I'm getting a signal from that Russian trawler." He listened, said, "Yes, I understand." To Forsythe, he said, "That chartered boat with the TV people sank. The Russians rescued them. All but one. A crewman was lost. They want to put them aboard us."

"Jesus," said Lovejoy. "This voyage is jinxed."

"What do I tell them?" asked Barnstable.

"Tell them yes, what the hell else can we say?" said Forsythe.

Sir Roger said, "Warn them to steam toward port. We don't have time for such a transfer."

Forsythe said, "Sir Roger, that is a Russian vessel. We can't make them do anything."

"But you can surely warn them of their danger."

"Her Captain can see the same sky we do," said Forsythe. "I don't mean to make light of the—relationship you have with your wife—but in all fairness, I can't use that kind of evidence to give suggestions to the Captain of a foreign vessel."

"You're being a fool," said the old sailor. "You're killing people, Mr. Forsythe."

"I hope not," said Paul. "Ray, give *Knipovich* our current position. Tell them that if we are finished with our work, we'll steam toward them. Otherwise, we'll be here."

"Yes, sir."

"Fools," repeated Sir Roger Lean as he left the bridge.

"He could be right," said Paul, to nobody in particular.

"It's Russian," said Beth Forsythe. "Look, there's the hammer and sickle."

"Let's get closer," said Dix.

"Not too close," said O'Keefe. "The currents here are fierce."

"What *is* it?" asked Janet Lovejoy.

"Before, I said it was a flying saucer," said Dix. "But now I recognize it, from some pictures I saw."

"And?" asked Beth.

"It's the Soviet space platform. The one that was supposed to have exploded last week."

The lens cloud seemed closer to the sea now.

Walter Wylie said, "Listen, kids, I think we're still in trouble. I didn't want to say anything before, but look at that goddamned cloud."

Wiggins said, "I never saw anything like it in twenty years out here."

Gloria Mitchel said, "Are there any life jackets on this tub?"

"You're wearing mine," said Wiggins without humor. She looked down at its plump shape and managed a weak laugh.

Jack Begley, standing near Postiglion, said, "That's a wave cloud. There's some kind of fantastic wind shear up there. The lens cloud is on the downwind side."

"Is it dangerous?"

"I never heard of it doing any damage on the ground. But those boys that fly gliders have gotten themselves caught in its lee, where the roll cloud is, and a few of them have found themselves sitting on bare air, with their wings torn off."

The producer said, "Do you think that might be the reason for some of the disappearances out here?"

Begley looked at him. "Mister, you're the guy who's making a movie about the Bermuda Triangle. Why don't you tell me?"

Raiko Nakamura, staring out the porthole of their cabin, said to Saito Osha, "My dearest one, what if we die?"

He said, "Foolishness, Raiko. This is my ship. It will endure any storm."

"Will it endure the evil demons of this bad place?"

"I do not believe in demons," he said. "I believe in my own measurements of stress and strength, I believe in what can be seen and evaluated by science."

Quietly, she said, "Can science measure love?"

"Of course not."

"Neither can it measure evil," she said. "And we are in a place of evil. Saito, I am frightened."

He held her. "I am here with you," he said.

"Give me your love," she asked.

"Gladly," he said, drawing her down to him.

Yellowtail was now as close to the metal object as O'Keefe dared.

Consulting his inertial guidance readout, he said, "It impacted right on top of my underwater highway."

Clicking off photographs as fast as she could operate the film advance, Beth said, "Is that what's squishing out from under? It looks like a layer of mud."

"Yeah," he said. "I guess that's what it was. But on the tapes, it sure as hell looked like concrete."

"Oh, my God," said Janet. "Look! There's a *body!*"

"Turn the sub a little, Ken," said Beth. "I need more light to get it."

"There's another one," said Dix.

Sickened, Beth said, "Ken, those are—"

"I know," he said. "Keep shooting pictures. This is too important to rely on the videotapes."

"I don't know about the rest of you," said Janet, "but I'm scared."

"Welcome to the club, baby," said O'Keefe. "Beth, do you have all you need?"

"I think so. But can't we recover—"

"No way. We've got to leave them here."

Distantly, a dull explosion trembled the water.

"What was that?" asked Dix.

"Hold on," said O'Keefe. Mentally, he counted the seconds. After ten had passed, he heard four more explosions, one right after the other. "Shit," he said. He tried the underwater telephone. It was dead. "We've been out of communication," he said. "We must have lost it when the power failed."

"What were those explosions?" Beth asked.

"Recall signal from *Lamprey*. They want us up there fast."

"Let me shoot a few more—"

"No," he said. "Time's run out. Here we go."

He turned the sub sharply and set out on a reverse course. In the television port, the bare cable contacted the hull again and made a bright arc as high voltage shot across the tiny gap between it and the metal. But this time, because the circuit breaker had been reset automatically, instead of blowing the safety system the short circuit began to drain the sub's battery power.

"Why aren't we going up?" asked Dix.

"Because if it's rough up there, we'll make better time down here. I've got the sonar reversed. We'll pick up *Lamprey*'s hull pretty soon, and then we'll surface."

"I don't believe what we just saw," said Beth Forsythe. "This is going to shake up the world."

"We've got to get it home first," O'Keefe said grimly.

"Ken," said Janet Lovejoy, "I think I'm going to be sick."

"Better not," he said. "Swallow hard."

"It doesn't help."

"Damn it, you crummy kid," he almost yelled, "you get sick and you may kill us all! Hold it in!"

Grimly, tears falling down her cheeks, she did as he said. After a while the spasm passed and her nausea was gone. But the coldness in her stomach from his harsh words remained.

"Paul, they're off course," said Ray Barnstable. "They're headed almost at right angles. They're already over the deep water, and it's getting deeper."

"Goddamned radios," raged Forsythe. "They're fine except when you need them!"

"Shall I set off some more charges?"

"It'd only confuse them more. Shit. Any word from the Russians?"

"They're on their way."

"Have you been able to raise the mainland?"

"Negative. All our radios are out."

Forsythe turned to the Captain, standing beside him, numbly. "Snap the hell out of it, Art. You'd better get everything loose lashed down. I think we're in for a blow."

"Sure," said Lovejoy. "Anything you say."

He meandered from the bridge. Forsythe looked after him and, seeing that Barnstable was near, stifled a curse. Instead, he said, "Ray, isn't there any alternative means of communication?"

"With the sub? Sorry, but no. The explosions were it. And they don't seem to be reacting to them properly."

"How about the mainland?"

"No contact at all."

"Okay, Ray. Do what you can. But how is it that we can still reach the Russians?"

"If I knew that," said the radioman, "I'd be writing Mr. Dix's book for him."

Joseph Horatio, peering up at the odd cloud, and sniffing the wind, took a swig of the clear overproof rum and coughed. He wiped his mouth.

"Lord," he said out loud, "I don't know why I had to come to this place, but if that's Your will, here I am. I hope You don't mind that I take a little drink. I may be an old man, but I ain't dead yet, and the flesh is weak."

He sipped again. The 180-proof rum was fierce in his throat.

The liquor seemed to free his mind and his tongue. He spoke again—perhaps to an unseen God, perhaps only to the waves, which were rising higher against the bow of his old sailboat.

"I think, Sir, I'm damned tired of living, if that doesn't displease You. I have seen all I want of men and women, and of the world. All of my friends are dead and gone, and wherever they are, I think it might be nice to join them, if You will permit. Do You hear me? Are You really there? I have always wondered, and I suppose one day soon I will find out. Until then, though, I will preserve my doubts and my rum." He sipped again. "Tell me, Lord, why did You kill Cap'n Slocum? Why did You let them shoot Mr. Lincoln? Why did You smite San Francisco with Your earthquake? Why did You sink Port Royal beneath the waters of Kingston Bay? I have never understood this. You were taught to me as a God of love, as a kindly observer of our deeds, bad and good. Yet You visit us with plague, with fire and pestilence, with pain and disgusting death. We try to behave as noble beings, but You repay the evil among us with riches and comfort, and torment the good with cancers and the pox. If You will forgive me, Sir, I do not think You have been able to create a good world, if that is what You had in mind. So if it is Your pleasure, I hope that You will soon relieve me of its burdens. I know that I am older than the ordinary person, and I have long awaited some word from You that there was a reason behind this, but You have not spoken. I have listened to the preacher-men, but they only babble of 'Thy will be done,' and give no sound reason for anything. I do not like this world any more, and if I have not spoken with You often before this, it is only because until now I have trusted Your decisions. I do not any more. Smite me, Lord. Because I no longer believe in You."

Horatio lowered his head and waited for the bolt of lightning to destroy him.

It did not come.

Instead, the wind began to rise.

The pilot of a Navy jet saw it first, approaching from the west. He hit the microphone button of his radio and began yelling, "Mayday, Mayday, this is Navy Nine-three-five. Come in, Jacksonville!" But he received no answer, and he was still screaming into his useless radio when something picked his plane up and hurled it almost straight down into the Sargasso Sea, where it broke into many tiny pieces that sank slowly, cradled by the still calm warm waters.

CHAPTER 23

"Half an hour, maximum," said David Lester as he fitted on his breathing mask. "I don't like the looks of that sky."

"Friend," said Moose Gregory, "you've turned into a real candyass."

"Half an hour," repeated the novelist, slipping down the boarding ladder into the welcoming sea.

Moose cursed, then told Lucia, "Honey, keep your baby blues on that compressor. We're not carrying reserve tanks."

"You can trust me," said the Italian girl. She patted the 300-cubic-feet-per-minute Ingersoll-Rand. The bracelet she always wore, with its tiny gold figure of an elephant, jangled on her wrist. Moose winced, but said nothing. He had given up screaming at her for wearing jewelry around moving machinery.

Lucia asked, "What shall I do if the weather gets worse before you come up?"

"Hit a paddle on the water hard three times. We ought to be able to hear it."

He fitted the full-face mask of the Desco carefully. He had never gotten used to it. A mouthpiece, an air tank, and a regulator were the underwater tools he had grown up with. This latest system, driving air down hoses to a free-swimming diver, was foreign to him. But he had to admit it was better for long periods below. There was no irritation by a mouthpiece, no risk of running out of air unless the compressor stopped, no decompression times to remember on your way up. The full mask gave a larger field of view, too. You could talk inside it, or hum, or even sing.

So why did he hate the Desco so much?

Pytor Bedovy let himself into the radio shack and uncaged the Morse code paddle. He switched on the transmitter, broadcast his code identification.

To the standard response "?," he answered, "We are again on station with the American survey vessel. Survivors on board. We plan to transfer them to the American ship. Instructions?"

They came back in a burst of code signals. "Keep close watch, but do not take action unless instructed from Moscow."

Bedovy transmitted, "Understood," and began to close down the radio transmitter.

He felt a cold draft on his neck.

When he turned, Captain Dimitri Ashkenazy was standing in the door, looking at him. His face was pale.

"It is too bad, Pytor," said Ashkenazy. "I also understand Morse code."

The power leakage within *Yellowtail*'s bowels was insidious, invisible. The voltage regulators strained, kept the declining direct current up to the required 220 volts, but with each passing minute, their capacity was reduced, and their overload increased.

The end came suddenly.

O'Keefe was saying, "If we don't pick up *Lamprey* in the next two minutes, I'm going to surface."

Dix began to reply: "Is that wise, if the waves—"

Then the lights went out.

With a whine, the air circulation system wound down and stopped.

"Don't move, anybody," warned O'Keefe. He groped for the emergency light. It was attached to his seat back, and when he found it, and switched on its cold neon bulb, the interior of the sub became a scene from a horror film. Faces were green, shadows were cast from below, and gloomy darkness filled all corners.

Unnecessarily, he said, "We've lost power. I'm going to try to surface."

He hit the emergency switch, which should have pumped seawater out of the oil-filled aft sphere. There was no sound of servos, no reaction of movement. The submersible seemed to float, dead still, in eternity.

"Shit," he yelled. "We're going down!"

Janet screamed. Beth reached for the girl, pulled her close.

"Quiet," she whispered. "Please be quiet. Let him work."

Dix said, "It's nearly seven thousand feet here. I saw the depth meter before the lights went out."

"Something must have shorted our main bus-bars," said O'Keefe.

"Don't you have backup power?"

"We should, but it's not responding."

"There must be *some* way to get this sub topside," said Dix.

Slowly, reluctantly, O'Keefe said, "No. I'm sorry, but there isn't." He looked down into the cold rays of the emergency light. "We're going all the way."

"Will the hull hold?" asked Beth Forsythe.

He did not look at her. "What does it matter? Without power, we'll never get up again."

"Maybe somebody'll come down."

"Seven thousand feet? No way."

"Fine," she said. "Give up, you spineless bastard! Let us all die because you don't have some *Sea Hunt* writer plotting the scene for you!"

Janet said, "Leave him alone!"

"Like hell I will. Come on, O'Keefe, put your head to work. You must have considered just such an emergency. Where's your contingency plan?"

"There's no way out," he said. Then, almost as an afterthought, he added, "Not for all of us."

"What does that mean?" Beth demanded.

"If we hurry, we can send one of us up. That's all. Just one."

The four looked at each other, and into their own

private souls, and fear was a blanket that enveloped them all.

The Navy jet had been halfway to Florida when it went down. *Tiger Shark* was closer to the crashed plane than to *Lamprey*. So it was Lucia de la Renata who next saw what was approaching. At first she stared, un-believing, then she begin to strike at the water with a paddle, screaming, "Dan! Come up! Come up now! Dan!"

Below, off the wreck, which was a dark hulk wrapped in torn fishing nets, the two divers heard her blows dimly. Moose Gregory pointed upward, Dave Lester nodded, and the two men prepared to surface. But they never did. Suddenly the masks and air hoses were ripped from their faces, throwing them violently against the wreck. The first impact broke Gregory's neck, and he died, belching air into the unforgiving sea.

Without his mask, David Lester started hopelessly for the surface. But it was more than two hundred feet, and he knew that he had almost no chance of making it.

Captain Arthur Lovejoy pointed at the flame orange float and said, "We're sitting almost on top of them. If we put a hook on that nylon line—"

"It'd snap," said Forsythe. "Ray, what's happening now?"

"They're sinking at the rate of twenty feet a second," said Barnstable. "It looks like they're headed for the bottom."

"How deep?"

Barnstable spoke into his handset. "A little over seven thousand," he reported.

"Their hull ought to hold, then," said Forsythe.

"But what about their air?" asked Lovejoy. "They've got four people aboard, remember."

"Six, maybe seven hours," said Forsythe. "Less if their scrubbers have been damaged."

"Radio for help," said Lovejoy. "We can get a Navy

CURV out here to hook onto *Yellowtail* and retrieve her."

"CURV?" asked Posty, who had joined them on the bridge.

"Controlled Underwater Recovery Vchicle," said Forsythe. "It's unmanned, so it can dive to great depths, with its functions handled by waldoes and TV viewing from topside. But the nearest one is in San Diego, Art, and even if we had radio communication—which we don't—we're out of time."

Lovejoy gripped Forsythe's wrist so hard that it shot pain through him. "Paul," he said harshly, *"do* something!"

"I can't," said Forsythe slowly. "Art, I know you're worried about your girl. But my wife's down there too. And there's absolutely nothing I can do."

Ray Barnstable said, "The Russian trawler's moving up on us, sir. She's blinking a signal. Their radios must be out too. They want to know if they can transfer survivors."

Forsythe waited for Lovejoy's answer. When it came, it was in a harsh voice.

"Tell them yes. We might as well save *somebody*."

Beth Forsythe said, "I'm as scared as anybody. But we've got to get my films up there."

"I agree," said Ken O'Keefe. "Who goes?"

She answered, "You. You've got the best chance of making it."

"No," he said. "Maybe I can do something with this sub. I'm the only one here who knows how to run it."

"If you think I'm leaving you, you're crazy," said Janet. "I mean it."

Beth stared at Anthony Dix. "That leaves it between you and me," she said.

"Ladies first," he said, trying to smile.

She hesitated. "No. I'm no good in the water. Maybe Keefer will figure out something for the rest of us. But you're strong and you've got a better chance of getting these cassettes up there than I have. I'm afraid you're elected, Mr. Dix."

She had placed the three 35mm high-speed Ekta-chrome cassettes in a plastic bag, sealed with a wire twist.

"Put on one of the breathing bottles," said O'Keefe. "Then crawl up through that hatch. Seal it behind you. Start breathing with the bottle, and open the other hatch to the sea. Once the chamber fills with water, let your-self out slowly. Don't go up too fast. No faster than your own bubbles."

"Why can't the rest of you do the same?" asked Dix, sweat beading on his forehead.

"Because once the sea's in the outer chamber, we have no power to clear it," said O'Keefe. "Come on, hurry up. We're getting deeper every second."

Dix hesitated. "I feel like a coward, leaving you."

"Just get those films into my husband's hands," Beth said harshly. Her voice broke. "And tell him I love him."

"Can't *you* go?" Dix said, almost weeping.

"Damn it," she said. "Get moving while you still have a chance!"

"Go, Dix!" urged O'Keefe. "We're getting deeper."

He helped Dix undog the upper hatch. "The other one works the same way. Remember, take it slow. Use the marker line to hold yourself down. Don't go up faster than your air bubbles, or you could explode your lungs."

"I—" began Dix.

"Now, damn it!" shouted O'Keefe. And, as the other man crawled into the upper chamber of the sub, he added, "Drink an extra beer tonight for me."

Paul Forsythe spoke on the short-range radio fre-quency to the Captain of *Knipovich*. The radios had started to work again, but contact was one-way. He could hear the mainland, but they could not hear him. "Do you have a submersible?" Forsythe asked.

"Why?" asked Captain Dimitri Ashkenazy.

"Our own is out of control and sinking," said Forsythe. "They must have lost power."

Ashkenazy, smiling a bitter grin at the events of the past hours, said, "My friend, we came here to spy on you, not to rescue you every eight hours."

"I understand that," said Forsythe. "But if you have a sub, I beg you to help us." He paused. "My wife is aboard that sinking vessel."

"Yes," said Ashkenazy, sighing. "I have a small sub. But its depth range is only three thousand of your feet. Below that, it would crush in. And my sonar tells me that the bottom here is seven thousand. I would offer it to you, but what good would it be to kill my own men? Please believe me, I would help if it was possible." He glanced at Pytor Bedovy, who sat, glaring, nearby. "If it was possible," he repeated.

"Thank you, Captain," said Forsythe. "We are sending our launch to pick up the survivors of the charter boat."

"Make haste," said Ashkenazy. "I do not like the look of this Atlantic sky."

Listening to the sound of the water pouring into the upper chamber of *Yellowtail,* O'Keefe said, "He's on his way."

"He'd better make it," said Beth, trying not to let her voice tremble. "Those pictures are more valuable than his worthless hide."

"Wrong," said O'Keefe. "Okay, we've solved a mystery. But I don't think *any*thing's worth more than somebody's life."

"Shut up," said Janet, pressing herself close to him. "Don't talk about lives, or mysteries, or anything. Just be still."

The sub lurched.

"He's gone out," said O'Keefe. "If he remembers what I told him, he'll make the surface."

Beth said, "I still don't understand. Why can't we put on these other air bottles and float up too?"

"Because," said O'Keefe patiently, "the air lock is full of water. If we open it now, it'll flood the sub, and we'll sink."

Janet looked at him. "But we're already sinking," she said. "So what does it matter?"

He stared. "Son of a bitch," he said. "You're right." He grabbed for the breathing devices. "Okay, listen good, because this is one exam that you can't take over again if you flunk."

The noise came first. It was like the sound of a hundred steam locomotives, charging at the ships which lay dead in the water. A full-throated growling that was as much a movement of air as it was a sound.

The sun was still bright. And while the odd lens cloud was now lower, there was no real wind yet.

There was nothing but the approaching sound, and a coolness to the air that reached *Lamprey* first, then struck the port side of the Russian trawler. On both ships, men looked around, wondering what had happened to change the air so suddenly.

It was still too soon for them to see it.

CHAPTER 24

To his dying day, David Lester would never know how he managed to rise more than two hundred feet, without an external air supply, and reach the surface of the Sargasso Sea that late December afternoon.

He followed all the expert teaching he'd paid so dearly for. He expelled air slowly as he ascended, careful to avoid the dreaded embolism of the lung that might result from trapped gasses expanding within his body. He fought down the impulse, caused by a build-up of carbon dioxide within his blood, to suck in the deadly seawater. He held his emotions icily calm, knowing that was his only hope.

And then his head broke water into the air, and he was able to gulp down delicious gasps of its spray-filled fragrance.

Only after he had quenched the near frantic craving for breath did he look around for the converted PT boat.

It was nowhere in sight.

The water had a glazed, greenish scum over it, as if it were a long stagnated pond. He could almost smell the rot and the decay.

Then he saw the object. It was a bit of wood, perhaps a yard in length. It bobbled gently on the glossy surface of the Sargasso.

Lester swam over, saving his strength.

The object was part of *Tiger Shark*'s transom. It had been torn violently into fragments by some unknown force which had left this little remainder of what had been a powerful and seaworthy boat.

And, clinging to it, was a hand, and a wrist, and part of an arm. Around the wrist was a bracelet with a tiny golden elephant. He had seen it every day, worn by Lucia de la Renata. The fingernails were painted bright red, but the flesh had already started turning to a greenish-blue, and the torn ends where the brilliantly white bones protruded were a grayish pink.

In the water, David Lester turned, and vomited.

In *Lamprey*'s launch, which had been lowered and sent over to the Russian trawler, Gloria Mitchel scowled at Pat Crosby. "You should have gotten some footage of *Little Judy* going down."

Glancing at Ellard Wiggins, who sat, silently, near the helmsman, Crosby said, "Sorry. I just wasn't in the mood."

"We'll see about your moods. Walter, tell him."

Wylie looked into his own soul and, his voice not quite true, answered, "I'm sorry, Glor. Pat's right. The world doesn't turn just so you can move up on Barbara Walters. We're too involved now. We have no right to provide tragedy so Procter and Gamble can sell soap."

Gloria raged, "I promise you, we're going to have some session when we get back to New York!"

"Do what you want, Gloria," said the producer. "Don't you see, your ambition doesn't matter any more? We're responsible for the death of a boy."

"Like hell we are," she said. "He took the same chances we did. And today, they don't kill the bearer of bad news any more. I will survive, Walter, and I'll be bigger than ever, because nothing is more salable than the heroine of a disaster. Ms. Walters may have ABC sewed up, but that leaves three networks for me to bargain with, and my contract is up this March. I'm at the peak of the market, and I'm going to make the most of it. You can take your Walter Cronkites, and your David Brinkleys, and your tippy-toes Barb Walters, and shove them, because I'm coming home with blood on my sleeve and grand larceny in my heart, and if you boobs don't want to play along, that's your big mistake. It's all show biz, and if you don't get it while you're hot, you won't get it at all. Didn't they teach that to you at good old Fuck U?"

"I think she's genuinely crazy," said Pat Crosby.

"Unfortunately," said Wylie, "that isn't a crime. Yet."

"This isn't going to be fun," said Kenneth O'Keefe. The two women in the sub with him had already donned their breathing mouthpieces and air bottles. "When I blow that hatch, the water's going to pour in. The light will go out, and you're going to get bounced around pretty good. Don't try to get out too soon. You'll only get yourselves mashed up against the side of the hatch." He held up a heavy wrench. "Wait until I hit this against the bulkhead two times, and then go. Remember what I told Dix. Don't rise faster than your air bubbles, or you'll get the bends. When you get top-side, inflate those life jackets. Not before. Repeat, don't pull those cords until you're looking at the sky, or you'll be dead. Do you understand?"

"Perfectly," said Beth Forsythe. "Come on, O'Keefe. Let's get on with it. I'm as scared as you. Like you said, we're getting deeper all the time."

O'Keefe placed the mouthpiece of his escape breather in his lips, bit down on its hard rubber, and said, muffled, "Here we go."

The noise was much louder now. Even those below deck had heard it, and come up to *Lamprey*'s topside. Aboard the Russian vessel, discipline was stricter, but some crewmen had either come to the deck, or jammed their heads through the narrow portholes.

In the launch, Wylie said, "It's getting ready to blow." He tightened his life jacket. "I hope we're on board before it hits."

"What a tiny man you are," said Gloria Mitchel. "I've only now realized it."

* * *

On board *Lamprey,* Paul Forsythe looked at the lens cloud that was hovering over them, heard the approaching sound of wind, and said, "Get that goddamned boat over here, Art. We're going to be hit by something."

Through a bullhorn, Lovejoy called, "Bring the launch alongside, on the double. Let's go!"

"This is no ordinary blow!" shouted Forsythe. "Ray, order everybody below! Now!"

Barnstable began broadcasting over the ship's loudspeaker system. "Emergency," he said. "Everybody below. Put on your life jackets, and remain in your cabins or the public rooms. Do not go on deck."

"What the hell is it?" asked Lovejoy. "Paul, I've been at sea all my life, and I never heard anything like that."

Forsythe said, "I never did either."

With the wind freshening, the launch slowed down. Gloria Mitchel turned to the crewman from *Lamprey* and yelled, "Why don't you go faster?"

"The faster we go, ma'am," he said, "the more water we take on board."

"Leave the kid alone," said Wylie. "He's just doing his job."

She replied, "Listen to the great sailing man."

When O'Keefe opened the hatch, the sea poured into *Yellowtail* like a million pounding fists. He and the two women were smashed against the hull, the controls, the seats, with a violence that left them gasping and fighting to keep the breather mouthpieces clenched between their teeth.

O'Keefe locked his legs around the back of his console seat, and waited for the forces of the water to subside. When they had calmed, he leaned forward and hit the bulkhead with the wrench, twice. The sound was muffled through the water, like a dull clanging far away. "Go," thought O'Keefe. "Get the hell out of here!"

Anthony Dix broke water just a foot away from the bright flame orange float which indicated *Yellowtail's* position. He spat out the breather mouthpiece, gasping, and shouted for help.

Bob Hart, on deck, saw him. The launch was already in the water on the other side of *Lamprey*. It would have taken five minutes or so to bring it around to this side of the survey vessel, even if he had direct communications with it, which he did not. So he threw a life ring, attached by a rope to the ship, to the floundering man in the water.

Dix caught hold of it. But he was unable to climb up the side of *Lamprey*, and Hart was not strong enough to lift him.

Hart shouted for help. Two crewmen and Forsythe joined him, and they hoisted Dix on deck.

"They're down there," he gasped. "No power. Sinking."

"Then why are *you* here?" demanded Forsythe, furious.

Dix choked, "These." He held up the film cassettes. "Your wife said they had to be saved. I had the best chance. I'm sorry."

Forsythe, still caught in rage, shoved him aside.

Arthur Lovejoy caught his arms. "Paul, there's nothing you can do. Get inside. Wait until this blow's over, and we'll get help down to them."

Enraged, Forsythe said, "What help? From where?"

"We'll think of something," said Lovejoy. "Get inside!"

The freight train noise was now so loud that it had to be shouted over.

Paul Forsythe allowed himself to be led into the enclosed bridge of *Lamprey*.

"Jesus," cried Arthur Lovejoy. "Look at that!"

Forsythe gripped the edge of the bridge console. "Turn into it," he ordered.

"But the launch—"

"We can't help them. Turn into it!"

Slowly, the helmsman turned *Lamprey* toward the west.

* * *

"God help us," said Arthur Lovejoy.

The two women and the man climbed up the underwater nylon rope like grotesque monkeys on a string.

Beth was first. She watched the air bubbles from her breather tumbling above her head, and forced herself to rise slower than they did.

Below her, she could see Janet, and below the girl, O'Keefe. They were all moving up the rope with a slow, measured progress.

Beth's lungs ached. She wondered why. But there was good reason for this. Pure oxygen is a specific cure for the common hangover. While *Yellowtail* had been fitting out in dry dock, several workers had availed themselves of the free hangover medication contained in her oxygen bottles. Beth was lucky; her bottle was still nearly a quarter full. Janet's held much less, and O'Keefe's was almost empty when he left the sinking submersible.

Still, they nearly made it to the top. Beth could see the shining mirror of the surface, reflecting everything beneath it, when she felt Janet's hand clutch her ankle. She looked down and saw O'Keefe, contorting in pain. Janet pointed, grabbed the mouthpiece of Beth's breather, and tore it away from her. Beth shrugged out of the harness and stroked toward the surface and real air.

But she kept her eyes in the water, and after gasping a breath, watched as Janet swam down to O'Keefe and passed him the air breather. He tried to use it, but could not, and then he began to thrash about, and the girl was struck by his elbow, and spun off into the gloomy water. She sank slowly, her mouthpiece flailing above her head. Beth Forsythe screamed, and tried to swim down to her, but she was not able to get more than a few feet below the surface of the waves. From the corner of her eye, as she watched Janet Lovejoy drifting toward the bottom of the Sargasso Sea, she saw Kenneth O'Keefe contorting, and then he began to sink too, and finally Beth was all alone.

LIMBO LEGENDS
THE YELLOW WALL: Paul Forsythe's Story

I have been going to sea for more than twenty years. I've heard all the tall stories, the ones that were true, and the ones that weren't. But nothing I've ever heard prepared me for what happened to us that evening of December 20, out in the Sargasso.

Everything had gone crazy. Our sub was sinking, with my wife on board. One survivor had surfaced, Anthony Dix, with three film cassettes she had given him to deliver to me. The sky was all wrong, and so was the sea. It was as if we were at the bottom of a large green bowl, which curved up around all the edges. We were out of radio contact with the mainland. A Russian trawler, the **Knipovich**, had picked up some television people and the skipper of a charter boat which had gone down, and was delivering them to us on our launch.

The temperature dropped thirty degrees within a few moments. And an unusual sound, you'd have sworn it was made by an old-fashioned steam locomotive, was rising.

We had already decided to head for port. Enough had happened to ruin the voyage. But then **Yellowtail** sank, and I'm not sure what we would have done next.

The choice was taken out of our hands.

I saw it approaching just as Ray Barnstable ran up from the radar room, shouting, "There's something coming at us! Due west!"

His words trailed away. He saw it too.

It looked like a yellow wall, that's the best way I can describe it. It was coming at us out of the setting sun, forcing a rising gale of air in front of it. The noise was almost unbearable.

The horizon was completely gone. Instead, there was this . . . thing . . . at least two hundred feet high, all foaming yellow water and mist. There's no way to know how fast it was moving, but from the time we saw it until it hit, no more than two minutes went by, so it was probably coming at us with a speed of at least three hundred miles an hour.

Naturally, I couldn't be everywhere at once, so much of what I now know was told to me by others, who experienced it.

We had to abandon the launch to its own fate. There just wasn't time to get it alongside, and our only hope for ourselves was to turn **Lamprey** into the wave. I gave the order for the turn as soon as I saw that mountain of water, and the engine room responded, reversing one prop, and going full ahead on the other. The helmsman helped with the rudder.

Just then, a lookout shouted, and pointed.

Beth, my wife, had surfaced near the submarine marker. She began swimming toward us.

If I continued our turn, we would be forced to run right over her.

Captain Arthur Lovejoy caught at my arm. "Paul, it's Beth!"

I shrugged him off. I could see her face now, staring up at me with disbelief as the bow of the ship came around toward her.

"You're running her down!" Lovejoy shouted.

There was only one chance I could give her. I signaled for both engines to go full speed astern. Our turn would continue, but it would slow our motion through the water.

Beth disappeared out of sight beneath the overhang of the bow. I had no way of knowing if we had hit her or not.

Lovejoy blasted the Klaxon horn three times. Those few men still on deck scrambled below.

One didn't although I did not know it at that time. He was Bob Hart, our Second Officer. He had seen Beth struggling in the water along our starboard side, and— snatching a boathook from its rack—he raced along the railing, leaned over, and just as she was kicking at the hull to keep from being pulled under into the props, managed to twist the boathook into her shirt. The frenzy of his fear and the urgency of the moment must have given him superhuman strength, because he hauled her up onto the deck like a flopping fish. She fell at his feet, clutching a broken collarbone, and he grabbed her arm and dragged her toward the shelter of the chain locker.

I was in Alaska when the tsunami storm wave wiped out the coastline back in the sixties. That was a hell of a wave, and destructive, but it was nothing compared to what I saw from the bridge of **Lamprey**. The Alaskan seiche wave was a wave, not a frothing wall of water that had the wrong color, and moved faster than most airplanes.

My stomach churned, with a slowly growing anguish over having lost my wife not once, but twice, and with a mounting certainty that unless the unexpected occurred, I had brought all aboard to their deaths too.

"Here it comes," said Lovejoy.

The yellow wave loomed up over us, higher than our radar mast.

"Hold her steady," I told the helmsman. If the wave broke over our bow, we would be forced under, and probably broken in half. But if we were able to climb up its sloping forward side, we might be able to let the mountain of water slip under us, just like a surfer topping a big one at Sunset Beach.

Lamprey's bow began to rise. "Hang on," I shouted, and just then we lost our luck. Although our bow didn't dig into the wave deeply enough to tumble us, or crush our back, it began to break and swept down our deck, ripping away superstructure and fittings as it went.

Metal and bodies were flying everywhere. We took all our casualties in those first few seconds.

The housing of the passenger and officer cabins was ripped back like the lid of a sardine can. The film group had gathered in William Postiglion's cabin, and when the port bulkhead and part of the overhead were torn away, the pilot, Jack Begley, was impaled by a section of deck railing that harpooned him through the stomach. The railing pinned him to a large clothes closet, and he seemed to be standing against it. Postiglion threw himself toward Begley, but his foot slipped and he fell at the pilot's feet. As he lay there, stunned, Begley's blood dripped on his head, giving him a clown's red fright wig.

He was slipping toward the torn bulkhead and the sucking water outside, when Anthony Dix locked his legs around the table, bolted to the deck, and caught Postiglion by one ankle. He held on grimly until the danger passed, while Posty screamed that his leg was being broken.

Saito Osha's cabin filled with water when the wave crashed down the door. He floundered in its salty turbulence. Frantically, he made sweeping movements with his arms, trying to locate Raiko. But she did not seem to be there.

Sir Roger Lean had an inside cabin, and although the wave swept through it, the water never got more than waist deep. He clutched at the top bunk's metal frame, and was merely battered around slightly, never in real danger.

Henry Frazier, worried about being trapped in the crew's quarters, had tried to make his way to the bridge. At that moment, the giant wave swept the deck, and all that was ever found of Frazier was one torn work shoe, wedged between the twisted housing of a winch and its cable.

As for **Lamprey's** launch, Ray Barnstable was looking at it when the wave struck. The small boat rode up the side of the monstrous yellow wall for a time, then as the angle of the wave bent overhead, the launch overturned and spilled its crewman and the four passengers into the frothing maelstrom. The crewman was never seen again. Ellard Wiggins' body was found a few hours later. Pat Crosby and Walter Wylie survived. Gloria Mitchel, who had made a frantic dive for the film package, was missing.

The Soviet vessel **Knipovich** fared worst of all. The trawler was lying broadside to the giant wave, and had no chance. She turned turtle instantly, and then the weight of millions of tons of cascading water broke her up. There were no survivors.

We on **Lamprey's** bridge saw much of this and, oddly enough, the wave seemed to part around us. We there were completely unharmed. As for **Lamprey,** damage was superficial. We still had power, we still floated. The pumps had to work overtime to get the water out of our holds, but the danger had passed with the yellow wave, which vanished toward Africa, leaving us adrift in the Sargasso, surrounded by wreckage and the vile-smelling yellow-green sargassum weed that had been ripped up from its beds and thrown over everything.

Beth found me on the bridge and, gasping with pain from her broken bone, hugged and smothered me with kisses.

"The film?" she demanded. "Did Tony make it with the film?"

"What film?" I asked, and then I remembered, and took the cassettes from my pocket. "This?"

"Paul," she said, "let's go home. Let's go to Washington."

"Sure," I said. "As soon as we count the dead."

It might have been worse. Jack Begley was gone, killed by the flying wreckage. Saito Osha found his beloved Raiko, half drowned, but alive and unhurt, clinging to a smashed door panel. One crewman, Henry Frazier, had been lost overboard. The skipper of **Little Judy** had drowned, and Gloria Mitchel was missing. So was our crewman who had manned the launch.

No trace of **Knipovich,** or any of the Russian crew, was ever found.

Sir Roger Lean said, thoughtfully, "I wonder about Joseph Horatio? Do you think he made it?"

"If he didn't," I said, "we'll never know. This is a big ocean."

"Tell me, Mr. Forsythe," he said. "Are you still so almighty sure that there's no such thing as the mystery of the Bermuda Triangle?"

"No," I said. "I'm not sure at all any more."

Beth developed her films within an hour after we got off the airplane at Washington's National Airport. I had left Lovejoy down in Florida to clean up the legal mess around our tragedy. Osha had agreed to put **Lamprey** into dry dock for repairs, and then, no matter what happened in Washington, we intended to do some more exploring. Except this time, it wouldn't be for minerals and oil.

To my surprise, President Howard Foster spoke with me directly, warning me that while he did not record his conversations, there was no guarantee that some other agency might not be doing so. He invited me for drinks that evening, and suggested that I bring Beth's photographs, which I had mentioned only briefly.

Her neck encased in a plastic cast, Beth said, "I'm going with you."

"Sunny, this may get rough. I'm going to call our President a liar."

She took my arm. "So what's new about that?"

The President examined the strip of unmounted transparencies carefully.

He put aside his magnifying glass. "Yes," he said. "That's the Soviet space platform. And those bodies are our astronauts."

"But how?" I asked. "Why?"

He unlocked a small drawer in his desk, took out a cassette recorder. "One of the frogmen found this in the capsule when they blew the hatch. It was marked, 'for the President only.' So he took it aboard the **New Orleans,** told Captain Walgreen what was involved, and had himself flown to Washington. That was when I decided to come down to Jacksonville to try and put the lid on what had happened. Listen."

He pressed the Play button.

We heard a voice, harsh because of the low fidelity

of the recorder, say, "Mr. President, this is Commander Pelham, on Apollo 19. If you're listening to this tape, it means that we have been able, that is, Colonel Jones and Dr. Loren, and myself, to stay aboard the Russian platform. I'm making this tape tonight, and if we can stow away up here, it'll be in the capsule with your name on it as Eyes Only."

There was a pause. "We've discovered, without the Russians knowing, that there's a dual purpose to this platform. One, the open purpose, is scientific research. But, Mr. President, the three of us have concluded that clustered around this craft are unmanned missiles, containing atomic warheads, which can be launched from either this vehicle or from the earth. Because of their earlier footprint, the Russians are unlatching nineteen minutes sooner than we are. During that time, we plan to go EVA, let our own Apollo make the return empty, and force our way into the Russian platform. I have located an emergency hatch that can be activated from the outside, so I don't think it will be too dangerous an attempt to get on board. Once there, our plan is to deactivate the missiles, or to send them into an escape orbit. I hope that we will be able to accomplish all this without creating an international crisis. If their destruction appears to be accidental, that will leave you with more options in your negotiations with the Russians."

Another pause. Some off-microphone conversation. Then Pelham returned.

"If we find that we are unable to do what we hope, I'm confident that we can detonate the warheads, or at least one of them. Dr. Loren says that he can run a sweep generator through all of the possible destruction sequences. If that is our only choice, we will do it at approximately eight P.M., so the wreckage will splash down in our territorial waters. I hope that won't be necessary. We estimate the life support systems up here will carry us for around two weeks. If you don't mind the suggestion, sir, it'd be nice if you could make a deal with the Russians by then, and send up a bird to get us home."

The President reached over and switched off the recorder.

"The rest doesn't pertain," he said. "Personal messages to their families."

"But it turned out that they couldn't deactivate the bombs," I said, choking down a quiet horror of what I had just heard.

"No. Instead, they had to detonate. And the blast threw the space platform out of orbit. It impacted in the Sargasso."

"But the bodies—those charred lumps found in the capsule?"

"Never existed. Just part of our cover story."

"My God," said Beth. "Those poor men."

"They did their duty," said the President. He paused. "Just as I had to do mine. That's why I blocked you from going out there, Paul."

"I understand," I said. "But, Mr. President, I intend to go there again."

"Why?"

"Because, and very reluctantly, I now believe there is some truth to those legends of the Bermuda Triangle. Perhaps they're natural forces we've never encountered on a serious scientific level. Or perhaps something else, beyond our understanding. Anyway, I'm going to refit **Lamprey**, and try to find out. Those power failures, the radio blackouts, the strange lights, the seiche waves." I looked at the President. "Are you going to block me again?"

Foster shook his head. "No. Premier Nabov and I have reached an—accommodation. Neither of us will bring any attention to the destroyed platform, or its ulterior purpose. And we'll keep a close eye on future Soviet space exploration. We don't plan any more shots that'll come down over water. From now on, the shuttle's our vehicle. So, for what it's worth, the Triangle is all yours, and welcome to it."

"Mr. President," said Beth, "do the wives know what their husbands did? That their deaths weren't just a stupid accident?"

"No," said Foster sadly. "I couldn't depend on their silence. I decided not to let them hear those last messages."

I saw, to my surprise, that there were tears in the President's eyes.

"It's a no-good job, isn't it, sir?" I asked.

"All the way," said the President. "That's why I'm always so surprised that so many men seem to want it."

EPILOGUE

Half unconscious, Gloria Mitchel floated in her life jacket through the long night. The yellow wave had gone past, and now she was drifting west, as the normal patterns of the sea re-established themselves.

Several times, she spoke, to no one in particular, repeating the punch lines of old jokes, and calling out names.

There was nobody to answer.

Just after dawn, when she came fully awake, still weak and groggy from her ordeal, she saw the old sailboat drifting out of the fog. Her memory searched back, and she remembered a conversation with William Postiglion.

"Mr. Horatio?" she called. "Joseph Horatio, is that you? Help me!"

The boat drifted closer, but there was no answer.

As the fog began to lift, she saw that the boat had been through a terrible mauling. The mast was cracked, and spars dangled. Sails were rent and torn.

But there was a man sitting at the tiller.

She called again. "Mr. Horatio! Help me!"

He did not answer; he did not even turn to look at her.

Slowly, Gloria swam toward the sailboat. She ached in every muscle, and her eyes were blurred.

"Goddamn it!" she shrieked. "I *need* you!"

But the man did not move.

She reached the boat. It took three tries, and every last particle of her energy, but she managed to drag herself aboard, stepping on the top of the rudder to help. She fell into the water-filled bottom of the boat.

Gasping for breath, she lifted herself with both hands and confronted the man at the tiller.

"You no-good bastard," she croaked, "why didn't you answer—?"

Her voice caught in her throat.

The tall black man had lashed himself to the tiller and to the transom. But the raging force of the water, failing to dislodge him, had instead torn the flesh from his face and body, until the bones showed whitely, and the dead-man's grin was all teeth and cheek-bones, and no lips at all.

Gloria Mitchel began to scream.

She was still screaming when the boat drifted further west, and a naked, trembling David Lester dragged himself aboard, his flesh puckered from long immersion in sea water.

He spoke to her, but she would not stop screaming. He tore bits of rag from Joseph Horatio's shirt finally, and plugged his ears, as he put the sailboat into some rough sort of order, and headed for port.

Near noon, Gloria stopped screaming. Her voice had gone.

But inside her head, she screamed still, and always would.

AFTERWORD

Naturally, *Sargasso* is fiction, but so much of it is taken from fact, and so many people have helped me in its research that I can't close this story without thanking them.

When I was in the Air Force, I spent two years at Patrick Air Force Base, which was once called the Banana River Naval Air Station. It was from there the ill-fated rescue seaplane took off seeking the missing five Avengers of Flight 19. The old-timers on base, and in the area, were full of tales, some improved by age, of the lost flight, and it was then that I first began to be interested in the mysteries of what was, then, not even labeled with its present name, the Bermuda Triangle.

So, with many thanks, I doff my sun helmet to:

Walter Cronkite, for providing the story with his inimitable TV coverage of the Apollo 19 splashdown.

Bill and Betty Claflin, of Cocoa Beach, Florida; over their friendly pub's bar I heard many an adventure.

Lieutenant Colonel Norman Levy, formerly of Cape Canaveral's Downrange Missile Test Range, for helping me with NASA search and retrieval techniques.

Major Bart Cummings, of NASA, for his expertise on communications systems. He did *not* reveal to me any hint of a time delay; that is the author's imagination at work.

Lieutenant (jg) Ray Bimonte, who increased my knowledge of sonar.

Herb Klein, former presidential aide, who got me behind the scenes of *Air Force One*.

All the good people of Bimini Island, in the Bahamas, and in particular, Marcel Jakes, who told me about the old man who could remember Lincoln's assassination, and who was still sailing the island streams.

And, finally, to the old man himself, whose real name I have promised not to reveal.

Without you, and the hundreds of others who spent their time talking with me, there would be no story.

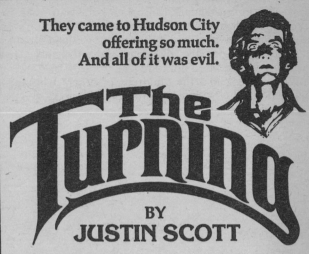

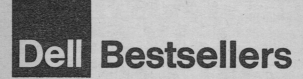

Dell Bestsellers

REMEMBER IT DOESN'T GROW ON TREES

ENERGY CONSERVATION -
IT'S YOUR CHANCE TO SAVE, AMERICA

Department of Energy, Washington, D.C.

A PUBLIC SERVICE MESSAGE FROM DELL PUBLISHING CO., INC.